The House of Many Lives

LK Wilde

ISBN:978-1-3999-3301-8

For Pete.

Chapter 1

The letter felt like it was burning a hole in Kate's pocket. As she ran along the platform, she could sense it there, leading her on its merry dance. What in the world would possess her grandmother to do it? There must have been a mistake. Either the letter was fake, or had been sent to the wrong address. It was too good to be true; good things didn't happen to people like Kate.

Kate hauled her bike onto the train and squished into a corner by the window. With no room on the luggage rack for her neatly folded bike, she leaned uncomfortably against it, pedals jabbing her legs as the train creaked out of the station. As the school holidays were finally over, Kate thought the train would be less busy. Not a chance.

Kate tried to look beyond the sweaty man in front of her to see who was travelling to the south west. She spotted a few grey heads. One couple had taken out their flask of tea and sandwiches before they'd even left Bristol Templemeads. She caught sight of a young couple, heads together, tongues locking them as one. Their slobbering made her feel sick. Newlyweds and nearly deads, that's who was travelling that day.

There should be a separate category, Kate decided, - *independent woman traveller*. It didn't have the same ring to it as the others, and if Kate were honest, she'd rather be in the newlywed category. Kate pulled down the window and let the smoggy city air cool her face. It was a good job she was small, or she might not have got on the train at all. It would be a long day if the train didn't clear before Bodmin.

Kate's feet ached like they were being held to a fire. She'd done a hellish fourteen-hour shift at The Sunbeam the day before. Kate was only supposed to be there till five, but one waitress had called in sick and she couldn't turn down the money. If it weren't for her good friend and workmate Flo, and the thought of a week's leave coming up, Kate may have walked out on the job half way through her shift. *What else could you do though?* Damn the voice of reason. That same voice had kept her working a dead-end job in a run-down hotel for the past ten years.

The Sunbeam was an awful name for a hotel, but then again, it was an awful hotel, so perhaps it was appropriate. Despite the name and two-star ratings on Trip Advisor, tourists flocked there. It probably had something to do with the price; fifty-five pounds for a double room including breakfast was unheard of in Bath. You couldn't get a cupboard on Airbnb for that.

Even worse than the name was the uniform. The manager, Silvia, insisted on all her *girls* wearing a uniform. Unlike the posh hotels where uniforms were flattering, the Sunbeam's chambermaids wore ill-fitting grey dresses, a large sun embroidered across their left breast. It looked like they'd been breast feeding and a baby had spewed its milk back up.

Hope your shift's going OK, she texted Flo. Kate felt a pang of guilt for leaving her friend behind at the depressing hotel. If anything, Flo deserved a run of good luck more than she did. Kate had never met anyone who worked as hard as Flo, who battled against the odds to keep her head above water and still kept a smile on her face and a good-natured stream of expletives ready to make Kate laugh. If it weren't for Flo's encouragement, Kate may never have summoned the courage to get on the train and deal with the contents of the letter.

Kate tapped her pocket to check the letter was still there. It could be her ticket out of The Sunbeam and its endless stream of hen and stag parties to clean up after. It could mean the end of stripping sheets stained with foundation and fake tan, clearing overflowing bins and scrubbing hangover stained toilets.

In an attempt to rest her legs, Kate perched herself on the bike's saddle. The wheels went from under her and sent her flying into Sweaty Man. He turned with a scowl, which became a sickly smile as he realised his attacker was a petite brunette. Gross. Kate smiled back through pursed lips and shuffled herself and her bike as far back from him as she could, a distance that could be measured in centimetres, if not millimetres.

It already felt like a long day and wasn't yet lunchtime. To save money, Kate had taken a bus from Bath to Bristol. The plan had been to cycle from the bus to the train station, but her phone battery had died, and without Google maps, she'd spent an hour cycling in heavy traffic before seeing a sign to the station.

Kate stuck her head out of the window as far as she could without risking decapitation. The air pounded her, clearing her mind of the cobwebs that had amassed over the past few months. The noise of the train and wind drowned out the anxiety she felt about making the journey. There was no turning back now, not until she had done what was needed. What would her mum think if she could see her now? She'd have a fit, or more likely drink half a bottle of vodka and swear at Kate till she passed out. *Poor Mum*, thought Kate, the familiar mix of sadness and anger twisting in her gut.

Green gave way to blue as the train snaked its way along the coastline. How old was she when she last made this journey? Five? Six? Kate could still taste the Spam sandwiches Mum had packed. She remembered the acrid taste as she'd taken a swig from Mum's water bottle, only to find it wasn't water at all. *Grown up medicine*, that's what Mum had called it. Kate remembered jumping up and down on the seat when she'd first spotted the sea. It must have been one of Mum's good days, as she'd laughed and cuddled her, singing *Oh I do like to be beside the seaside,* until the woman in the seat behind asked her to shut up.

As the train arrived at Dawlish, the sandwiches and flask couple got off the train. Kate took her chance, pushing past Sweaty Man to secure a seat for both her and her bike. There was no smile from him this time. The scowl was back. Kate rested her head against the window and closed her eyes. She'd barely slept the previous night. Maddie had come round. Unlike Flo, who thought the letter equalled adventure, Maddie spent the evening trying to insist she come with Kate in case she was travelling to meet a con artist, or worse, an axe murderer. The thought had been planted in Kate's mind and at two a.m. she'd finally given up on sleep and done a thorough google search of the solicitor to check he was legit. It all seemed above board, and besides, she doubted a con artist posing as a solicitor would choose Bodmin as their base.

Kate must have fallen asleep, for when she opened her eyes the train was pulling out of Plymouth station. The passenger numbers had thinned, but she could still hear the sucking and slurping of the newlyweds. She put her headphones on and selected the latest Beyonce album. A guilty pleasure, but she needed a bit of female sass. She needed to feel in control.

Her favourite song was interrupted by the message tone on her phone. Alex. She didn't open the message, just swiped across the screen and hit the delete button. There was nothing he could say that would be helpful today. Kate spent the time it took to reach Liskeard imagining all the things he might have said. Perhaps he was getting bored with Jess, though it seemed unlikely with her bouncy castle boobs and energy of a Duracell bunny.

A crackling announcement over the train's tannoy informed her they would shortly arrive at Bodmin Parkway. Kate put on her backpack and carried her bike to the door. As she stepped off the train, she wondered what it would be like to have someone there to meet you. Not one of those people who hold out signs at airports, but someone there just for you, waiting with open arms. That was another thing that never happened to people like her.

Kate unfolded her bike and pedalled out through the station and into the nearby woods. Her phone had charged on the train and she checked the route again. It would be just her luck to get lost in a town as small as Bodmin. The woods gave way to a country lane, her muscles screaming as she forced her pedals to turn against the steep incline. A valiant two-hundred metres were covered before Kate gave up and pushed.

It wasn't long ago that a thirty-mile bike ride would be a regular occurrence. But Alex insisted the bike he'd bought for her birthday belonged to him, so she'd left it at his house along with her pride. Weeks of eating ice cream and drinking gin (she didn't even like gin) had taken their toll on her fitness, something she vowed to resolve at the earliest opportunity.

The ride into town was pretty, helped by sunshine and a gentle tailwind. Her memories of the town were vague, but Kate couldn't remember there being so many hills the last time she had come. Mind you, that was twenty years ago and her mother had hailed a taxi for the three mile drive into town. Kate remembered the awkward encounter with the driver as her mum tried to haggle the price of the journey down. *It's funny what sticks in your mind,* she thought, making the most of a downhill stretch to get back on the bike and pick up some speed.

Kate couldn't afford a taxi fare. She'd be walking if it wasn't for a well-timed Facebook ad that enabled her to get a decent bike for a very reasonable price. That was the trouble with working in hospitality. Not only were the hours crap, the pay was too. At least the waiting staff got tips. No one tipped the skivvies who cleaned poo from the toilet and scooped dirty towels from the floor.

Kate pushed on through another patch of woodland before coming out at an industrial estate. *Welcome to Bodmin,* she thought, cycling past dreary looking squat warehouses and pebble dash huts. Soon, the industrial estate was behind her, and she reached yet another hill. The cycle route signs took her around a park and she found herself in the centre of the town.

Pushing the bike slowly along the town's main shopping street, she noticed how many shops were empty, big boards outside announcing *For Sale* or *To Let*. But she also saw signs of life, well-kept flower beds, historic buildings, signs advertising community events. Perhaps she wouldn't write the town off just yet.

Chapter 2

Kate looked up at the grand building in front of her and gripped the crumpled letter in her hands. She'd spent weeks ignoring the solicitor's emails, convinced they were just another in the gathering pile of spam she received on a daily basis. Kate was certain she had no long-lost relatives in Nigeria, or Australia, or Hungary, and even if she'd been stupid enough to fall for it, she didn't have the one thousand pounds in her bank account the *solicitor* needed to release the funds. But this was different. Cornwall. She did have a relative here. And they'd sent an actual, paper letter. Who did that these days? Not scammers, of that she was certain.

Kate wiped her sweaty palms on the closest she had to smart trousers, stepped forward, and rang the bell.

"Hello?" came a crackly voice through the intercom.

"Oh, yeah, hi. I'm Kate, Kate Trenain, I have an appointment at one-thirty."

"Come on in."

The door buzzed and Kate pushed it open. She took a deep breath and stepped inside, swearing as her bike caught on the door and pulled off a strip of ancient paint. She was hit by the smell of wood polish and fresh flowers, coming, she realised, from a plug-in air freshener in the corner of the room. In front of her sat an enormous desk, slightly too orange to be made of actual wood. The woman behind it looked up as Kate entered, failing to hide her surprise at the bike in Kate's hand.

"Morning," said a smiling, plump woman with bleach blonde hair and a button missing from her too tight shirt.

"Morning, I'm here for a one-thirty appointment, but I'm a bit early."

"No problem at all. Take a seat. Tea? Coffee?"

"Tea please."

Her bladder was fit to burst after all the tea she'd drunk on the train, but accepting seemed the polite thing to do.

"Milk? Sugar?"

"Just milk, please."

"No problem. I'll be back in a tick. Oh, and could you tuck that bike behind my desk? Could be a health and safety hazard."

"Sure," said Kate, standing to move her bike. Her legs groaned at the movement. She'd forgotten how many hills there were here, and how few cycle lanes, for that matter. City life had spoiled her.

A door creaked open and an enormous man appeared, bending to move beneath its frame. Kate took in his three-piece suit, pink, flowery shirt and felt her cheeks redden at the mud stained skinny jeans she counted as smart-casual wear.

"Miss Trenain, good to meet you," he said, reaching her in two strides and crushing her hand in a warm handshake. "That's a Cornish name, if ever I heard one. How long since you were last here?"

"Twenty years."

"Goodness me, the place must have changed a bit since then."

Kate nodded politely. From what she'd seen in the hour she'd been in the Duchy, not much had changed at all.

"Right, come on through."

*

An hour later, Kate found herself standing with the

giant solicitor outside the thinnest house she had ever seen. It had taken less than five minutes to walk there from the solicitor's office, and she could've done with a longer walk to wrap her tired brain around what had just happened. The house was hers. Nanny Cornwall, as Kate had known her, had left it to her in her will. The same Nanny Cornwall who cut Kate and Mum out of her life after Dad died. The same Nanny Cornwall who yelled at them in the street never to set foot in her house, or town, ever again.

Keys jangled as the solicitor pulled them from his pocket. "Shall we?"

"Just a sec." Kate parked her bike up against the railings and spread her arms wide. She leaned against the house, her fingertips touching each end. "It's smaller than I remember," she said, smiling for the first time that day.

"Wait till you get inside. It's a Tardis. Trust me."

Kate did trust him. The man reminded her of a teddy bear she'd had as a child. She stepped back and let him open the front door.

"Ladies first," he said, motioning for her to lead the way.

Kate stepped through the door and was hit by a musty smell mixed with lavender, and a sadness that weighed down on her chest and made it hard to breathe. She walked straight into the living room. A scruffy armchair nestled in one corner, a lace cloth covering the head rest. It faced a sofa that when Kate sat down, pinched and prodded her with springs fighting their way through its fabric. On a dark wood table sat a book and a pair of reading glasses.

"Are you all right Mrs Trenain?"

Kate couldn't speak, not even to correct him that she was a Ms, not a Mrs. She didn't trust herself to open her mouth. What would come out? A cry? A scream? A howl seemed the most likely option. The owner of the reading glasses had been her closest living relative. As an adult, it should've been up to her to take care of her, move past the memory of that awful last meeting and try to mend frayed family ties.

"Come on, I'll show you around."

Kate followed the solicitor (*call me Bob*) out of the sitting room and into a narrow hallway. To her left, stairs covered in threadbare carpet led upstairs, and in front was another door.

"The dining room is through here, and the kitchen."

Bob bent down as he went through the door. The dining room felt wider than the sitting room, a lot wider.

"See what I mean about a Tardis? This place is so deceptive from the outside."

Despite the width, the dining room felt oppressive. Swirling red and brown carpet met thick, yellowing wallpaper. Even the ceiling was a swirling mess of Artex and cobwebs.

"I suppose you'll want to strip the house, do it up and sell it on?"

Kate nodded. Her mind was swirling as much at the ceiling and all she could think was that she needed to get out, get rid of this horrible mass of sadness as quickly as she could. Bob moved into the kitchen and Kate followed. Despite herself, she had to admit that things were looking up. Bob chatted on about new kitchens, Homebase deals and local builders. Kate could see why; nothing had changed in the kitchen since at least the fifties. It wouldn't appeal to a modern family at all, but Kate loved it.

The kitchen was long and thin, and it took an awkward dance with Bob to move around the space. Kate opened a cupboard and found it filled with tins and packages. Several flies were dancing around the oven, and against her better judgment, Kate opened the door. Flies. Flies in her mouth, flies in her nose and flies tangled in her hair.

"Open the door, open the door," Kate said, lips pursed to prevent any more fly supper.

The solicitor opened the door and mercifully a cloud of flies danced their way out of the kitchen.

"What the hell is in there?" Kate said, peering into the oven. She pulled out a casserole dish and held it at arm's length, throwing it in the sink and turning on the tap.

"When did you say she died?"

"Six months ago."

Six months it had taken for them to track Kate down. Six months where the house had been home to nothing but flies and God knows what else. The familiar loneliness tugged at Kate and she resolved she would die surrounded by family and friends. How to make that happen she didn't know, but she'd make it happen somehow.

"Do you want to take a look upstairs or in the garden?"

"Let's look at the garden next please," said Kate, desperately needing to be out in the fresh air.

To begin with, the garden looked like any ordinary yard. In one corner was a stone outbuilding, or *workshop,* as Bob called it. They peeked inside and several spider webs joined the flies in Kate's hair. It was filthy, but in one corner stood a toilet and sink.

"You can never have too many toilets," Kate said.

Bob laughed, but after giving the toilet a closer look, the smile dropped from his face and he turned a little green around the gills.

The rest of the yard was filled with large pots of dead plants. A rotten table and chairs stood against one wall, ivy slowly taking it over.

"It's not a bad space, considering we're in the middle of town."

"No, you're right, but you haven't seen the rest yet."

"The rest?"

"Yes, follow me."

Bob led Kate down the side of the outbuilding to a series of crumbling steps. She followed behind him, and at the top, grabbed hold of his arm.

"This... this belongs to the house?"

Bob smiled at her and threw his arms out wide. "All yours."

Kate let go of his arm and began pushing her way through the long grass mixed with brambles. The garden was narrow, but stretched upwards for what felt like miles. As she tore away some of the long grass, Kate could see where beds once lay, and beneath the brambles she caught the occasional scent of a rose.

"You never came out here with your grandmother?" asked Bob, slightly out of breath as he raced to catch her up.

"No. I only remember visiting her once. We had a cup of tea in the sitting room I think, though I was too small to remember much about it. I never asked you how she died?"

"Cancer. Years of smoking eventually took their toll."

"Was it quick?"

"Not from what I heard."

"Why did no one tell me? Was she all alone?"

"I don't think anyone realised she had any family. She had a large network of friends, mainly from church and the WI. They took it upon themselves to look after her in her last few months."

Church? WI? A vague memory of a hunched old lady with a down-turned mouth flitted through Kate's mind. She couldn't reconcile the image with a woman who had a large network of friends.

"Can you tear yourself away from the garden to have a look upstairs?"

"Lead the way."

The pair scrambled back through the thick undergrowth and by the time they made it to the yard, Bob had sticky weed clinging to his suit and Kate had several tears in her jeans thanks to all the brambles. The house was even more oppressive after the excitement of the garden, and Kate took a deep breath before climbing the stairs.

The upstairs rooms were spacious, yet they contained the same awful carpet and wallpaper as downstairs. At the front of the house was a double bedroom, with another behind it. A bathroom came off the second bedroom. The suite was peach. Dirty, cracked tiles covered the floor and the tiles around the bath were covered in mould.

"No shower, but it would be easy enough to fit one, I imagine."

"I think I've seen enough," said Kate. "Shall we head back to your office and finish off the paperwork?"

"We could, but I'd say you've had quite a shock. How about we go somewhere where they serve something stronger than Sarah's dishwater coffee?"

"Sounds like a plan."

Stepping out onto the street, both Kate and Bob blinked in the late summer sunlight. It was yet another reminder of how dingy the house was. Bob set off along the street, Kate trotting beside him to keep up. He pointed across the road .

"Don't have far to walk to your local."

"That's a definite bonus."

"Right, come on, the kind of decisions you're facing require strong liquour."

Kate laughed and followed Bob across the road and into the pub.

Chapter 3

"So," said Bob, placing a pint of Tribute and a glass of Sauvignon Blanc down on the table. "What are you going to do?"

"Drink my wine and wait to wake up from this bizarre dream?"

Bob laughed and took a sip of his pint. "But seriously, I guess you have a life up in Bath that would be hard to leave. Will you do the house up, or put it on the market as it is?"

Kate tried not to look at the foamy moustache lying above Bob's lip. She swilled the wine around in her glass, wondering if the titchy flat she could barely afford, Flo and Maddie, her only friends, and an ex who lived around the corner were worth sticking around for.

"Sorry," said Bob, taking her hesitancy for indecision. "It's a big thing to take on. I didn't mean to pry or push you in any way."

"No, no, it's not that. I was just thinking about my life back in Bath. I'm not sure there's much keeping me there anymore."

"No partner?"

"No... well, yes... not really."

"Sounds complicated."

"It is." Kate thought about Alex, in the house she once

shared with him. Would Jess be there now, sitting in Kate's chair, drinking tea from Kate's mug? Perhaps if she answered Alex's calls, she could find out, but she wasn't ready to speak to him yet. "You know what? I'm going to keep it. Come on, sell Bodmin to me before I can change my mind."

"Crikey, that's a challenge if ever I heard one. You know the town's reputation?"

"Yep. But that can't be the full story."

"No, you're right, of course. There are loads of great things about the town and its surroundings. I sometimes think it's good it has such a bad reputation, it keeps the town real, you know? We're never overrun with tourists like other parts of Cornwall. There's a real, stable community here."

"And why did you choose to live here?"

Bob laughed and took several swigs of his beer. "Long story."

"Sorry."

"No, it's fine. Well, I was born here, but like most teenagers, I left as soon as I could. University, then a job in London, marriage, the prospect of kids on the horizon. But when life doesn't work out how you expect, sometimes all you want is to come home."

"What went wrong in London?"

"My wife died."

"Oh, I'm so sorry. I shouldn't have pried."

"It's fine, don't worry, it's been ten years now. I like talking about Ellie. It keeps her memory alive."

"Yes, I understand that. There's no one around who knew my mum, and sometimes I just need someone to remember her with. How did your wife die, if you don't mind me asking?"

"An undiagnosed heart condition. She was far too young to go, but life's crap sometimes and she was dealt a bad hand. I stuck it out in London for a couple of years after she passed, but my parents were getting frailer and it seemed a no-brainer to come home."

"How long have you been back here?"

"About eight years. It's embarrassing really. I'll be forty soon and I'm still living with my parents, but it suits us all for the moment."

Kate choked on her wine when he mentioned his age, but disguised it with a cough. She'd placed him in the fifty to fifty-five bracket. It must be the grey hair and beer belly. Either that or she was less perceptive than she thought.

They chatted a while longer before Bob announced he really must get back to the office. After the informality of their drink, it surprised Kate when he reached out to shake her hand. He promised the paperwork would be completed within a week, but left her with the keys in case she wanted to get quotes from builders in the meantime.

Kate waved him off down the road and let herself into Nanny Cornwall's house. It felt strange calling her Nanny Cornwall, but stranger still to think of her as Moira. Kate couldn't think of the house as her own yet despite the papers in her bag proving that yes, it really was. Her stomach rumbled, and she realised it had been hours since she'd eaten. The Indian takeaway was so close Kate could almost smell it. In twenty minutes she was back in the house, curled up in an armchair, eating food from tin containers and drinking a bottle of Tiger.

With a full belly and mind dulled by beer, Kate began idly picking at a loose piece of wallpaper. She gave it a gentle tug and it came away easily in her hand. Too easily. Her hand rubbed against the wall, coming away cold and damp. It was no surprise the house was damp. This was Cornwall, after all. Pound and dollar signs flashed in front of Kate's eyes as she heaved herself up and began inspecting the walls more thoroughly. There were patches of mould on almost every wall. She'd hoped to live on the thirty thousand pounds of savings her grandmother had left with the house, but that figure was slipping away fast as she added up all the work needed to make the house habitable. How had her grandmother coped for so long? On top of the cigarettes, the damp must have played havoc with her lungs. Once again, Kate felt a creeping guilt at her lack of contact with the old woman.

Kate pulled a notebook and pen from her backpack and began jotting down all the things that needed doing. She went from room to room, floor to ceiling, and by the time she'd finished, three pages of her notebook were full on each side. The only room not in need of a complete refurb was the kitchen. If Kate was the one living in it, nothing would need changing. People paid thousands to get a retro-style kitchen just like the one she already had. It needed a good clean, though.

Underneath the sink, Kate found more cleaning products than she could possibly need in one lifetime. It took a while to get the boiler to work, but once it did, she had hot water running from the taps in no time. *Electric, gas, water, phone and broadband.* She noted the utilities down in her notebook so she'd remember to contact the providers the following morning. Then she set to work.

Three hours and four beers later, the kitchen was clean enough that it was no longer an attractive fly habitat. With their scrubbed fronts, the Formica cabinets and worktops looked pretty cool in her opinion, and glasses sparkled from their wall-mounted cabinet. Pleased with her progress, Kate found her phone in the bottom of her backpack and decided she needed to hear another human's voice. With no signal or Wi-Fi Kate wandered outside.

"Hello?"

"Hi Maddie, you OK?"

"Yes, I'm fine, but what the hell are you doing calling at eleven at night? Is everything OK?"

"It's eleven? Shit, I'm sorry, time has flown today."

"Where are you? What are you up to?"

"You know that letter I told you about? It was genuine. I'm officially a home owner."

"What? But I didn't think you had family?"

"Well, I had a Nan, and it turns out she liked me better than I thought as she left everything to me in her will."

"Everything? How much are we talking?"

"Don't get too excited. I'm not a millionaire overnight. She left me a small, damp-riddled house in a town everyone hates, and thirty grand, that will probably all be swallowed up making the house less of a death trap."

"You sound pretty ungrateful to me. I'd be jumping for joy if I'd been left a house by a long-lost relative. It doesn't matter if it's a state. When you sell it, you'll have enough to buy a nice flat."

"That's what I wanted to talk to you about. I'm not selling it. I've decided to move in myself."

Kate was sure Maddie had let out a stream of expletives, but at that moment a police car with screeching sirens drove past and she missed it.

"Where are you? Sounds like you're in an episode of *Line of Duty*."

"I'm outside, on a bench, wrapped in a blanket. I don't get any signal in the house."

"Right, so the house is damp, mouldy, in a horrible town *and* has no phone signal. Remind me why you want to live there again?"

"Got to go," said Kate, unable to find any sane reason for her decision.

"So you wake me up with momentous news, a massive life decision, then say you've got to go?"

Kate felt the events of the day hit her like a ton of bricks and she let out a loud yawn. "Sorry, it's been a mad day. Can we talk tomorrow? I'll probably stay here the rest of the week then hire a van at the weekend to come and collect my stuff, not that there's much in my flat."

"Don't go booking any vans yet. I've got the rest of the

week to talk you out of this crazy plan. Speak tomorrow, love you."

"Love you too."

Kate hung up the phone and returned to the house. She didn't fancy sleeping in Nanny Cornwall's old bed which, for all she knew, the old lady had died in, so gathered up some blankets and made her way to the sofa. It was no more comfortable to sleep on than it was to sit on, and Kate spent the entire night tossing and turning. The few times she managed to sleep, she was woken by the sound of drunks singing and fighting in the street outside, sometimes at the same time.

At five, Kate gave up on sleep and went through to the kitchen to make a coffee. She'd boiled the water in the rusty old kettle before remembering she was lacking both coffee and milk. Kate slipped her boots on over her pyjamas and wrapped a blanket around her shoulders. Back on her favourite bench, she googled local shops and found out there was a twenty-four-hour garage at the bottom of the hill. The coffee would be crap, but better than nothing.

Half an hour later, Kate was home with a machine Costa coffee in one hand, a bag of doughnuts in the other, and a jar of instant coffee granules in her coat pocket. Not the healthiest of breakfasts, but needs must. On her way through to the kitchen, she caught her reflection in the mirror and let out a snort. God knows what the poor garage attendant must have thought of her. Her bobbed hair stuck out in light brown tufts around her head, and her hazel eyes were framed by enormous black circles. Her coat was open, showing a fetching swatch of unicorn pyjamas that she bought for their irony, and one of the buttons had come loose, exposing half a breast.

With the kettle re-boiled and a second coffee made, Kate pulled a dining chair outside and sat in her new yard. It was cold enough to need a blanket over her shoulders, but the air filled with birdsong. After a hellish night on the sofa she'd been wavering over her decision, but the birds confirmed she was doing the right thing. At least that's how she took it; for all she knew they could be yelling at her to bugger off out of their garden.

As the sun rose and the air warmed, Kate picked her way along the path she'd made yesterday until she reached the top of the garden. It was only September, but already the leaves were beginning to turn. Kate spotted apples on a trees and picked one from its branch. She took a bite and immediately spat it out onto the grass. She'd need to learn to cook a crumble.

Kate looked around, surveying her new kingdom. In her mind, she saw a large vegetable patch, rose bushes and a wildflower meadow. There must be courses you could take to learn about plants, and if she was careful with her inheritance, she'd have the time to do it. Life would be a far cry from her relentless work at the hotel, unsociable shifts and crap pay. Yes, she thought, this could be the life for me.

Chapter 4

Three days into her new life and the house was unrecognisable. Fuelled by beer and takeaways, Kate had pulled up the downstairs carpets and taken them to the dump, stripped the wallpaper in the front room, and was halfway through the bedroom walls. Hiring a van early had paid off, the alternative would have been a skip.

Kate was just settling down to a fish supper and bottle of beer when there was a knock at the door. For a moment she considered ignoring it, after all, she didn't know anyone in town, so it was most likely Jehovah's Witnesses or some charity collector. Curiosity got the better of her, and she opened the door. Kate smiled at the sight of Bob, dressed as before in a smart three-piece suit, but this time he'd even added braces to the ensemble.

"Good evening. I thought I'd come and see how you're getting on. I brought a couple of papers I need you to sign if thats OK?"

"Sure, come in. Chip?"

"Better not, I'm watching my weight."

Bob set the papers down on a coffee table and Kate went off to grab a pen from her bag. When she returned, she noticed her chip supply diminished and Bob licking salt and vinegar off his fingers. She pretended not to notice and scrawled her signature in the allotted spaces.

"That's great, thanks. So, how are you getting on? Looks like you've had a busy few days."

"Yes, I thought I may as well get stuck in. I've had a builder and an electrician round."

"Oh?"

"Yes, good news...ish. I need a new boiler, but the electrics are all fine and most of the work is just cosmetic."

"No damp?"

Kate laughed. "Oh, plenty of damp, but your bog standard, Cornish-house-sitting-empty-for-six-months kind of damp, not costs-thousands-to-fix damp."

"That's a relief."

"Yes, it means I can afford to replace the hideous peach bathroom suite upstairs and get some decent furniture in here, too. I may even have enough left over to live on for a few months, but I'm not getting ahead of myself."

"Do you need help with anything?"

"Is that a genuine offer or a polite offer?"

"Genuine."

"Well, I wouldn't want to get your lovely suit dirty, but if you are up for helping, this sofa could do with a trip to the dump."

"No problem. Just let me know when you want to go."

"Now?"

"Now?"

"Just say if it's a problem, I expect you've got a lot on."

"No, just an evening watching Eastenders and Midsummer Murders with my aged parents. A trip to the dump sounds more fun."

"Alright then, if you're sure."

The sofa was heavier than Kate thought, and there was no way she could've moved it herself as she'd first planned. After much huffing and puffing they finally got it loaded into the back of the van, followed by the armchair, two boxes of bric-a-brac, a crate full of out-of-date food Kate had removed from the kitchen cupboards, and the old mattress from Nanny Cornwall's bed. Bob kept his jacket on the whole time, despite having to continually dab his forehead with a handkerchief.

"Aren't you hot in that?"

"No, I'm fine," said Bob, sweat beading on his brow.

Kate thought Bob was a very strange man, but strange in the best possible way. All her friends were a bit odd and surely after two hours of heaving furniture, she could class Bob as a friend.

When they returned to the now empty living room, it felt enormous. Kate wished she'd waited to get the furniture out before attempting to take up the carpet as it would have been a damn sight easier, but logic was never her forte.

"These boards look in pretty good condition," Bob said, scuffing up some of the dirt to get a better look.

"Yes, I know. I don't think I'll replace the carpets, just sand down the boards and give them a coat of varnish."

"I could help with that if you like?"

"That's very kind of you, but you've already done more than enough. Fancy a beer?"

Bob looked at his watch and shook his head. "Sorry, better get back. Mum gets antsy if I'm not home for dinner."

"Ah, OK." Kate hadn't had Bob down as a mummy's boy, but perhaps she'd got him wrong.

"I can come over at the weekend?"

"Thanks, but I'm heading home this weekend to collect my stuff and tie up a few loose ends."

"OK then, see you around."

"See you."

Bob let himself out, and the room felt even bigger with the large man removed from it. As darkness fell, Kate realised she had made an error. With the sofa gone, and the mattress heading for landfill, she had removed all options for a semi-comfortable nights sleep. Weary from all the lugging of furniture, Kate trudged up the stairs into what had been her grandmother's bedroom. She had found a blanket on top of a large wardrobe, but hadn't had time to explore further. Perhaps there would be something resembling bedding inside it.

The wardrobe doors opened to reveal her grandmother's old clothes. Hangers clicked against each other as Kate threaded shirts, blouses and jackets along the rail. Tomorrow would be a charity shop trip, she decided. At the far end of the wardrobe Kate found a dress. She pulled the hanger off the rail and laid it out on the bare base of the bed to get a better look. Silk slipped across her hands, undamaged by the passage of time. The dress was floor length, cut away at the back with delicate beads across the bodice. When had her grandmother had the chance to wear such a beautiful gown? It would probably fetch a good price on eBay, but it was too precious to let go. Kate replaced it in the wardrobe, pulling out all the dull everyday clothes and piling them up on the bed ready for the charity shop.

In the three days she'd been there, Kate had given little thought to the woman who once inhabited the house, and who had passed on a quarter of Kate's genes. But the dress raised her curiosity, and she began removing boxes from the base of the wardrobe. Most contained boring paperwork from years ago, gas bills, receipts, *life admin* Maddie would call it. Certain there was nothing of importance, Kate fetched a bin bag from the kitchen and began filling it with paper ready for recycling.

Beneath the boxes of papers, Kate found a set of photo albums. She held a thick, worn velvet book in her hands, thumbing through the pages. Most of the photos had been taken either in the house itself, or around the town, from what she could tell. Kate recognised a young woman with dark hair as soon as she saw her. The resemblance to Kate was striking and tugged once more on the guilt of estrangement.

Kate lowered herself onto the wooden floor and took her time. Strangers' faces grinned out of each page. Nanny Cornwall had her arm around a different man in every photo. What struck Kate the most was the house. She saw it only as bricks and mortar, but in the faded photographs it was a place full of life. It was a far cry from the prim matriarchal portrait of Nanny Cornwall painted by her mum. At the back of the album was an envelope, fresh white, unlike the yellowing photographic paper. Kate stared at the envelope in her hands, her own name *Katherine* marring white with black. Her hands shook as she tore the seal and pulled out a piece of thick cream paper.

Dear Katherine,

I suspect the correct etiquette would have been to leave this letter with my will, but I don't want it being read by a stuffy solicitor type. If you've found it, the house will now be yours, and I will be gone. We never had a chance to get to know one another in life, but I hope by being here, you will develop a sense of who I really was. Not the person your mother made me out to be. Sorry, if I'm dead, it's time to let bygones be bygones. I shall be more careful with my words going forward.

The truth is, I did want to know you. I wanted to be part of your life. Please don't solely blame either myself or your mother for our estrangement, we were equally to blame. I never forgave her for taking your father from me, and she never forgave me for taking him back from her. Two stubborn women are an unfortunate combination, and we were both stubborn all right.

Anyway, enough about the past. You are reading this in your present. You may have decided to sell the house, which is entirely your right. But something makes me think you'll stay, and if you do, I have some requests;

-The house has welcomed many people over the years (as you'll see from the photographs). In recent years I've

not been able to maintain my 'open house', but you bring with you a fresh start. Fill the house with love and laughter, and wine (or beer or whisky, if that's your tipple of choice).

-Spend your life doing what you love. The money I've left you won't go far in today's world, but it will buy you some time. Don't settle, don't chase money, find what brings you fulfilment and pursue that above all else. Remember that fulfilment is different from happiness. This modern obsession with being happy is a recipe for disaster. Life is full of sadness, but that makes the moments of joy shine all the brighter.

-For all I know, you might be married, but if you're not, don't settle for any man. Find someone who treats you well, who loves you as much as you love him (or her if that's your persuasion). Remember, relationships take work. Another terrible modern idea is that of the 'perfect man'. Trust me, dear, such a thing doesn't exist. People are fallible. Rate kindness above all other qualities.

Here endeth the lesson. In other words, these are the things I wish I had told you in person, but never got the chance. Speaking of which, I'll quickly add in one final request- DON'T HOLD A GRUDGE! I did, and it cost me you.

Anyway dear, I expect you have a lot to be getting on with. That old sofa needs replacing, for starters. Go well, be kind, and have a wonderful life.

All my love,

Moira (Nanny Cornwall)

Kate folded the letter carefully and laid it on the floor in front of her. The last thing she wanted was to smudge the ink with her tears. The woman who wrote it sounded like someone she would have wanted to know, to spend time with. Quite how she would fill the house with love and laughter when she didn't know a soul in the town and spent most nights crying herself to sleep over Alex, she couldn't say. But at least she had something to aspire to. The thought of finding out more about Moira sent a shiver of excitement through her.

Kate wiped her eyes on the back of her sleeve and packed the photo album and letter away to return to later. There were practical matters to attend to. She could wallow in her emotions once she had a house that looked less like a bomb site and a comfortable place to sleep that night. Having failed in her mission to find anything resembling bedding, it looked like she'd either be sleeping on bare floorboards, or a trip to the local supermarket was in order. The hired van was more than earning its keep.

Chapter 5

After the solitude of house clearing in a small town, the noise, smells and bustle of the city hit Kate's senses like a freight train. Since arriving back in Bath, the word she'd uttered most was 'sorry', jostling against people as she navigated the busy streets like a ball in a pinball machine. Kate parked the van as close as she could to her flat, but needed caffeine before she could face the task of dismantling her old life.

Half an hour after arriving, Kate settled herself down on a set of endless steps and took a sip of her Americano. The steps emitted a faint whiff of urine, but Kate ignored it, taking a large bite out of a bagel, and wiping her chin as cream cheese and sweet chilli sauce dribbled down it.

Maddie had been in regular contact all week, giving Kate a hundred and one reasons why leaving the city was a bad idea. Some came close to persuading her, but being back in Bath brought no twinge of regret. As soon as Kate entered its boundary, the old, familiar feelings returned. *You're not good enough, Kate. You're too anti-social, Kate. Why can't you sort your life out, Kate?* Perhaps in Bodmin she'd be kinder to herself. It was worth a try.

Licking the final stickiness of the bagel from her fingers, Kate abandoned the steps and began the short walk to her flat. There was a reassuring familiarity to the streets, but the memories they held were not happy ones, despite the beauty and grandeur of their architecture. The road climbed upwards and Kate found herself outside a tired Georgian building, divided into twelve flats many years ago. She pulled a key from her pocket, took a deep breath, and stepped inside.

Kate had taken the flat for two reasons; money and light. It had been the cheapest flat she could find, remarkably so for its central location. She knew there would be a reason for the price tag, which there was. It was a studio, which Kate always thought sounded romantic, like she should be creating vast oil paintings inside it, but in reality it just meant all she had to her name was one room. The enormous windows at either end were magnificent, but their magnificence was dimmed by the moss that framed each pane, peeling wood squishy beneath her fingers. If someone wanted to break in, they'd have no trouble; none of the window locks worked. Kate had consoled herself by thinking how useful it would be if she ever forgot her key.

The flat looked tired and empty. Alex had persuaded her to get rid of most of her furniture when she moved in with him, and after he kicked her out, she'd never got round to replacing it. A pine bed stood against the wall in the middle of the room. It doubled as a sofa, and Kate had bought massive cushions to go along its headboard for when she was reading or watching TV on the laptop. A matching orange pine kitchenette lay against the opposite wall, cupboard doors hanging awkwardly from their hinges, black filling the spaces between tiles where white should have been.

Kate began taking clothes from the flat pack wardrobe she'd bought from Argos. She thought of the sturdy old wardrobe in Bodmin, standing the test of time better than this flimsy combination of wood and calico ever could. Kate knelt down beside her bed and pulled a shoe-box from under it. All her memories of family were shoved into the one box, a pitiful reminder of how dysfunctional family life had been. In friends' houses, family portraits adorned the walls, certificates from music exams and swimming competitions stood proudly on polished cabinets. All Kate had was one manky shoe box covered in dust.

The thick layer of dust and grime flew up into a cloud as Kate blew across the lid. Inside the open box lay a handful of photographs. She took the closest one, a picture of her dad. She could barely remember the man who smiled so happily out at her. He must have been in his late teens or early twenties when the photo was taken, for there were no drug-ravaged signs on his face. He had a full set of teeth and his muscular body was a far cry from the thin shell he would occupy a few short years later. He stood bare chested, hands on his hips, clothed in a tight pair of swimming trunks and squinting against the sun. Kate wasn't sure where the photo had been taken but it would have been somewhere in Cornwall. He'd only left once, a foray so disastrous he'd returned home only six months later.

Beneath the beach photo was the only photo she had of them as a family unit. It was her first birthday and both her parents squished their faces close to hers, a birthday cake with one candle on a table in front of them. Her parents were smiling, her mum looked beautiful, long shiny hair falling across a paisley dress, red lipstick highlighting her full lips and perfect teeth. The only sign of disquiet was the glass of wine in her hand; the poison which would eventually take her the same way as Dad, but not before it had put both mother and daughter through twenty years of torture.

Kate enjoyed a drink, but her dark family history sat like a stone on her shoulder and she had only ever been drunk once. It had been at uni, and the experience scared her so much it was weeks before she risked another drop of alcohol. A memory flashed through Kate's mind, hauling Alex up the steps to their house, just making it through the door before he vomited all over her. He'd been mortified the next morning, made her breakfast in bed despite his huge hangover. He could be sweet like that. God, she missed him.

Kate wondered if she were a witch, for at that very moment her phone vibrated, Alex's smiling face staring out from the screen. Her thumb hovered above the green icon, but she opted for red and cut him off. The phone buzzed again. Perhaps there was no harm speaking to him once, to say goodbye. Kate was setting off on a new adventure. Unlike the previous few months, she actually had some news that didn't make her sound like a desperate loser. She hit the green button and pulled the phone to her ear.

"Hello?" Alex sounded surprised.

"Yep, what do you want?"

"Oh, hi. I wasn't expecting you to pick up."

"So you called for no reason."

"No, not at all. I wanted to hear your voice."

"Why? You've got Jess's squeaky voice in your ear all day now. Isn't that enough?" That was the thing that had tormented Kate the most after their split. How could he have left her for someone with a voice so high pitched it could break glasses? Surely that would be a deal breaker for any sane human being?

"There's no need for that."

No need? Kate felt there was every need, the familiar anger of the past few months bubbling up once more. Kate waited in silence until Alex was forced to break it.

"Look, Maddie told me you're leaving. What the hell are you thinking, Kate? Is this a reaction to us?"

Bloody cheek of the man. "No, Alex, it's not. Funnily enough I'm not still pining over you and basing all my life decisions on my toad of an ex." That wasn't strictly true, not the pining bit anyway, but she wouldn't give him the satisfaction of letting him in on her true feelings.

"So what happened? You're not really going, are you?"

"I've got a house, is what happened. And yes, I am going. I'm leaving today."

"But you can't!"

"Really?" Kate spat the word, despite the deep breaths she was taking to remain calm.

"No, I didn't mean... I just meant..."

"Spit it out."

"I've still got your jumper. You know, the mustard one I bought you for your birthday? I thought you might want it before you go?"

Kate loved that jumper. She regretted leaving it behind to spite him every time she felt a chill in the air. A nice thick jumper would be useful in the draughty Bodmin house.

"You can post it to me."

"Come on, Kate, don't be ridiculous. Posting it would cost a fortune. Can't you come over and collect it?"

"Fine. It shouldn't take me long to pack up here. I'll be over around two-ish."

"Great, it will be good to see you again..."

Kate's thumb hit the red button and cut him off.

Chapter 6

It only took a few hours to clear the house, load the van and leave the flat presentable enough to get her deposit returned. Kate checked her watch. One-thirty. She decided to head straight to Alex's rather than hang around the depressing flat longer than necessary. Alex was spitting mad when she rented a flat on the next street to his. Kate enjoyed watching him squirm every time she bumped into him in the corner shop, small victories and all that. A few times she saw Jess in there, but found a good hiding spot nestled between the wine and frozen ready meals. It would be too humiliating to confront the upgraded woman in Alex's life.

Kate's steps slowed as she neared the house, a house that had been her home for the best part of a year. Tears pricked her eyes as she remembered Alex talking about starting a family, what colour they could paint the nursery. They even argued over baby names. Sadness was no use to her now. She needed to turn it into fighting fuel, anger. Far crueller than his affair had been Alex's ability to raise her hopes. She had truly believed she would get the kind of family she'd longed for. How gullible can a person be?

He must have spotted her from an upstairs window, for before she reached the door, it was flung open. There he stood in his M&S lambswool jumper and chinos. (Never trust a man in chinos was Flo's motto.) His hair had that carefully coiffured just-out-of-bed look that, from experience, Kate knew would have taken him the best part of an hour to perfect. She wondered if he'd been away, as his face was bronzed, making his blue eyes all the more startling.

Before she could stop him, Alex grabbed her by each arm and planted a stubbly kiss on each cheek. He held her at arm's length, studying her face. Kate looked away, refusing to meet his intense gaze.

"Darling, you look so tired. What's all this nonsense about moving away? Mid-life crisis?"

"You said you had my jumper?"

"Don't be like that. How about a coffee? You can tell me all about your plans."

"I'd like my jumper please, then I need to be on my way. I'm meeting Maddie in a bit."

"Oh, you know what Maddie's like, always late. Come on in, I can't remember where I put the jumper, so you may as well have a coffee while I look."

Kate knew that was bollocks. Alex was a neat freak, on at her all the time about her mess, despite how hard she had tried to tidy up after herself. She contemplated waiting on the doorstep, but part of her was curious about what Jess might have done with the place.

"I'll come in while you look, but you can forget about the coffee."

Alex tutted and turned back into the house, waving his arm to signal she should follow. The hallway was as immaculate as ever, the deep green walls, crisp white skirting boards and polished parquet floor showing no hint of the furious row that had unfolded there the day she left. The mirror's glass had been replaced, and a new vase filled with fresh lilies stood in place of the one Kate had smashed.

So far, the only sign of a new female inhabitant was a pair of expensive running trainers on the oak shoe rack. It was no surprise Jess was a runner. You'd have to be a proper exercise freak to keep a curvy figure as trim as Jess's, although Kate wouldn't have put it past her to have a bit of surgical help on the side. Alex was keen his women kept themselves in shape. Kate thought of all the wasted hours she spent with him in the gym while secretly longing to be out on her bike or hiking through the Somerset countryside. Alex didn't count walking or cycling as proper exercise. Kate resolved to do as much walking and cycling as she could once settled in Bodmin.

"Give me a sec. I'll have a look upstairs. Make yourself comfortable."

Kate watched his back retreating up the staircase, then wandered into the living room. She'd forgotten how beautiful the room was. Large moss and mould-free windows looked out onto the street, covered with dust free shutters to maintain privacy whilst letting in the light. The deep blue sofa housed expensive cushions, faced by a green velvet over-sized armchair. The walls were white, each filled with an enormous abstract painting in colours complementing the furniture. Tall, lush plants stood in expensive pots and a polished silver lamp hung languidly from its stand.

When they first met at university, Kate assumed Alex was gay. It turned out he was just a well-dressed metrosexual with an eye for interior design. Nothing had changed in the room since Kate's departure, and Kate was wondering if Jess even lived there when she noticed a banal romance novel tucked neatly under the coffee table. Kate moved back through to the hallway.

"How are you getting on up there?"

"Fine, be down in a minute."

Kate sighed and checked her watch. It was lucky she arrived early, as this was taking far too long. The door to the kitchen diner was open. Kate peeked her head round. Nothing had changed here, either. The clean white lines of the kitchen fed through to a glass dining table that could seat eight. Kate remembered the laborious dinner parties

Alex held regularly, always coming up with some reason or other why her own friends couldn't be invited.

Kate strode through the kitchen to the French doors at the back, flinging them open and welcoming the fresh air on her face. She loved this garden once. It had been her sanctuary when the clean lines and exacting standards of inside became too much. The garden was still beautiful, lovingly tended by an old chap who lived on the same street. He was expertly green fingered, and Alex gave him free rein. He had no interest in outdoor spaces as long as they complimented his Insta-ready interior.

Kate sat down on the garden step to wait. This garden was the thing she missed most about the house, but she had her own garden now. It might not be up to much yet, but it was bigger than Alex's and would be even more magnificent, given time.

"Found it," said Alex, wandering in to the kitchen with the jumper held aloft. "Ah, your favourite spot. I miss coming home and finding you sat there."

Kate shrugged and let the comment wash over her. She stood up, locked the patio doors, and moved to take the jumper from Alex's hands. He twisted his arm back and Kate was left scrabbling in mid-air.

"Stop being a dick. Give it to me."

"I miss the fun we used to have."

"Yeah, well, you've got a new playmate now. Give me it Alex, or I'll leave right now and you can put it in the post."

"Fine," he said, handing her the jumper without letting go. Kate tugged at it, but Alex kept hold, pulling her closer till she could smell the scent of mint on his breath. Had he been up there cleaning his teeth for her? Alex moved forward in an attempt at a kiss, but Kate moved her head round and his lips caught the edge of her nose.

"Don't contact me again."

Kate stormed out of the house, slamming the door behind her, hopefully with enough force to knock the new vase from its stand. How dare he? Hadn't he hurt her enough already without playing stupid games? The worst part of their encounter was how much she wanted to kiss him back. He was so familiar. He was all the family she had. Kate shook her head to push the thoughts away. She strode off along the road, pummelling her sadness and frustration out on the pavement beneath her.

*

"He did what?" Maddie's cup was halfway to her lips, her mouth open wide with shock.

"Tried to kiss me. He kept me waiting ages too, all part of his game, though what game he's playing is anyone's guess."

"Tell me you didn't kiss him back." Maddie's forehead was creased, her cup still poised in mid-air.

"Of course I didn't kiss him back... Though part of me wanted to." Kate looked down at the flowery table cloth, refusing to meet Maddie's eyes.

"Katherine Trenain, don't you even think of going back there. It's taken months for you to start putting yourself back together again. Suddenly, you leaving seems a better idea than I first thought."

"I'm not as stupid as you think, Maddie. Of course I won't go back to him. But, you know, it's hard. He was all I had when Mum died, then all that mess with uni. He supported me through it all."

"But think of all the ways he hurt you. There was always something in it for him. It suited him to have you meek, feeble, and eternally grateful."

"I think you're being a bit harsh."

Maddie raised her eyebrows. Kate changed the subject, and they drank the remainder of their coffee amid more comfortable topics, like what colour Kate would paint the walls of her new home.

"Oh, I nearly forgot. Look what I found." Kate pulled Moira's letter from her bag and passed it to Maddie.

Maddie read in silence, and when she looked up, her eyes were blurred with tears. "Oh my God, your granny sounds amazing. You are going to follow her wishes aren't you?"

"I'll try, but as I barely know a soul in the town, it may take me some time before the house is *filled with love and laughter*. God, that sounds like something you find on one of those home trinkets."

"What about Airbnb?"

"How do you mean?"

"Well, that would be a good way to get people into the house, and it would give you an income while you figure out what you want to do."

"Hmm, I'm not sure I like the sound of strangers in the house while I'm there. What if they're nutters? Or murderers, or rapists..." Kate shuddered.

"You wouldn't have to share all the house. They could have part, you could have part. Win-win."

"Maybe..."

"Look, there's no rush, have a think about it. In the meantime, when can I come and stay?"

Kate laughed. "Any time you like, you know you're always welcome."

"How about the weekend after next?"

"Really? You'll come and visit?"

"Of course I'll come and visit you. Come here."

Kate and Maddie attracted bemused looks from other customers as they bent over the table and wrapped their arms around each other.

"Thanks for being there for me," said Kate, settling herself back in her chair.

"Always, my friend, always."

*

Maddie walked with Kate to the van to wave her off. She cupped her hands and peered in the back. "Bloody hell, is that all you've got to take?"

"Yeah, hardly seems worth hiring a van. I could've managed with a Fiat Panda, though the van's come in handy for my multiple trips to the dump. I'm on first-name terms with the blokes there now."

"Wow, your new life sounds thrilling."

Kate gave Maddie a good-natured punch on the arm, then drew her into one last hug.

"I'll miss you. Be good while I'm gone."

Maddie laughed. "When am I ever good? Listen, get your Wi-Fi sorted ASAP so we can Face Time. I don't like the thought of you sat on a bench at all hours."

"It's at the top of my to-do list."

"Good. Now drive carefully. I know how jittery you get after a couple of coffees."

"Shut up." Kate smiled at Maddie as she climbed into the van. "See you in a couple of weeks. Love you lots."

"Love you too."

Kate pulled out into the busy traffic and headed west.

Chapter 7

Kate paced up and down the hallway, wringing her hands. It was stupid to be nervous, It was only a takeaway and a few beers, but Bob's approval mattered. He was her only friend in town and this was the first time she had truly made a place her own. To her untrained eye it looked good, but what if she was mistaken, if her mis-matched furnishings screamed 'cheap' rather than 'eclectic'?

Bob had been a huge help the first couple of weeks after Kate had officially moved in. He'd done four more dump runs for her, helped strip wallpaper, even cleaned out the manky outside loo. But for the past week, she'd asked him not to come round. Kate needed to do the finishing touches herself. It was important she prove to herself she could do it.

While the plumbers were clearing their tools from the newly improved upstairs bathroom, Kate headed into town to Bob's office. She could just as easily have sent a text, but she felt awkward around the plumbers, having offered tea so many times it had become embarrassing. Kate was used to working for other people, not having them work for her. Bob was out when she arrived, but Kate left a message with the receptionist who seemed relieved she'd not lugged a bike in with her this time.

Keen not to get in the way at home, Kate headed to the bakery and bought herself a pasty. Her mum used to say she had hollow legs, for she ate enough to feed a family but never put on weight. Pasties would need to be rationed, though. Earlier that morning, Kate caught her reflection in the mirror and noticed she was getting a bit squishy round the middle. *Cuddly,* as Flo would say. It was hard, though, when the smell of freshly baked pasties filled the air all around town.

Kate took a photo of her pasty and sent it to Flo. Moments later, her phone pinged with a laughing emoji and *not again!!!!!* There wasn't much about city life Kate missed so far, but not being able to share a McDonald's breakfast with Flo, or walk round to Maddie's for a glass of wine had taken some getting used to. Flo couldn't afford the time off to visit, and Kate had put Maddie's visit off for a couple of weeks, despite Maddie's protests that she wanted to help. When her friends came, Kate wanted them to see a finished home, not a dusty building site.

Kate's phone pinged again, this time with a message from the plumbers:

All done. Put the key through the letter box. Will email the invoice.

Thanks x she replied, immediately regretting the kiss on the end. She didn't want either Roger, in his sixties, or his spotty teenage apprentice getting the wrong idea.

No problem xx

Oh dear. Kate slipped her phone away, hoping that would be the end of her correspondence. The phone pinged again, but she ignored it. She wrapped the half-eaten pasty up in its paper bag and headed home. Back inside her own four walls, she checked her phone and with relief found a message from Bob- *8 OK?* She sent back a thumbs up before taking the stairs two at a time to see the finished bathroom. It was covered in a fair amount of dust, but all traces of peach were banished.

*

Twenty past eight and still no sign of Bob. She put the

curry in the oven to stop it from getting cold and stared out of the window. It was only twenty minutes, but he always arrived on the dot and she was starting to get worried. Another ten minutes passed before, finally, she saw his battered VW pulling up outside. Bob's choice of car was a mystery to her. Surely solicitors earned a packet? Maybe he didn't like to flash the cash.

"Sorry, sorry," said Bob, flustered and sweating as he bumbled into the house.

"Don't worry about it. Everything alright?"

"Yes, yes, just a bit of bother at home, nothing to worry about."

"Do you want to talk about it?"

"No, I'm starving. Let's eat."

"Fine, but then I need your honest opinion on the house."

Bob laughed and looked around the living room. "I'm not sure why you want my opinion. I don't know the first thing about interior decor. It used to drive Ellie mad when she'd try talking to me about paint charts. I couldn't get past the names to take it seriously- *Mermaid Net, Mayonnaise, Spruce Dust*- I mean, what's that all about? Whatever happened to light yellow or dark blue?"

"OK, I get it, but you're the first person to see my handiwork and believe it or not, your opinion does matter to me. You've been a good friend since I got here."

Kate swore Bob blushed at the compliment, but he could have still been red in the face from all his rushing around.

"Well, this room looks ace. I love the sofas."

"Fifty quid on eBay."

"Really?"

"Yes, there weren't many takers for purple velour sofas, but I think they look all right calmed down a bit with a throw?"

"Yes, yes, they're great." Bob flopped down on said

sofa. "Comfy too, perfect for snuggling up with a book."

"That will be my reward for getting it all finished. I've given myself tomorrow off for reading, lounging, and nothing else."

"Good for you. These tables are... interesting."

"Do you think they're too much?" asked Kate, looking at the tables she'd lovingly covered in nature photos from a magazine. She was still picking PVA glue from her skin despite finishing them four days ago.

"No, they go well with the sofas. Now, how about some grub?"

"Alright, alright. Make yourself comfortable in here. I'll bring dinner through."

Kate appeared a few minutes later, two plates rammed with food, naan bread and poppadoms balanced precariously on top. "Can you grab the beers?" she asked, nodding to the two bottles balanced beneath her arm.

"So you haven't got a dining table yet then?"

"No, not yet. I haven't decided what to do with the dining room yet. I've had an idea, but you might think it's mad."

"Try me," said Bob, through a mouth full of rogan josh.

"It's my friend Maddie's fault. She suggested it when I was up in Bath to collect my stuff."

"Spit it out woman, your food's getting cold."

"I've been thinking about doing Airbnb, you know, in this house..."

A look of confusion spread across Bob's face, and Kate couldn't be sure, but she thought he looked sad. "Oh, right, I see. Well, yes, go for it. Bodmin probably would've been a bit dull for you, anyway. Yes, not much going on for young people. YOLO, as the youth say."

"Bob?"

"Yes?"

"Stop blabbering, and just so you know, no youths I've met say YOLO these days."

"Oh."

"Look, you've got the wrong end of the stick. I don't mean renting out the entire house, just some of the rooms. Like a B&B, though I'm a crap cook, so I won't be offering breakfast."

"Ah, I see. Well, it's not the worst idea I've heard. But would you be comfortable sharing your home with perfect strangers?"

"I wouldn't necessarily have to share it. I've been thinking about how it could work. I'd have the downstairs and guests could have the upstairs. The back bedroom could be en-suite as the bathroom leads off it, and the front bedroom could be a sitting room, with tea and coffee, microwave, etcetera. The sofa could even be a sofa bed, and..."

"Sorry to interrupt you, but wouldn't that leave you without a bathroom?"

"Well, yes, but there's the outside loo that you so carefully de-spidered for me. I had the plumbers take a look, and they said it would be easy enough to get a shower fitted in there as the plumbing's already set up."

"But you'd have to go outside every time you need a wee."

"It wouldn't be the end of the world. I've always enjoyed camping. But seriously, toilet aside, what do you think?"

"It would certainly be in line with the open house your grandmother talked about, plus you'd be getting an income from it. On balance, I'd say it's a rather sensible plan."

Kate smiled. She'd shown Bob Moira's letter, confident that he wasn't the usual *solicitor type* she had written disparagingly about. He'd even had the good grace to laugh at that part. "Well I'm pleased you approve. Now get your food down you. I'm itching to show you around."

*

Despite Bob's ignorance over interiors, he oohed and

aahed in all the right places as Kate led him round the house. He was particularly impressed with the new bathroom; white, shiny and complete with bath and overhead power shower.

"That's an interesting choice of flooring..."

"I had a cork floor in my house when I was little. We weren't living there long as the landlord kicked us out, but I remember our time there as mostly happy. I have so few happy memories from childhood I thought it would be good to be reminded it wasn't all bad. And anyway, it will go well with the pot plants I plan to put in here. Do you like it?"

"Yes, I do. It's unusual, but in a good way. I love the exposed floorboards everywhere too. You've done a great job sanding them down."

"Thanks. I just hope it's not too noisy when guests are here."

"When do you hope to start taking guests in?"

"Well, there's furniture to buy for the guest sitting room, and I'll need to set up my room downstairs, but once that's done, I should be all set."

"Well, let me know if you need any help. You might want to get a lock fitted to your bedroom door."

Kate was touched by Bob's concern. "Yeah, I was thinking I may get one fitted to the door through to the dining room. It would also stop people trying to use the kitchen and I'd feel like I had a bit more personal space."

"I could do that for you if you like?"

Kate would have accepted his offer, but at that moment Bob's mobile started playing Bon Jovi's Living On a Prayer and he excused himself from the room. Through the door, Kate could hear him getting more and more frustrated.

"Argh, stupid phone signal."

"Try the bench outside," she called through the door. "That's where I go to make calls."

"Thanks," Bob called back.

Kate heard his footsteps pound down the newly varnished staircase. Only when the door clicked did she make her way downstairs herself, curling up on a purple sofa and covering her legs with one of the new fuchsia throws. Summer was long gone, and it was becoming very chilly in the evenings. Kate wrote herself a note on her pad to call someone about the fire. Ten minutes after he'd gone outside, Kate peered out of the window to see if Bob was still there. He was sitting on the bench, hands flying wildly around him as he gesticulated to whoever was on the other end of the phone. Bob looked back towards the house and Kate whipped her head away. The last thing she wanted was to seem like a nosy neighbour.

Kate waited and waited, but Bob didn't return. Reluctant to be caught spying, she picked up a book and pulled the throw tighter around her knees. She was finishing a chapter when a knock on the door made her jump. Kate opened it to a red-faced Bob, wringing his hands.

"Oh, hi. Sorry, I thought you'd gone home. Is everything all right?"

"Bit of trouble at home. I'd better be off."

"Anything I can help with?"

Bob surprised her with a peck on the cheek. "That's very kind of you, but I need to sort this out myself."

"OK, see you soon," she said, but he was already striding towards his car and she wasn't sure he heard.

Chapter 8

Kate flung the door open and threw herself in Maddie's arms. "It's so, so good to see you," she said into a mouthful of blonde curls.

"Anyone would think it had been a year. I saw you a month ago!"

"I know, but it feels like a year. Let me look at you." Kate held Maddie at arm's length, relieved to see she hadn't changed. She was makeup free, wearing a crop top, baggy jeans and a chunky knit cardigan. She could have stepped off the pages of a Boohoo catalog, if catalogs were still a thing. "You look amazing."

"So do you."

Kate laughed, she was in her cleaning clothes which consisted of a baggy old jumper and torn skinny jeans. Not torn in a cool Maddie way, torn in a falling apart with no money to replace them kind of way. She probably had a spider family in her hair, as it had a familiar sticky feeling when she ran her hands through it.

"Are you going to let me in? I'm dying to see inside, and it looks like it's about to piss it down."

"Sorry, yes, come in."

"Wow!" said Maddie, stepping into the sitting room.

"Good-wow, or what-the-hell-have-you-done-wow?" asked Kate, scrutinising her friend's face for clues about her true feelings.

"You're joking, right? This looks amazing!"

Kate smiled, and her shoulders dropped. "Come on I'll give you a tour."

Kate led Maddie through to what used to be the dining room. "This is my bedroom. The guests will be upstairs."

Maddie threw herself onto the iron bed Kate found in a reclamation yard and spread her arms and legs in a star fish. "I love what you've done with the photos."

Kate was proud of her photo wall. She'd got hold of the frames by scouring the many charity shops in town and had been surprised by how good they looked against the pale pink wall (rose blush, if she was going to use the technical name). "You don't think it's too studenty?"

"No, not at all. It's classy. I love that you've got your old photos up. Look at your dad in those trunks! It doesn't make you too sad, does it? Having them looking down on you when you're trying to sleep?"

"No, I wondered if it would, but it felt right somehow. They've been hidden in a box for so long, but coming here feels like a fresh start, like I don't need to hide away that part of me anymore."

"Pleased to hear it. Now come on tour guide, what's next?"

"Feast your eyes on this, madam," said Kate, pointing through to the kitchen.

"Oh. My. God," said Maddie, practically lying on the kitchen worktop and stroking the Formica with her palms. "Is this original?"

"Yes, seemed too good to rip out. You like it?"

"Love it."

"OK, prepare yourself. This is my bathroom..."

"What the..." Maddie looked on open mouthed as Kate opened the back door. "You have to take a piss in the garden?"

"Sort of. Come and see."

Kate had done her best to tart up the outside loo. The plumbers had been back to fit a shower, and she'd white washed the walls and put up a floating shelf covered in plants. Still, the resident spiders claimed it as their home, and there was nothing she could do about the temperature.

"But this is like going back to the dark ages," said Maddie.

"Best close your mouth. There's plenty of spiders here that might climb in." Maddie clamped her mouth shut. "I'll show you the garden when it's stopped raining."

"Does it ever stop raining here?"

"Not often," laughed Kate, leading her back inside. "Now, up here is the guest suite."

"Ooh, how posh."

Kate showed Maddie the guests' living room, complete with sofa bed, TV, a small table and chairs. The kitchenette consisted of a cabinet she'd found at the dump and repainted, microwave, kettle and toaster. The only new items she'd bought were a selection of colourful bamboo crockery, which had cost more than the all the room's furniture put together.

Maddie seemed impressed with the upstairs. Once again, she flung herself down on the bed in the guest room.

"That's my Nan's old bed."

"God," said Maddie, jumping up. "It's not where she died is it?"

"No, I checked. It's a new mattress anyway, and new bedding, Marks and Sparks, don't you know?"

"Don't you go turning posh on me. I love how simple it is up here."

"Yes, I thought neutral was the best way to go, more stylish."

Kate had painted the walls white. White bedding would be a pain to keep clean, but she'd taken the plunge, deciding it looked more upmarket. The odd Kate flourish could be seen in the colourful prints on the walls, and plaid throws on the bed and armchair.

"The bathroom's lovely," said Maddie, poking her head in.

"Thanks. You're my first guest, so you can test out the facilities and let me know what you think. Now, the most important question... beer or wine?"

Maddie looked at her watch. "It's not even twelve yet! Wine, please."

*

"Seriously though, Kate, you've done an amazing job here."

The two friends had been settled on the purple sofas for a couple of hours, and were finishing the dregs of a bottle of Sauvignon Kate bought for the occasion.

"Thanks, it's been a lot of work, but Bob's been a great help."

"Bob?" asked Maddie, wiggling an eyebrow.

"Oh no, nothing like that. He's way older than me, weirdly under the thumb of his mother, and has a beer belly."

"Beer belly...hubba-hubba..." said Maddie, wiggling both eyebrows in her classic party trick.

Kate threw a cushion at her and shared the last dribbles of wine between their glasses. "He's been a good friend. In fact, he's my only friend."

"You need to get out more."

"I know, and I will. Now that the house is sorted, I'll have more time."

"Has it cost a bomb?"

"No, not really. The boiler and bathroom were expensive, but I got all the furniture second hand. I've got enough cash left over to see me through a year if I'm careful, six months if I'm not."

Kate had a talent for being thrifty. That's what happened when you grew up the way she had, searching for food in the cupboards and only finding bottles of vodka.

The school had known her situation and without the free school breakfasts and lunches, she probably would've starved. Kate still burned with the shame of relying on other people's kindness and determined never to be in that position again.

"So, what are we doing tonight?" asked Maddie, chucking the last of her wine down her neck.

"I thought maybe we could go for a drink at the local, then come home and watch a film?"

"You're serious, aren't you? Bloody hell, Kate, doesn't this town have any clubs?"

"Maddie, we're thirty-year-old women. We're too old for clubbing."

"We'll never be too old for clubbing, dear," said Maddie, putting on her best old lady voice.

"I don't even know if there *is* a club."

"That's what our best friend Google's for," said Maddie, pulling out her phone.

*

"Seriously? That's what you're wearing?"

Maddie stood in front of Kate and did a twirl. "What's wrong with it?"

Kate couldn't find the words to describe how inappropriate Maddie's outfit was. Sparkling sequined hot pants, a neon green boob tube, and three-inch stilettos. "Have you looked out of a window lately? It's pouring with rain and blowing a gale."

"So?"

"So maybe you should wear something a little more... practical."

"Practical? Kate, we're going to a club, not on a hike."

Kate sighed, very much wishing she could choose the second of those options.

"Aren't you going to get changed?" Maddie asked, wandering through to the kitchen and grabbing a beer from the fridge.

"What do you mean? I am changed."

"You're going like that?"

Maddie seemed just as horrified with Kate's outfit as she had been with her friend's ensemble. "What's wrong with what I'm wearing?"

"What's wrong with it? You look like a nun!"

Kate moved over to the mirror. Until Maddie appeared like a glitter ball, she'd been pleased with how she looked. Admittedly, the black jeans had seen better days, but her cream floaty shirt was real silk, her best charity shop find to date. She'd managed to scrape her bobbed hair back into a ponytail, and had even gone to the trouble of applying eyeliner. "I like how I look."

"OK, fine, I'm not going to argue with you on my first night here. Come on, let's call a cab."

"It doesn't look far on Google maps. Why don't we walk?"

"In these?" asked Maddie, sticking a foot so high in the air Kate could see she wasn't wearing any knickers.

"All right, book a cab." Kate fancied a walk. Her head had been pounding since the wine at lunchtime and she'd hoped fresh air might work where ibuprofen so badly failed.

Maddie hadn't stopped with the wine. She'd moved to G&Ts as they'd sat flicking through magazines, then on to the beers Kate had bought for the weekend. There were only two left now, so she'd need to make another Sainsburys trip in the morning. Maddie's drinking worried Kate, but they'd spoken about it in the past and Maddie had assured her she only drank at weekends, so at least that was something.

A beeping horn signalled their taxi was waiting. Maddie tottered ahead of Kate and slurred instructions at the driver. She tried engaging him in conversation, but it was ten o'clock and he'd already had enough drunks bending his ear for one night. Unimpressed with the driver's monosyllabic answers, Maddie turned her attention to Kate.

"You know I met Alex for a drink last week."

"What?"

"Ooops, he told me not to say anything, silly me."

"What are you doing meeting Alex behind my back?"

"It's not like you have any claim over him anymore."

Kate stared at her friend. She'd forgotten how Maddie could get after a skin-full.

"Anyway," said Maddie in her annoying sulky voice, "he only wanted to talk about you."

"Me?"

"Yeah, seems things aren't quite as rosy with the boobalicious Jess as we'd thought. He said he missed you."

"Well, I don't miss him."

"You sure? From the looks of you, it's not like you intend to go out on the pull any time soon."

Kate stared out of the window. It would be a long night unless Maddie snapped out of the mood she'd got herself in. The only thing worse than being drunk, Kate decided, was being sober as a judge and out with people who weren't.

The taxi arrived at the club all too soon. Kate resented paying the driver for what would have been a twenty-minute walk in sensible shoes, but handed over the cash and even left a tip, as she felt sorry for him. Maddie fell out of the taxi and Kate rushed round to her side to help her up.

"Look Maddie, are you sure you're up for this? We can go back home for you to sleep it off if you'd prefer?"

"Don't be stupid. Let's go. Woohoo!"

Maddie had her arms in the air, dancing to the music barely dampened by the club's stone walls. Kate prayed the bouncers would view Maddie as too inebriated to be let in, but one look at her skimpy outfit and they let her in without even taking the entrance fee. Kate had no such luck, shelling out again for a night out she really didn't want to be on.

Kate stepped into the club and immediately wanted to run away. All five senses were assaulted in that first thirty seconds. She could barely breathe amongst the fug. Flashing neon lights tortured her head, the ache pounding in time with the too-loud bass. Her low-heeled boots stuck to the floor with every step, and the smell - oh the smell was the worst. She supported the smoking ban when it came in, despite being a smoker herself at the time. Now she wished she could smell stale cigarette smoke. It would be a vast improvement to the combination of beer, sweat and vomit that filled her nostrils.

Kate looked round for Maddie, eventually spotting her in the middle of the dance floor, surrounded by sweaty men in shiny shirts. Was she twerking? Kate flushed on Maddie's behalf. She wondered if she should intervene, as Maddie rubbed her bum against an acne ridden teenage boy, but she decided any intervention would be unwelcome. The club was heaving with bodies. Kate pushed her way through the throng and found herself a place to sit in the corner of the room. She had a feeling it was going to be a long night.

Chapter 9

Kate put her head in her hands. She could have sobbed there and then, on the sticky red sofa that smelled of puke. She wondered if her head might actually explode. Each beat of the bass line stabbed at her brain like a knife. Things turned from bad to worse. The whole club had their arms in the air, jumping up and down, singing 'Yellow Submarine' at the top of their voices. All the incredible Beatles songs the DJ could've picked, and he'd chosen the only one Kate couldn't stand. For a moment, Kate wondered if she'd died and gone to hell.

"Kate? Kate!"

Was someone calling her name? Kate lifted her head up and saw a swaying man in front of her. She saw the polished shoes first, then the tailored trousers, pressed shirt, and braces. "Bob? What are you doing here?"

"What?" he shouted. "Can't hear you!"

"Let's go outside."

"What?"

"Let's go..." Kate gave up trying to shout above the racket and grabbed Bob's arm, weaving him through the throbbing mass of bodies towards the exit. Out in the fresh air, she took a large gulp of air. Beside her a couple were leaning against the wall. If the bloke tried to stick his tongue any further down the girl's throat, he might get stuck in there. She pulled Bob further away from the building till she could hear herself think.

"Bob, what are you doing here? I didn't have you down as a clubber?"

"Not a clubber," he slurred. "Colleague's stag do. Had to come. Didn't want..."

"Bob, are you OK?"

Bob had turned an alarming shade of grey, sweat beading his brow as he began to shake.

"Bob?"

Bob held up a hand to stop Kate from talking. Next thing she knew, he'd disappeared behind a bin. The bin was too small to hide such a large man, and Kate watched his shoulders heaving up and down as he brought up whatever vile booze he'd consumed that evening. When he was done, he leaned against a wall, wiping his mouth on his expensive shirt sleeve.

"Sorry about that," he said, giving her a weak smile as he staggered over.

"Don't worry about it, happens to the best of us." Actually, Kate thought, it didn't happen to her. Only once, and that was when she'd been spiked.

"Need to get home."

"I don't think you're in a fit state to be going anywhere. Come back to mine. You can sleep on the sofa."

"Thanks, Kate, you're an angel."

"Hmm, I'm not sure about that. Let me try calling Maddie. I don't want to leave her on her own in there." Kate thought it unlikely Maddie would hear her phone ringing, but if she could avoid going back into that sweat pit, she'd try anything. She took her phone out of her bag and saw three missed calls and a text from Maddie.

Met someone. B hme latr. By xxxxxxxxxxxxxxxcccxxxccc

Kate took a deep breath. The message had been sent an hour ago. So Maddie had left her for the sake of some bloke.

She could have got a decent night's sleep after all, rather than sitting in the corner of a club like some loser, waiting for a friend who wasn't even there.

Kate turned her attention back to Bob. "Come on," she said, "put an arm round me. You seem a bit unsteady on your feet."

Bob's arm was surprisingly heavy. Kate felt like a walking stick as he leaned his whole weight on her. She had to practically drag him along the pavement to keep him moving. As they waited to cross a road, he bent over to kiss her cheek, but missed, nearly choking on a mouthful of hair. Kate was grateful for her sensible boots as they trudged their way along the high street. It was busy on the main street, groups of girls staggering arm in arm, a gaggle of teenage boys half hidden inside a shop doorway.

At her front door, Kate propped Bob up against the wall and fished her keys out of her pocket. Thank goodness she'd given Maddie a spare, or she'd have to wait up for her.

"Come on, in you come." Kate guided Bob up the front steps and to the purple sofa. She prayed he wouldn't throw up again. Purple velvet would be a nightmare to clean.

The arm of Bob's shirt was stained lime green where he'd wiped his mouth. Bob was already snoring away, but Kate carefully undid his shirt buttons and somehow managed to wriggle his arms out and roll him enough to get the shirt free. She avoided looking at him semi-naked and was glad she'd left the light off.

Kate fetched a bucket from the kitchen and placed it beside the sofa. She grabbed a throw from the spare sofa and tucked Bob into it as a mother would a child. Her body was screaming for sleep, but at least the fresh air had gone some way to ease the pain in her head. Back in the kitchen, Kate coated the arm of Bob's shirt with stain remover before putting it on a wash cycle. She let herself outside, brushed her teeth in the outside bathroom and flopped on her bed, falling asleep in seconds, her silk shirt creasing beneath her.

*

A large figure appeared at the end of Kate's bed and she let out a scream.

"Sorry, sorry, didn't mean to wake you, or scare you, for that matter. I'm just making my way to the facilities."

"Bob? Are you alright? What time is it?"

"Yes I'm fine thanks. It's eight thirty."

Kate flopped back against the pillow. She was known as an early riser, any time after seven counting as a lie in, but she was relieved she'd been able to get some sleep. She sat up again and smiled at Bob. "You go use the loo. I'll get a pot of coffee going."

"You're an angel."

Kate laughed. "You said the same last night."

"I did? Oh." Bob shuffled out of the room, blushing as he went.

Kate got up and pulled her dressing gown on. Shit. Maddie. She had no idea if she'd made it home or not. With her feet slipped into a pair of thick socks, Kate crept up the stairs. If Maddie was home, she'd need her sleep, and Kate knew from experience how grumpy she was if she didn't get enough of it. Kate tiptoed along the landing and gave the bedroom door a gentle nudge. She breathed a sigh of relief to see Maddie comatose on top of the duvet, still in the clothes from the night before. She breathed a second sigh of relief to see she was alone in the bed. At least she'd not brought a random man home with her. Kate closed the door with a quiet click and headed back downstairs.

With the coffee brewed, Kate poured out two cups and took them to her new table and chairs in the yard. It was a cold morning, but the sun was shining for a change, and she decided Bob could probably do with a bit of fresh air. She'd just settled herself down when a sheepish-looking Bob emerged from the outhouse. He was topless, and Kate flushed as he caught her looking. Bob wrapped his arms around himself and shivered.

“I thought some fresh air would do us some good. Here,” she said, holding out a blanket.

“Cheers,” said Bob, sitting himself down and wrapping the blanket around himself.

“How are you feeling?”

“As rough as a badger’s bum.”

“That’s a new one on me,” laughed Kate, sipping her coffee. “If you need a toothbrush, there’s a spare new one in the basket by the sink.”

“I already found it. Sorry, I should have asked, but I’ll replace it today.”

“Oh, don’t worry about that. I’d say you need a quiet day of sleep and a Netflix box set.”

“Look, Kate, I’m really sorry about last night. I’m not usually like that. I hope I didn’t say… or do anything too embarrassing?”

“You don’t remember what happened?”

“I don’t remember leaving the club at all. I had no idea where I was when I woke up this morning.”

“I don’t know how to tell you but…” Kate looked at the horrified expression on Bob’s face and decided he was too fragile for teasing. “Don’t worry, I’m just messing. Apart from calling me an angel, you didn’t say anything at all. In fact, I’m sure I heard a snore as we were walking up the high street. I’ve never seen anyone sleep-walk before.”

“That’s such a relief. It’s the first time I’ve ever blacked out, you know. A bloody terrifying experience I never want to repeat.”

“Oh, I forgot, you were sick. That’s why you don’t have a shirt. I’ve washed it and it’s in the tumble dryer. Shouldn’t be long till it’s done.”

“Thanks, I’m sorry you had to deal with that.”

“No problem. You said it was a stag do?”

“Yeah, a bloke from work. I hate stag do’s and I don’t even like the bloke, but felt I should show my face. The plan was to go for a quick pint, then slip away home. Then they started plying me with shots and the rest, as they say, is history."

"Ah well, we live and learn."

"What about you? How come you were there? I didn't have you down as the clubbing sort, either."

"I'm not, but unfortunately my friend is. Remember I said Maddie was coming to stay? She decided we should go out, though I lost her after five minutes and spent most of the night sitting on my own."

"Did she make it home all right?"

"Yeah, I've been up to check on her and... oh, speak of the devil."

A crumpled, wan looking Maddie appeared from the kitchen. Her hair was sticking up, clumped together in places by God knows what. She still had on her makeup from the night before, but her mascara had smudged around her eyes and she looked rather scary.

"Come and sit down," said Kate. "I'll grab you a cup and you can get some coffee down you."

Maddie downed her coffee in three gulps. "I needed that."

"So, come on, spill the beans. What happened to you last night?"

Maddie groaned. "I'm such an idiot. You know that bloke I was dancing with?"

"Not the spotty teenager?"

Maddie groaned again and put her head in her hands. "He was twenty actually, but yes, him. We hit it off and got a bit frisky. I stupidly went back to his, but by then I'd sobered up enough to know I was making a terrible mistake. He smelt gross too."

Kate laughed. "I think most of the people in there smelt gross."

"No, not sweaty beery gross... a sort of raw meat kind of gross."

"Raw meat?"

"Yeah, I remember him saying he works making pasties...Ginsters, I think he said. Hopefully that explains the smell."

"If you'd said he works for any of the local pasty makers, I'd tell you he's a keeper, but Ginsters? You're well rid." Bob took a sip of his coffee and grinned at Maddie.

"Sorry," said Maddie, looking confused as if she'd just noticed there was someone else sitting at the table. "Who are you?"

"Bob. Pleased to meet you," he said, holding out his hand for Maddie to shake.

Chapter 10

Kate plumped up the pillows for the hundredth time that day and straightened the already straight handmade soaps lying on the new fluffy towels. The first guests were due to arrive in a few hours, and she wasn't sure what to do with herself in the meantime. Maddie and Bob had helped her list the house online over the weekend. They'd made a good team once Maddie's hangover subsided, and she got used to finding a strange, half-naked man in Kate's garden.

Bob insisted on cooking them breakfast before he left, despite his fragile state. After a plate of bacon, sausage and eggs, Maddie declared him her new best friend and tried to persuade Kate to let her move in so she could be closer to Bob. If she hadn't known Maddie was joking, she would've been worried; no way could she keep up with Maddie's lifestyle of work-hard, play-hard. Kate didn't mind the working, it was the playing she struggled with.

Kate gave the bathroom another glance over. Spiders were sneaky beasts and it would be just her luck for one to whip up a web in the hours before the guests arrived. Next, she moved through to the guest sitting room. The flowers on the table were giving off a beautiful scent. Glass jars were filled with ground coffee, a choice of teas and luxury biscuits. It was impressive, but Kate knew she'd have to find a way to cut her costs if she was ever to make a profit.

The hands on her watch ticked slowly round, still two

hours to go. If she went round the house checking again, she was more likely to make a mess than find one. Instead, Kate settled herself in her room and flicked through film options on her laptop. It would have to be a comedy. She didn't want a tear jerker and the guests arriving to a red eyed emotional wreck of a host.

Five minutes into the film, her phone pinged with a message-

Hope it goes well with the guests. Thinking of you x

Thanks, I'll let you know how it goes x she replied.

Kate smiled at the message. Bob was a sweetie, like a giant teddy bear. She didn't feel he'd completely opened up to her yet, though. It was true he'd been very open about his past and he had no qualms talking about his dead wife, but she still knew very little about his current life. She had half expected he might invite her round one day. After all, he'd been to her place often enough, but the invite never came. And every time she asked after his parents, he brushed away the questions, changing the subject as quickly as was polite.

Kate checked the sound was up on her phone in case the guests called and settled herself down for ninety minutes of escapism. She realised within the first ten minutes that *We Bought A Zoo* was a risky choice, but it was too late. She was hooked. Before long, a pile of sodden tissues lay beside her and her nose was red from all the blowing. Kate checked her watch. Still another hour before they arrived. That left plenty of time to paint concealer around her puffy red eyes.

A knock came on her bedroom door and Kate froze. Someone was in the house. She paused the film and grabbed the nearest weapon. A hairbrush was an unlikely weapon against intruders, but it was the best she could do, and who knows what damage those bristles could inflict? Sitting on the bed seemed a vulnerable position, so she raised herself to standing and tried to still the shake in her legs.

"Hello? Who's there?"

The door opened and an auburn head poked around it.

"Are you Kate?"

"Yes. Who are you? What are you doing in my house?"

"I'm Sarah, your guest. This is Mark." Sarah pushed the door open wider to reveal a scrawny-looking boy with glasses. Sarah, in contrast, was ruddy and well built. They reminded her of Jack Sprat and his wife.

"Oh, oh, hi, nice to meet you." Kate dropped the hairbrush onto the bed and rushed forward with an outstretched hand. Sarah gave it a hearty shake. Mark's hand felt cold and damp, like a limp fish.

"We knocked and rang the bell, but there was no answer."

"Oh, God, I'm so sorry. Have you been waiting out there long?"

"Fifteen minutes" "Five minutes" said Sarah and Mark simultaneously. Kate noticed Sarah jab her partner in the ribs before giving a hearty laugh. "Let's meet in the middle and say ten." She grinned at Kate, who struggled to take her eyes off Mark as he rubbed at his elbow-dented ribs.

"Well, I can only apologise. I'll have to get the doorbell checked. I'll show you to your room. Do you have much luggage? I can take it for you if you like?"

Kate knew she was babbling, but couldn't stop the verbal diarrhoea. Sarah insisted they didn't need help with their luggage, before handing both backpacks to Mark. They were almost as big as him, and Kate was worried he'd topple backwards as he wrestled them up the stairs. Sarah and Mark were hard to read, but seemed happy enough with their accommodation and Kate left them to settle in, instructing them to find her if there was anything they needed.

Kate returned to her position on the bed and tried to get back to the film. Above her, she could hear every footstep and the sound of voices, or one voice to be precise. It had taken all of thirty seconds to see who wore the trousers in that relationship. A thud came through the ceiling as bags were plonked on the floor. It was a strange feeling, knowing strangers were just upstairs. Kate felt like she was eavesdropping on them, an intruder in her own home. She gave up on the film, clicking the laptop shut. Perhaps in the kitchen she'd feel more at home.

Kate was making herself a cup of tea when Mark appeared like a shadow in the doorway.

"Um, hi. Sarah asked if you've got a key for us? And if you can recommend anywhere to have dinner?"

"Oh, sorry. I'll grab the keys. I totally forgot."

"No problem," said Mark, pressing himself against the wall to let Kate pass.

Kate handed him the keys and ran him through the selection of pubs and restaurants in town.

"Thanks, and, ah, in your experience, which, ah, is the best, ah, value for money. And ah, do they have gluten-free options? Sarah's trying to stay off wheat. Sorry." Mark stood wringing his hands, his face a deep shade of red. Kate wasn't used to people being ill at ease in her company. The poor chap looked as though he'd been sent into the lion's den.

"Well, I've not actually lived here that long myself, so I've not had time to try many of the restaurants. Tell you what, I'll give my friend a call. He's a local, lived here most of his life. I'll pop up and see you when he's given me some more info."

"Thank you. Ah, one last thing, um, Sarah wondered if, um, you had any extra, um, towels?"

"Oh, sorry, I thought I'd left them on the bed?"

"Um, you did, yes, um, but she likes to have one for the upstairs and one for the, um, downstairs." Mark flushed furiously as he indicated precisely what he meant by upstairs and downstairs.

"Oh, OK, no problem. I'll bring some extras up when

I've got the restaurant info. Should only be a few minutes."

"Great, thanks," said Mark, shuffling out of the kitchen and up to the guest quarters.

Kate grabbed her phone and was just letting herself out into the garden when Mark appeared at her shoulder once more.

"Um, sorry to bother you again, but do you have the code for the Wi-Fi?"

"Yes, sure." Kate scribbled the code onto a piece of scrap paper and indicated to the garden. "Back in a mo, I get a better signal out there."

Mark gave her a shy smile and made his retreat upstairs. Kate swore her way up to the top of the garden. She prayed Bob had his phone on him and could help her out. She did a little victory dance after he answered on the second ring.

"Hi, you alright?"

Kate groaned. "What have I done? Bob, I'm so unprepared. I thought I'd got everything ready but I forgot to give them keys, and the Wi-Fi code. I didn't even hear the door, they just let themselves in. They appeared outside my bedroom. Now they're asking about value for money places to eat and gluten free options and I really don't know what I'm doing. Help me!"

"Kate, calm down. Let's go through this one step at the time. Do they have keys and the Wi-Fi code?"

"Yes."

"Good. Are they pleased with their room?"

"Yes, once they'd got towels specifically for their genitals."

"Sorry, what?"

"Doesn't matter. Look, do you know anything about the restaurants or pubs in town? I don't have a clue."

Bob ran off a list of every eatery in town, good and bad points, those that had veggie options, those that catered for food allergies, those whose hygiene ratings were a lie and best avoided.

"Wow, I never knew there were so many places to eat here. Look, can you WhatsApp me the list ASAP? I don't have anything to write with out here."

"Where are you?"

"In the garden. I made an excuse about signal to come out here, which is sort of true except I could've FaceTimed you. I think I've made an error with the exposed floorboards. I can hear everything they're doing through the ceiling. I could probably hear their conversations if I listened carefully enough. And that means they can also hear me, hence why I'm stood outside in the rain, talking to you."

"Ah. Right, well, you get yourself back indoors and I'll send you the restaurant pros and cons straight away."

"Thanks."

Kate hung up, took a few deep, calming breaths and made her way inside. She was seriously doubting the wisdom of opening her home to strangers. *Teething problems*, she told herself, copying out Bob's list of eateries onto a piece of paper, before searching for another two towels among the clean laundry. Mark was standing at the kitchenette, making two cups of tea. He gave Kate a shy smile and when she offered him the towels and list, suggested he pass them directly to 'the boss'. Kate assumed he meant Sarah, who, when she entered the bedroom, was sprawled out on the bed, book in hand.

"Oh, thanks, that's great."

"No problem. Anything else you need?"

"No, I think that's all for now. I'll send Mark down again if there's anything else that crops up."

I bet you will, thought Kate, marvelling at the dynamics of some relationships. She pitied poor Mark, being bossed around like a skivvy. Worse than the pity though, was recognition. She'd never been like him, had she?

Chapter 11

Mark placed the steaming cup of coffee down on the table beside his fiancée.

"Well, that was a poor night's sleep," said Sarah, taking a sip of her coffee. She promptly spat it out over Kate's new M&S bedding. "For goodness' sake, Mark you could've told me it was that hot. I've only gone and burned my mouth. Can you fetch me a water please?"

"Sure, have some of mine."

"No thanks, fresh please," said Sarah, handing him her glass. Mark got up once more and filled her cup from the tap in the bathroom.

"You did run it till it was properly cold, didn't you? I hate it when it's luke warm."

"Thanks, Mark," Mark muttered under his breath.

"What did you say? I didn't catch that."

"I said yes, dear, I ran the tap till it was cold."

"Good."

"How come you didn't sleep too well?"

"It's this bed," said Sarah, staring at him open-mouthed as if the answer was obvious. "Didn't you notice how hard the mattress is?"

"I thought it was very comfortable." Mark hadn't slept well either, but it was nothing to do with the mattress. Sarah had been snoring like a rhinoceros most of the night, whatever claims she made about insomnia.

"I don't get this modern obsession with mattresses like rocks. I've never slept as well as I did when I lived with Mum. She knows a good mattress when she sees one."

Mark thought of his soon to be mother-in-law's house, all frilly curtains and squishy beds. The heating was on all year and the coffin sized bed he was made to sleep in gave him a bad back every time. Sarah was still talking, and Mark tuned back in time to hear the words *bad review*.

"You're not going to leave her a bad review, are you? What about all the extras; coffee, soaps? She went to a lot of trouble to recommend where to eat and find the extra towels. I'd say she deserves five stars."

Sarah wasn't pleased he'd offered an opinion, and Mark tuned out as she listed all the reasons why a three star review would be generous. He resolved to leave the review himself before Sarah got the chance. The thought of the small defiance made him smile, and his thin chest puffed out a little.

"What are you smiling at?"

"Nothing, dear." Mark realised his jaw was so tight it was beginning to hurt. Had he been grinding his teeth again in the night? He wished they'd not fallen into the habit of calling each other *dear*. It reminded him of his grandparents. "I wondered if you'd like to visit Bodmin Jail today? I've read some reviews. It sounds great."

"You leave the activities to me, dear. You know what you're like. Remember Ibiza?"

Not this again, thought Mark, his jaw clenching up once more. Ibiza was their first trip away together, to the quiet side of the island, obviously. He'd tried to take the initiative and booked a wine tasting event, only it had turned out to be more of an eighteen to thirties pub crawl and he'd never been allowed to forget his mistake.

"We'll go on a bike ride today, take a little ride along the trail they've made from the old railway line. Then a pub lunch, a wander round the town, then catch the train down to St Ives at five."

"We don't have our bikes, though."

Sarah sighed in a *do I have to think of everything* sort of way. "We'll hire them, obvs. Shouldn't cost much for a couple of hours." She grabbed a handful of clothes and disappeared into the bathroom to dress in privacy. Mark couldn't understand why. It wasn't like he'd not seen her naked before. Mind you, those occasions were few and far between, his mind trawling back through the previous four months before he settled on a memory of sex.

It had been Sarah's idea to come to Cornwall, and Sarah's idea to stop off in Bodmin. *Break the journey,* she'd said, though Mark would have been happy to head straight down west. If he were honest, he'd have preferred the Lake District, but that idea had been poo-pooed, just like all his others. Before heading off on their holidays, he'd been made to endure Sunday lunch with Sarah's parents. He tried his best with Frank, Sarah's dad, but the poor bloke was a shell of a man, flinching every time his wife Margaret barked orders at him. He could barely hold a conversation and seemed to have no interest in anything other than pleasing his wife. 'Happy wife, happy life', he'd muttered as he got up on an errand for the hundredth time in the two hours they were there.

Sarah came back into the room looking the spitting image of her mother. "What do you think?" she asked, doing a twirl. "Mum was going to take these to the charity shop, but they've got plenty of life in them yet. She gave me one of Dad's shirts for you. Want to try it on?"

"Um, it may not be the best choice for cycling," Mark said, wrapping his arms round himself to protect his faded Hitchhiker's Guide T-shirt from being forcibly withdrawn.

"No, you're probably right. You can wear it tonight when we go out for dinner."

"Great."

“Can you go downstairs and ask the woman about leaving our bags here?”

Mark inwardly sighed, then made his way back downstairs. He paused outside the door to their host’s quarters. He felt awkward disturbing her yet again. This must be at least the fifth time he’d been to see her. At this rate, she’d start to think he had a thing for her. He knocked quietly and waited for the woman to appear.

“Just a sec,” Kate called through the door. She appeared moments later in a dressing-gown, a towel wrapped round her wet hair. Mark blushed, feeling like a perv despite the greying dressing-gown being the least attractive thing she could be wearing.

“Hi, um, we were wondering if, um, it would be OK to leave our bags here, um, just for a few hours while we go for a bike ride?”

“Oh, OK. Yes, sure. Do you know roughly when you’ll be back for them?”

“Our train is at five, so four at the latest.”

“OK, well I may be out, so hang on to your keys, then leave them on the coffee table once you’ve collected your bags. That OK for a plan?”

“Yes, thank you so much.”

Kate smiled at him and closed the door. Mark was sure he heard her whisper *bugger* as the door clicked to, but he could’ve been imagining it.

*

“Hurry up,” Sarah called as Mark chased after her, a ball of hot, sweaty effort compared to her unflappable resolve. He didn’t have her pegged as a decent cyclist. The only exercise she’d done in their two years together was running for a bus.

“Sorry,” said Mark when he finally caught up with her. “It’s... much... harder than... I thought.”

“Dear dear, I didn’t realise you were this unfit,” said Sarah, shaking her head. “You’ll have to do something about that when we get home. I need my man in prime condition."

For all the running around you make him do? Mark kept his thoughts to himself and plodded on behind her.

"You got a puncture, mate," yelled a portly Lycra-clad man as he whizzed past.

"Crap." Mark got off his bike and checked his tyres. Yep, there it was, the back wheel sagging with a lack of enthusiasm shared by Mark himself. He could see Sarah's back disappearing round a bend, and trotted along, bike in hands, trying to catch her up. He found her resting her bike against the fence of a small train station.

"What happened to you? I've been waiting ages!"

Mark checked his watch. She couldn't have been there longer than five minutes. "Look, why don't you go back to the pub we passed and get a drink? I'll wait here and find someone to help me with this puncture, then come and join you."

"How long will you be?"

Mark sighed. "I don't know, Sarah, as long as it takes?"

"No need to snap," said Sarah, retrieving her bike and heading off down the path with a curious backwards glance.

Mark gave the useless bike a kick. What had got into him today? He stopped a couple of blokes who, if their outfits were anything to go by, looked like they knew their way around a bike. They pored over the tyre, muttering to themselves. Eventually, after prodding, poking and spinning the wheel round hundreds of times, they stood up.

"Sorry mate, in my expert opinion, that tyre's screwed."

"You mean it can't be fixed?"

"No, needs a new inner tube. Sorry, buddy. Hope it's not too far home."

Mark shouted a thank you as they sped off. The thought of returning to Sarah with an unfixable bike was as tempting as sitting down in the patch of nettles beside him. Mark turned to look at the train. He couldn't, could he? He jumped over the fence and jogged over to a man in a smart blue uniform, whistle in hand.

"Um, excuse me. Where does this train go?"

"It's the end of the line, sir. It's turning back to Bodmin Parkway now."

"Could I buy a ticket, please?"

"You'll need the conductor for that. If you hop on, he should be around shortly."

"Thanks."

Mark paused at the door, feeling the slightest pang of guilt, but not enough to stop him climbing up and pulling the door shut behind him. A whistle blew and plumes of steamy smoke filled the air around him. There was a lightness to his body that Mark hadn't felt for a long time. He laughed, quiet chuckles at first, followed by loud, shoulder shaking guffaws. The woman across the aisle held her child close, throwing a worried look his way. He mouthed *sorry* to her and pulled himself together. Thank goodness he'd got his shoulder bag with him. Mark pulled out his phone, typed a short message, then as soon as it read *sent*, switched his phone off, closed his eyes, and smiled.

*

Sarah tapped her fingers against the wooden picnic bench. She wasn't one for daytime drinking, but as the minutes clocked up to sixty, her resolve broke and she ordered a large glass of wine. Twenty minutes later, the wineglass was empty and the tapping fingers had been joined by jiggling legs. Where had he got to? Sarah checked her phone for the umpteenth time, but no matter how high she raised it above her head, she couldn't find a single bar of signal.

Sarah sighed and collected her bike, cursing Mark and his stupidity under her breath. She pushed the bike through the car park and down a steep slope. A family was coming the other way, but Sarah pressed on, hearing *bitch* from a teenage boy as she forced them to press into the bush on the side of the narrow path.

Half a mile down the track, Sarah's phone burst into life, the jangle of a message tone nurturing both relief and annoyance. What scrape had he got himself into this time? Sarah unlocked her phone and read the message. She read it again, and again, wondering if it was a practical joke.

I've left on the train. Going back to London. You'll need to collect my bike from the station nearest the pub. Enjoy your time away. Please don't contact me again. Mark.

Both phone and bike fell from Sarah's hands, the pedals tearing a line of red into her skin as they dropped to the ground. This had to be a joke. With shaking hands, Sarah picked her phone out of the mud and dialled Mark's number. *I'm sorry, but the person you have called is unavailable. Please try again later.*

Chapter 12

Kate was finishing up cleaning the bathroom when a knock came at the door. Her watch showed six o'clock. About time, she thought, trotting down the stairs. She was ready for an apology. All day she'd been waiting for them to come and get their bags. They had a key, but the thought of strangers letting themselves in when she wasn't there didn't sit well and as a result, she'd been waiting in all day.

Kate opened the door to a dishevelled looking Sarah.

"I'm here for the bags," said Sarah, her voice an angry slur.

"Yes, sure, come in. Did you miss your train? I thought it was leaving at five?"

"Bastard got the train himself. Left me to pick up his shitting clothes in his shitting bag."

"Sorry, I don't understand. Has something happened?"

"None of your business," said Sarah, trying to heave both bags onto her back, stumbling and falling into the coffee table.

"Woah, careful there. It looks like you could do with a coffee?"

Sarah sniffed and nodded her head. The heavy bags seemed to take the fight out of her, and she plonked herself down on the sofa, head in her hands. "Milk, two sugars, and not too strong," she managed to mumble.

"Right, back in a mo."

The woman was obviously distressed, and as Kate stirred the coffee, she tried to guess what could have happened. Whatever it was, it hadn't stopped Sarah being the most demanding guest she'd encountered over her many years in hospitality. They weren't even like that at The Sunbeam, and Kate had thought those guests were the dregs of the British tourist industry.

"Here you go," said Kate, laying a mug of coffee down beside Sarah. "Would you like to talk about it?"

Sarah shook her head. She picked up her coffee, blew across the top, took a sip, then grimaced.

"Do you need me to call you a taxi?" Kate asked, praying the answer would be yes.

Sarah looked up at her, confused. "A taxi? To where?"

"To the station. I thought you were headed for St Ives?"

"Missed the train."

"Yes, I realise that, but there must be others. Would you like me to check?"

Sarah nodded, and Kate began searching train times on her phone. The two women sat in silence, the only sound Kate's fingers tapping her phone, and Sarah taking small sips from her mug.

"OK, it looks like there's another train in an hour. Is your partner waiting somewhere nearby? You probably need to text him to let him know, or you'll miss the next one, too."

"He's gone."

"Pardon?"

"I said he'd gone."

Sarah looked up, her eyes swimming in tears. The bravado was gone, and in its place Kate saw a vulnerability that tugged at her empathy.

"What happened?" Kate asked, sitting down beside Sarah and placing a hand on her arm.

"He left me. Right there on the Camel Trail. Got on a train and headed back to London. Bastard."

"Oh dear, that sounds a mean thing to do. Had you had a falling out?"

Sarah looked at Kate in surprise. "No? Why would we have fallen out?"

"Sorry, um, it's just there must have been a reason for him leaving?"

Sarah dug her phone from her pocket and showed Kate Mark's message.

"Shit. That's pretty brutal. And he didn't say why he'd gone?"

"No."

Here they come, thought Kate, as one fat tear trickled down Sarah's face. One was followed by another, and another, until Kate had Sarah held in her arms, sobbing like a baby. At first they were angry tears, directed solely at Mark. According to Sarah, he'd been a wet blanket, fun straw, crap at conversation, crap in bed, crap at cooking, crap at everything if Sarah was to be believed. The angry tears were followed by self-pity. What had Sarah ever done to deserve such treatment?

Sarah's tears stopped abruptly. She blew her nose loudly, throwing her used tissue on the floor, and looked Kate square in the eyes. "What do you think?"

"Me? I only met you both yesterday. I don't think I'm qualified to give an opinion."

"But you must have formed one. Everyone is judgmental to some degree. Did he come across as an arsewipe to you?"

"Um, not that I could tell?"

This was clearly the wrong answer, as Sarah huffed and folded her arms tight around herself. "So if he didn't seem like an arsewipe, how did he come across?"

"Well..." Kate realised she would need to choose her words carefully. "He seemed rather devoted, if I'm honest.

He kept running errands for you and didn't once complain."

"Why should he complain? What's wrong with asking him to do stuff for me?"

"Nothing... it's just I've not met many men who would be so..." Kate wanted to say hen pecked, but felt this may not go down well. "So... obliging."

Sarah humphed and glared at Kate. "So you think it's my fault he left me?"

"I didn't say that."

"You implied it."

"Look, Sarah, you asked for my opinion. I told you I wasn't qualified to give one, but you insisted. Don't shoot the messenger."

Sarah looked up at the ceiling. Kate wondered if the tears were about to resurface, but instead she took a deep breath and launched into a rant.

"My mum says you need to put men in their place, let them know who's boss. It's worked for her. She's been married thirty-eight years. I don't hear my dad complaining. No, Mark just wasn't man enough. That's the problem. Do you know he left his bike for me to take back? Imagine that! Ha! He toddles off on his steam train and there's me, looking a right loser, wheeling two hire bikes for miles back to Bodmin. What kind of a man does that to his woman? Plus, he'd got a puncture, so I had to explain that to the hire guy, who made me pay extra. I'll be sending Mark a bill for that, I promise you. Men are useless, spineless creeps. I'd be better off a lesbian."

Kate breathed a sigh of relief when Sarah finally stopped to take a breath. She discreetly checked her watch, and could've hugged the taxi driver as he sounded his horn outside on the road.

"I think your taxi's here. I'm sorry how things have turned out for you. Hopefully, you can salvage something from the holiday. Time alone may help you reflect on what went wrong."

"What went wrong was that I trusted that sly bastard."

"OK, well, um, yes, that may be true. Do you need a hand with your bags?"

Kate would've happily carried the bags all the way to Bodmin Parkway if it meant getting her house back any time soon.

"Yes," said Sarah, handing Kate both enormous backpacks.

Kate wobbled her way to the taxi. The driver leaped out when he saw Kate struggling and helped her deposit both bags into the boot of the car.

"What will you do with Mark's bag?" Kate asked, as Sarah climbed into the car.

"Leave it on the train."

"Right, OK. Well, have a good journey."

Kate slammed the door and waved the taxi off. As soon as they were out of sight, she went back in the house and opened a beer. What a day. It was horrible seeing someone so upset, yet she couldn't help rooting for Mark. It took a lot of guts to stand up to a bully, and Kate was in no doubt that Sarah was a bully. It was possible she didn't realise, but Kate had seen how nervy and anxious Mark had been. No one should be made to feel like that in a relationship.

Kate thought back to her own dating history. There'd been a couple of boys at school she'd gone out with briefly, but Alex was the only one who fell into serious relationship territory. He'd treated her well, hadn't he?

A niggling doubt crept over Kate as she remembered the first time she'd introduced Alex to her friends. That was in the days when Kate had a large social circle and plenty of people vying for the 'best friend' category. She'd been nervous to introduce Alex into the group, but certain that when they got to know him, they'd all love him as much as she did. He'd been OK with the women, but not the blokes. That was unfortunate as Kate had plenty of male friends, all of whom showed her a brotherly protectiveness.

A long buried memory came flooding back. Two men fighting. One had been Alex, but who was the second man? Oh yes, Tom, who she sat next to in lectures. Kate couldn't remember how the fight had started, but was sure it had something to do with her. Tom could be brittle on the outside, and happy to disagree with anyone he could to cause a bit of friction. No wonder Alex had been pissed off with him. After the fight, she'd taken Alex home to her place and nursed his wounds. He'd made her promise not to talk to Tom again, and consequently, all her other male friends had sided with Tom and given her a wide berth.

Alex had been open with her from the start about his own insecurities. He'd been in love with a girl from school. They planned to get engaged until she had cheated on him with his best friend. An experience like that was bound to make you wary. Kate enjoyed his possessive jealousy at first. Yes, it had been hard letting friends go, but if it was a choice, she'd always put Alex first. But over the years, her friendship group had been whittled down so much, Maddie and Flo were the only ones who'd stuck it out.

Now Kate thought about it, Alex had held onto plenty of his female friends. It hadn't been a problem at the time, but now, here she was living alone at thirty with only a handful of people she could call on. And there he was, in his beautiful Bath townhouse, a packed diary of social engagements and a new companion filling the void Kate had left. Had she been a mug? Not as much a mug as Mark. The thought brought some comfort, and Kate cracked open another beer and turned on the TV.

Chapter 13

What a joy it was to have a free Sunday morning. Kate had forgotten the luxury of it, having been rostered on at The Sunbeam every weekend she could remember. She woke early, made a coffee and crawled back into bed with her book. It was eleven before she got up to shower and face the day. Bob had texted the evening before and Kate gratefully accepted his offer of company.

Kate opened the door to Bob at twelve and took a double take at the jeans and polo shirt he was wearing.

"What happened to the suit and braces?" she asked, as he followed her through to the kitchen.

"It's the weekend."

Kate laughed. "I know, it's just weird seeing you in normal clothes. I'd begun to wonder if you slept in that suit."

Bob laughed and filled the kettle for her. "I was pretty young when I joined the firm. Needed to make myself look more middle-aged."

"Well, you certainly managed that."

Bob flicked Kate with a tea towel and she chucked a wet sponge at him in return.

"You make the coffee. I've got something for you in the car."

Bob reappeared moments later, carrying a full carrier

bag. "I thought you might need cheering up after your experience with those guests."

"Ah, that's sweet of you," said Kate, taking the bag. "I must admit I'm wondering what the hell I've let myself in for."

"It's just teething problems, don't worry."

"Oooh," said Kate, pulling a bottle of wine from the bag. "This doesn't look like an Aldi special. Oh, and there's mint Aero, that's my favourite chocolate in the world!"

"I know, Maddie told me."

"Hang on, what's this?" Kate pulled a beautiful hardback book from the bag. The cover was a blaze of exotic flowers and birds. She flicked through the blank pages and eyed Bob with curiosity. "Are you suggesting I take up journaling?"

"Ha, no. That's for your guests."

"The guests?"

"Yes, you're going to fill it with all the information they need. You can start with the boring stuff, Wi-Fi code, contact details etcetera etcetera, then give them tips about all the great things they can do round here. You know, places to eat, places to visit."

"But I don't know any of that stuff."

"And that's where I come in. Think of me as your local tour guide. We start today."

"Today?"

"Yep, I'm taking you for lunch. You'll need sensible shoes, it's a bit damp out there."

*

In hindsight, wellies were a bit over the top, Kate decided, as they strolled along the tarmacked path beside the old jail.

"That's on our list for next weekend," said Bob, pointing up to the sombre looking stone building.

Kate shivered. "It looks a bit depressing."

"Think yourself lucky. I was going to take you on an

overnight ghost tour, but I'm not sure they're running now the place has been done up. I'll ease you in with the museum, don't worry."

"Thanks."

They strolled on past a park that quickly gave way to woodland. A narrow stream trickled along beside them and squirrels chased between the trees, following them along the path. The track was busy, cyclists in Lycra whizzing past, couples walking dogs, runners sweating heavily, distracted by the airpods in their ears, young families waiting patiently as toddlers collected sticks and jumped in puddles. Several times Bob said a friendly *Hi, how are you?* to people they passed.

"You know everyone here," said Kate, after they'd stopped for a brief conversation with an older couple.

"Well, I still know quite a few people from when I was a kid, and now, as a solicitor, I deal with all sorts from the community."

"Is it weird knowing people's secrets?"

"It's not that exciting, I promise. If anything, I prefer the boring stuff. There's nothing worse than dealing with a divorce, that's the absolute pits. On the rare occasions I know less than flattering things about people, you'll be able to tell."

"How?"

"They'll very deliberately avoid my eye, pretending not to see me. More often than not, I wouldn't recognise them anyway, but they give themselves away."

"I'll have to look out for that," said Kate, stopping at a spot where the river widened enough to need stepping stones across it.

"I used to play here as a kid," said Bob. "Mum would bring me and my mates down here after school. There used to be a rope swing over the river. We always got wet, but Mum would just laugh. The other mums weren't quite so relaxed about the amount of washing it created."

“It must have been a lovely place to grow up.”

“Yeah, it was really. You never appreciate it when you’re young, though. And as a teenager, all you want to do is get away as fast as you can. Me and my friends used to come down here when we were in our teens and plan our escape.”

“Are many of them still around?”

“Nah, not really. Out of the six or seven in our group, a couple of them dropped out of school and have about ten kids between them, but I don’t see them anymore, not much in common these days. The others all left and never came back. Most went to London, one’s in Sydney and one works for a big oil company in Bahrain. We meet up at Christmas when they come back to visit their parents. What about you? Do you still see anyone from school?”

“No, I wasn’t exactly popular back then.” Kate grimaced as she remembered the lonely lunch hours and long routes back from school to avoid the bullies. “Funnily enough, not many people want to befriend the kid with nits who stinks.” Kate laughed to lighten the mood, but Bob was looking at her with a frown.

“That must have been tough.”

“It is what it is. Mum couldn’t look after me properly. It wasn’t her fault. It got a bit easier as I got older and could do my own washing, but reputations follow you, and by the time I got to secondary school, my card had been marked. Uni was different. No one knew me there so I could start afresh.”

“You’ve still got friends from your uni days?”

“Only Maddie. I fell in love in my second year, you know what it’s like, friends don’t seem as important all of a sudden. Then I dropped out just before finals and that sealed the deal where rocky friendships were concerned.”

“Why did you drop out?”

“Look, can we change the subject to something happier?”

"Well, here's the turn off to the pub. Saved by the beer."

"I think you mean bell, but I'll take it."

Bob led Kate up a steep slope, through a large car park and into a quaint old pub, complete with roaring fire and the smell of roast beef. The pub was busy, but they arrived just as a couple were leaving and managed to secure two armchairs by the fire.

"I hope you're taking notes for your guest book," said Bob, laying two pints down on the table.

"I'm taking plenty of mental notes. I'll write it all up later."

"Good. So how am I doing on my first day of tour-guiding?"

"Six out of ten."

"Six? Why only six?"

"Well, I reckon if you went and got us a plate of roast dinner from the carvery, your score would suddenly climb higher."

"Haha, your wish is my command."

"I don't like sprouts," Kate called to Bob's departing back.

"I know, Maddie told me," he called back, raising his hand in the air with a thumbs up.

Bloody Maddie, thought Kate as she snuggled into the armchair, pint in hand. *Was there anything she hadn't told Bob?* The warmth of the fire made her sleepy and her eyelids were drooping heavily by the time Bob returned with loaded plates.

"Wow, that's a lot of food. Consider your tour-guiding score raised to a ten."

"Why thank you, madam," he said, giving a little bow. "So, when are you next guests arriving?"

"Guest, singular. She's coming on Wednesday. It was a good idea to start in low season, I don't think I could cope with having guests back to back."

"Did the last guests leave a review?"

"Yes, I have a feeling the chap, Mark, left it. It was a rave five stars and I can't see the woman ever giving me that."

"Well, that's a great start. You'll have bookings flooding in before you know it."

"I'm happy for a trickle at the moment. It still feels a bit weird having other people in the house."

"You'll get used to it, and you know you can always call if there's trouble."

"Thanks. You've been a really good friend since I arrived here."

"It's all part of the service. I'll be adding my tour guide moonlighting to your final bill."

Kate looked at him in horror, then realised he was joking. "Idiot," she said, flicking a green bean his way.

*

The walk home took almost twice as long as the walk there, both Kate and Bob feeling snoozy after two pints of Doom Bar. They'd finished their meal in companionable silence, the kind of silence Kate usually only achieved with Flo. Conversation had picked up on the walk home, but half way back Bob's phone pinged and his face tensed up.

"You go on ahead," he said. "I just need to make a quick call."

Kate sped up her pace, wondering if the call was a sensitive work matter. She looked back once, and saw Bob gesticulating in the air, before rubbing his temples. By the time he caught her up, he looked deflated, like he'd shrunk several inches.

"Are you OK? A problem with work?"

Bob looked at her, his face flickering with an unidentified emotion. "Um, yeah, that's it. A problem at work. Do you mind if we speed up a bit? I really need to be getting back."

"Yeah sure. It seems a bit off though, them calling you

on a Sunday. Surely you're entitled to a weekend like everyone else?"

"Can you just drop it please, Kate?"

Bob's words stung Kate like the nettles at the side of the path. She was only trying to be a supportive friend. They walked the rest of the way back in silence. Not the comfortable silence of earlier, but a jarring, awkward silence, neither of them wanting or knowing how to break the deadlock.

"Sorry I snapped earlier," said Bob as they arrived back at the house. "I'll text you about next weekend, and I promise to be in a better mood."

"OK, see you then," said Kate, leaving him at his car and letting herself in the house.

She hoped Bob would be true to his word. Sullen Bob was like a bear with a sore head, and she'd rather explore the town herself than encounter that version of him again.

Chapter 14

On Wednesday morning, a knock on the door sent Kate into a blind panic. She checked her watch. It was only nine-thirty and her next guest wasn't due to arrive till three. Had they got their wires crossed? Kate thought of the unmade bed and empty biscuit tin upstairs and opened the door with caution, wondering how she could put the guest off for a couple of hours.

The woman stood before her was tiny, and Kate, at five foot five, towered over her. She was clutching a bunch of flowers in front of a sky blue twin-set, and her neat silver hair had pink tones running through it.

"Hi, you must be Gloria. I'm sorry, but I wasn't expecting you till this afternoon."

The woman looked startled and took a step back from the door. "Sorry, dear, I think you've got me muddled up with someone else."

"You're not Gloria?"

"No, dear."

"Oh thank God for that."

"Why? What has Gloria done?"

"Nothing, I'm just not quite ready for her yet." Kate was now thoroughly confused, as seemed the other lady, clutching her flowers with one hand and patting her permed hair with the other. "Sorry, how can I help you?

I'm not interested in religion, if that's what you're here for?"

"Religion? Well, I wouldn't be so quick to write it off, but no, that's not why I'm here."

Kate fought the urge to close the door, as the old lady studied her from behind thick, red-rimmed glasses.

"Are you Katherine Trenain?"

"Yes, I am, but no one calls me Katherine."

"Oh, I see. Well, dear, what do they call you?"

"Kate. Sorry, how can I help you?"

"Moira asked me to come and check on you."

"Moira? You mean my grandmother?"

"That's the one."

Great. An early guest would have been better than this poor, confused old biddy. "My grandmother's dead."

"Yes, I'm fully aware of that, young lady."

"But, you said she asked you to call round?"

Kate remembered the spiritualist church she'd seen down the road and hoped the woman wasn't bringing a message from the dead. Her confused brain couldn't handle that.

The old lady narrowed her eyes and pointed a finger at Kate. "You think I'm mad, don't you?" Before Kate could reply, the lady burst into noisy laughter, clasping her chest and sending petals flying to the ground. She wiped the tears from her eyes. "Oh, this is a hoot. Moira hoped we'd get on. I'm Joy, by the way." She held out a hand for Kate to shake. "Well, aren't you going to invite me in? I'm dying to see what you've done with the place."

"Um, well, OK then," Kate said, as Joy pushed past her into the living room.

"My, my, this is all a bit different." Joy went around the room, picking up photo frames, stroking her hand over the purple sofa. She even poked a finger into the soil of a pot plant, presumably to check it was well watered.

"So, um, you knew my Nan? Do you think she'd

approve? I hope she's not turning in her grave."

Joy laughed again, and Kate smiled. The laugh was so at odds with the woman's age. She sounded like a teenage girl with her high-pitched chuckle and occasional snorts. "God no, she'll be dancing in her grave. She always said she wanted to do the place up, but in the end she ran out of energy. Now, how about that cuppa?"

Kate couldn't remember offering tea, but decided it was easier not to argue. "Sure thing. Milk and sugar?"

"Four sugars, please, dear. Just don't tell my doctor."

Joy followed Kate to the kitchen. As she walked through the door, her hand flew once more to her chest, but this time there was no laughter, just eyes shiny with tears. "You kept it," she said, her voice a small croak.

"Yes, I thought the kitchen was lovely and a terrible waste to replace it with some crap modern version."

Joy grabbed hold of Kate's arm and looked around the room. "I can see her here. Not, you know, like a ghost, just memories," she added quickly, presumably not to add fuel to the doolally fire.

"Was my Nan a good cook? I don't remember much about her."

Joy's eyes twinkled. This time instead of tears, they brimmed with mischief. "Moira struggled to boil an egg. She used to buy Sainsbury's Taste the Difference cakes for the WI meeting and pass them off as her own. No, her time in the kitchen was spent making cocktails."

"Cocktails?"

"Yes, she was very creative, you know. She would have made a wonderful barmaid. Always coming up with new recipes. I've never been so ill as the time she plied me with some dreadful combination of marmalade, gin, and rhubarb liquor. Most were a success, though."

"Blimey. You must have known her well then?"

"Best friends we were, ever since our first day of primary school. Seventy-five years we were there for each other. Now... now I'm on my own. Except I've got you now, haven't I, dear?" Joy threw the bunch of flowers down on the worktop and wrapped her arms round Kate's waist. Kate stood still as a statue, thoughts of madness once more returning. The kettle boiled, and Kate extracted herself from Joy's arms.

"Let's take our tea out into the garden," said Joy.

"Are you sure? It's pretty cold out there?"

"I know, but I could do with a smoke. Those flowers are for you, by the way. You might want to put them in a vase before they wilt."

"Thank you, that's very kind," said Kate, pulling a pint glass from the cupboard and filling it with water. Joy looked horrified. "I'll put them in a proper vase later," Kate added, and Joy's face softened.

"So," said Joy, holding a mug and cigarette in the same hand. "How are you finding Bodmin? I expect a pretty young thing like you has made lots of friends already."

"Not exactly. It took me a while to get the house sorted, then I've been setting up a B&B business, so there's not been much time for socialising. I've befriended the solicitor who dealt with Nan's will. He's offered to show me around a bit."

"Oh, has he now?" said Joy, raising and wiggling an eyebrow.

Kate laughed. "Not like that. He's just a friend, and much older than me, so not a romantic contender."

"Very wise, dear. Woman usually outlive men, so best get yourself a younger model unless you want to end up alone. Neither Moira nor I took that advice and both of us ended up lonely old bags. What's the name of this solicitor chap?"

"Bob Carter."

"Little Bobby Carter, hey. He can't be that much older than you. I remember him as a little boy. His mother was a gentle soul, but I'll never forget the anger on her face the time he pulled down his shorts in the old methodist chapel and peed all over the floor." Joy began to laugh, but it was ill timed as a lungful of cigarette smoke went down the wrong way and Kate feared for a moment Joy might choke to death.

Joy ran through a series of embarrassing anecdotes that Kate banked in her brain for a later date, then moved on to talking about Moira. It was strange, hearing her Nan spoken about as a young woman, and Kate hung on Joy's every word.

"What happened with your dad broke her heart. She was never the same after. On the outside she was as jolly as ever, but her eyes lost their sparkle."

"Yes, Mum would never talk to me about him, but I was given the basics."

"Ha, I bet she told you it was suicide?"

"Yeah..."

"Moira didn't believe a word of it. He'd gone out drinking with a bunch of low-lifes on one of the north coast beaches. Up on the cliffs they were, getting hammered and taking God knows what. They were all so out of it, none of them noticed him go over the edge. Now, if he'd done it on purpose, don't you think he would have made more of a song and dance about it?"

Kate wasn't sure that was how these things worked, but let Joy continue.

"Even if he had stepped off on purpose, his brain was so addled he wouldn't have known what he was doing. Moira could never believe he'd leave her on purpose, or you. He adored you, and your mother."

Not enough to stay off the drugs, thought Kate, once again keeping her thoughts to herself.

"Of course, Moira blamed your mum, you know, for not straightening him out. I told her, it's not a woman's place to change a man, but Moira thought the sun shone out of that boy's arse, so she was having none of it."

"Mum blamed Nan for bringing him back to Cornwall. She thought if he'd stayed with us in London, things would have turned out differently."

"Nah, sometimes there's no going back. Even if he'd got off the drugs, who's to say what damage he'd already done to himself. Moira thought she was doing the right thing, bringing him back here. She tried to lock him up, you know?"

"No, I didn't know."

"Well, fat lot of use that did. He just climbed out the window and got himself mixed up with a bad crowd. Bad clings to bad, whatever town you're in. Bodmin, London, he could've gone to Timbuktu and it wouldn't have made the slightest difference." Joy stubbed out her cigarette and stood up. "Well, I've taken up enough of your time and dragged you the wrong way down memory lane. I think I'd better get going before my tongue loosens again. Thanks for the tea, I'll see myself out."

"Joy? Would you like to come round again? I'd like to know more about Nan, and you knew her better than most."

Joy let out a chuckle. "Not better than most, dear. I knew her better than anyone, better than she knew herself. Of course I'll come round again, but next time, make sure you've got something stronger than tea for me, eh?"

"Of course," said Kate, "though I can't promise cocktails."

Joy waved a hand and disappeared through the door.

*

The weather took a turn for the worse. Kate spent the afternoon locked in thoughts of her parents. She'd only ever got her mum's side of the story, and it was good to get a fresh perspective, however brutal it might feel at the time. Staring out of the window, Kate saw images from her childhood rather than the rain and wind buffeting plants outside. It took her a moment to realise the noise she could hear was not the wind, but a banging on the door. She leaped up and ran to open it.

Kate could only make out the round shape of a woman, drowning in a large, unflattering rain mac. This was no time for polite introductions as Kate ushered the figure inside out of the rain.

"Gloria, pleased to meet you," the woman said, peeling off the rain mac and holding out a wet hand. She balanced a full carrier bag beneath her arm and shook off the coat's water onto the floor.

"I'm Kate. Pleased to meet you. Would you like me to take your luggage?"

Gloria moved the carrier bag to her chest and held it tight to her body. "Not this. But yes, you could take the suitcase, if you don't mind?"

"Not at all. Your room is this way."

Chapter 15

Gloria woke early. She crept across the bare boards of the floor and opened the thick corduroy curtains. Despite winter clawing its way into autumn, the sound of birdsong still floated through the window. The sky looked ominous, thick wisps of black streaked across grey. Gloria sighed. It wasn't an appetising day to be plunging into the estuary, but that was what she was here for and she couldn't back out now.

Tiptoeing across to her suitcase, Gloria pulled out the fluffy slippers she took everywhere with her and crept through to the sitting room. She made herself a fresh coffee in the cafetiere, and returned to the bedroom to await the arrival of dawn.

It was an angry light when it appeared. There were no bright flashes of colour, no oranges, fuchsias or pastel pinks, just an ominous illuminating of the thick clouds. Like someone had turned a spotlight on beneath them. As the first patters of rain hit the windowpane, Gloria pulled the duvet around her and swallowed the last of her coffee. She propped herself up against the iron headboard and closed her eyes.

Gloria wouldn't describe herself as a spiritual person, but the many years attending her parish church had instilled a deep faith, and if there was ever a need for prayer, it was now. Her lips moved silently in a one-sided conversation. She prayed the turmoil within her would cease, that today would be a fresh start, but most of all she prayed for forgiveness. No voice in the sky answered her, there was no lightning bolt, no message placed on her heart, but when she opened her eyes, she felt much calmer than when she woke, and today, that was enough.

Gloria pulled out a cereal bar from her bag and took birdlike bites. Her stomach groaned for the cooked breakfast it truly desired, but she couldn't risk a big breakfast before heading into the water. She was doing this alone, and on a late October day, there would be few people around to save her if anything went wrong.

With her stomach briefly sated, Gloria reached into her suitcase and took out an unflattering combination of jogging bottoms, T-shirt and hoodie. Today was about warmth, not style. *Slut.* For a moment she felt her mother with her, giving her opinion freely about Gloria's appearance. She ignored her mother's voice, pulled her hair back into a scrunchy, took a dry bag from her suitcase, and filled it with all she would need. Then, with the carrier bag firmly in her arms, Gloria crept downstairs and out of the house.

In five minutes she was leaving the town, guiding her car through open countryside. The wide road gave way to fields on either side and her breath caught as she glimpsed a snaking river in the distance. She turned off the wide road onto a narrower, winding lane, tall hedgerows on either side. Gloria fired off a quick prayer that she wouldn't meet anyone coming the other way. She had never been a confident driver, and lacked the spacial awareness to take the road at anything above a crawl. Her mother had known her fear behind the wheel, of course. Gloria suspected that was why she had chosen this particular spot.

Gloria reached the outskirts of Fowey and breathed a sigh of relief at her proximity to the destination. She bypassed the town, driving along a newly tarmacked road until she finally saw the sign to the car park. There were no other cars in the car park, but Gloria's face still burned at the five minutes it took her to manoeuvre the car into a space.

She took the dry bag and carrier bag from the boot, leaving her handbag hidden under a blanket and tucking her keys beneath the front wheel arch. The air around her was cold and damp. No wonder there were no other takers for the car park. Gloria took her time walking down the wooded path, remembering the small child who'd skipped down it decades before. That same little girl had tripped in her excitement, grazing her knee so badly blood had streamed down her leg, collecting at the bottom in her white sock. She remembered her mother, usually so fierce about appearance, taking off her scarf and dabbing it on the wound. The scarf had been ruined, but it was never mentioned. Instead, when they'd reached the bottom of the hill, her mother had stopped at an ice cream stand and bought Gloria a Ninety-Nine.

Gloria stopped on the path, lost in her memories. Perhaps her mother hadn't chosen this place to torment her. Perhaps the memory of that one precious day had been equally precious to her. The thought that her mother's final act might have been a kind one was too much, and a choke escaped Gloria's mouth. She took a deep breath. *Pull yourself together.*

The beach was smaller than Gloria remembered, but just as beautiful. *Readymoney*. Her mother had chosen it for its name, telling Gloria a visit there may bring them luck. It didn't.

The tide was at its highest point, leaving a thin strip of sand to hug the stone wall. On either side, trees the colour of flames guarded the bay, rising steeply away from the water. She'd forgotten about the trees, but they must have been here all those years ago. Back then, all she'd been aware of was the sand. It had been her first time at the seaside, and she could still remember her giddiness at feeling warm sand beneath her toes.

Gloria wasn't built to glide through water. Even as a child she had been short and plump, more jellyfish than mermaid. Her mother insisted on her learning to swim, patiently holding her under her stomach, reassuring Gloria that she wouldn't let go. She had let go though, and Gloria had sunk like a stone. It had been another forty years before she attempted swimming lessons again.

Gloria pulled a changing towel from the dry bag and stripped beneath it. The beach was deserted and she could've stripped without it. But the house perched on the cliff had its lights on, and she wasn't prepared to give its inhabitants a laugh. Once naked, Gloria unfolded the wetsuit from her bag. Her mother would have shrieked with disdain at the sight of a wetsuit, but this was October in Cornwall, and Gloria had no intention of leaving with hypothermia.

Gloria sent up a prayer of thanks that there was no one to see the wetsuit fiasco. The size sixteen she'd ordered appeared too optimistic. She could barely get the thick folds up one leg. Having come too far to give up, Gloria squirmed on the sand, a fish out of water, struggling with metres of neoprene. With her arms firmly in, Gloria switched from fish to monkey as she hopped about the sand, trying to get the wetsuit done up. She should have brought a friend with her to do the zip. Gloria mentally ran through her friends list. No, there was no one she trusted enough to share this moment with.

By the time the wetsuit was on and zipped, Gloria was sweating profusely. She rolled up the legs and arms which were flapping around and making her look like a clown. The water was calm, and Gloria decided to chance her bobble hat, pulling it tightly on her head so she wouldn't lose it.

Gloria walked to the water's edge, dipping her toes in and recoiling at the water temperature. A pontoon lay in the middle of the bay, a new addition since the last time she was there. It was as if it had been laid there just for her. The perfect place to do what she had come for. She stuffed the carrier bag safely in her orange dry bag and, once it was secured, stepped into the water.

Freezing salt water shot up the legs of Gloria's wetsuit, taking her breath away. She pressed on, knowing if she paused, her rational mind would send her scurrying for the shore. Deeper and deeper she walked until she stood on tiptoes. Gloria spread her arms wide and lifted her feet from the bottom. In an instant, Gloria realised her mistake, her limbs flailing in panic, held vice-like by her black second skin. She should've practiced swimming in the wetsuit, then maybe she could have mastered the technique.

Gloria closed her eyes, treading water, trying to bring calm to her racing heart. She tried a few tentative scoops of doggy paddle, and found she could make progress this way, however slow that progress may be. As Gloria grew more confident, panic was replaced by calm. She may not look elegant to the outside world, but the way the water supported her body felt wonderful. She felt weightless, freed from the insecurities and frustrations of her aging body.

After half an hour of paddling, Gloria reached the pontoon. She could picture the joy on children's faces as they leaped from it in the warm summer months, but she was not there to play. Gloria hauled herself up on to the thick plastic and retrieved her dry bag. It was heavy, and she hoped the swim back would be easier without pulling the weight behind her.

Sat cross legged, Gloria placed the carrier bag in front of her. She pulled down its sides to reveal a thick cardboard box. Shaking her hands to rid them of water, Gloria laid them on the box, stroking its smooth surface. The wind had picked up a little, and she opened the lid with care, not wanting the contents whipped away until she was ready. Inside the box lay grey powder, all that was left of a life.

"Well, Mum, here we are. I've done what you asked,

now I suppose this is goodbye."

There had been many times over the past few years that Gloria had longed for that moment, longed for the relief it would bring. But now the moment had arrived, she found she didn't want it. Instead of the release she'd hoped to feel her body was being dragged down by a heavy sadness. All those wasted opportunities, all the things left unsaid.

As Gloria sat contemplating the box, the light around her changed and the sun broke through the clouds. *Thank you,* she whispered, her head tilted to the sky. The sun turned the grey ash silver, and Gloria knew it was time. She raised herself to standing, holding out her arms to steady herself against the swaying pontoon. Once steady, Gloria reached down for the box. She filled her palm with ash, held it high above her, then opened it, allowing the wind to carry it away. Her hand dug in for another and another before finally, Gloria grabbed the whole box and, with a cry, tipped it out into the air. The wind caught it, swirling dancing flecks of ash momentarily suspended, before dropping to the water and laying on it like a pool of ink. She watched as what was once her mother disappeared beneath the surface. *I love you,* she choked, the realisation startling her. How long had it been since she said those words? Twenty...thirty years?

Gloria dropped to her knees, her gaze fixed on the water. Was her mother looking down on her? Was she finally proud? She felt now would be the right time to cry, but her eyes remained stubbornly dry. *Oh well*, she thought, *Mum would approve of that*. She had never been one to enjoy public displays of emotion.

A gentle fluttering filled her chest, and Gloria smiled. Today was a day of endings, but endings brought beginnings. She had no idea what the future would bring, but she was ready to embrace it. Gloria blew a kiss to her mother's resting place, crawled to the edge of the pontoon and plunged herself back into the water.

Chapter 16

Kate waited till eleven before creeping up the stairs to check on her guest. The poor woman resembled a drowned rat when she arrived, and Kate hoped she hadn't become ill because of it. Kate knocked tentatively on the door, but there was no answer.

"Hello?" she said. No reply. "Hello?" she tried again.

Kate opened the door a crack and peered around it. A sigh of relief escaped her as she saw the well-made bed and suitcase tucked in the corner of the room. At least there wasn't a dead body waiting for her. The guest must have been up and out very early, as Kate had woken at seven and hadn't heard anyone moving about upstairs. The woman had booked for two nights, but given no clue as to her plans while she was in town. Kate found solo female travellers intriguing. There must be a reason why she was alone. At the same time, she admired their courage. She'd spent several evenings alone in restaurants when Alex had been held up at work, and it hadn't been much fun.

Kate was making herself crumpets dripping with honey when the front door clicked open and she heard the guest return. It was a tricky balance to strike between friendliness and allowing guests their space, but as their interaction the previous day had been minimal, Kate decided to wander through and say hello.

Gloria was carrying a bright orange bag that looked the

type used by wild swimmers. Her hair was damp, pulled back by a scrunchy Kate felt should have been left in the eighties.

"Hi, how are you? Did you sleep well last night?"

Gloria nodded and smiled. Her smile was dazzling, changing her entire face. For the first time, Kate noticed Gloria was actually rather beautiful, in a plump English rose sort of way. It was impossible to guess her age.

"I slept very well, thank you. It's a lovely mattress you've got up there."

"Thanks. Have you been out for a swim?" asked Kate, signalling to the orange bag.

"Well, sort of. I was scattering my mother's ashes. She wanted them scattered at sea, but as I get terribly sea sick, swimming seemed the least bad option." There was that dazzling smile again.

"Goodness, I'm so sorry, that must have been a hard thing to do."

"Not as hard as I was expecting. It was rather cathartic."

"Oh, well, that's, um, good? Can I get you anything?"

"Actually, I feel in need of a drink. A drink drink. Is there a good pub nearby?"

"Yes, there is, practically opposite. They've got several rooms there, so you should be able to find somewhere quiet."

"Thank you, but I'm not sure I really want somewhere quiet. I don't suppose you'd like to join me?"

Gloria's hands twisted in front of her, and Kate wondered if she was feeling shy. Going for drinks with guests wasn't what she'd planned, if anything she'd hoped to keep them at arm's length. But then again, after what Gloria had been through that morning, surely one couldn't hurt. "Yes, OK, why not? Are you ready now?"

"I'll just pop upstairs for a shower if that's OK? I have seaweed and goodness knows what else clinging to me."

"A shower sounds necessary, then. Just give me a shout when you're ready."

"Will do."

Half an hour later, there was a knock on Kate's bedroom door. Gloria stood there, looking like a different person from the bedraggled woman who'd walked in earlier. She was wearing a cashmere dress that skimmed her ankles, a leather jacket and pointy black ankle boots. Her silver hair was swept back in a stylish chignon, and her lips were coated in shimmering pink.

"Wow, you look amazing! I feel pretty under-dressed."

"Oh don't worry, you look fine. I had to get out of those awful joggers, I felt such a slob."

Kate pointed to her ripped jeans, scuffed boots, and bobbly jumper. "I think I might be letting the side down," said Kate. Gloria laughed and hoisted a handbag onto her shoulder, indicating they should be off.

Gloria insisted on buying the drinks and arrived at their table with a bottle of wine. "I thought we may as well get a bottle. Unless you've got somewhere you need to be later?"

"No, nowhere."

"What is it you do, work wise, I mean?"

"Currently not much. I run the Airbnb, but I've not lived in the house long and I'm still trying to figure out what to do."

"Have you had many guests so far?"

"You're my second. I've not got many bookings as it's low season."

"That can't keep you very busy. I'd go mad if I had too much thinking time."

"What do you do?"

"I'm CEO of a logistics firm."

"Wow."

"Ha, it's not as exciting as it sounds, but it keeps me out of trouble."

Kate felt suddenly inferior, not just in clothing, but life in general. "Shall we have a toast to your mum?"

"What a lovely idea. To Mum!" Gloria clinked her glass against Kate's.

"Were you and your mum close?"

Gloria winced at the question. "No, we hated each other most of our lives."

"Oh, sorry."

"Don't be. Hate's probably too strong a word. We didn't understand each other. I resented her, and I suspect she was jealous of me. She never did much with her own life and I think my success shone a light on that."

"She must have been proud of you though, I mean, CEO? That's not something women achieve every day."

"It was down to hard work. The thing is, Mum was much cleverer than me. She was the first in her family to go to university. Everyone had high expectations of her."

"So what happened?"

"I did. She got pregnant in the first term, the father scarpered and I, according to her, ruined her life."

"I'm sure she didn't really think that."

"Oh, she did, believe me. Trouble is, I don't think she'd have been any happier if I'd gone down the marriage and kids route. I don't think anything would've pleased her. She did love me, in her own way. That's what today was about."

"Really?"

"Yes, she left instructions for me to scatter her ashes in the only place we went on holiday. A place we went to one happy summer when I was little and no threat to her insecurities. We were happy then."

"God, that must have been so hard for you."

"I thought it would be, but actually, it was great to be reminded of happy times. I played my part in the relationship too. As soon as I could, I left home, hardly ever visited, created a new life for myself that didn't involve her. It's no wonder things were broken beyond repair by the time she needed me to look after her. Anyway, enough about me. Do you get on with your mum?"

"My mum died a few years back."

"Oh I'm so sorry. She must have been pretty young?"

"Yeah, early forties. Years of alcoholism finally took their toll. She wasn't a bad mum, she just had her demons. I grew up knowing I was loved, even if it was in a chaotic, confusing kind of way. I still miss her, ten years on. It's like I've been standing still all that time."

"Well, moving to Cornwall's certainly not standing still. It's funny, you know, I'm not sure you ever grow out of needing your mum, whatever they're like."

Kate and Gloria sat in silence, pondering their pasts. "My mum was eighty when she died. That feels young these days, doesn't it? I remember when sixty seemed ancient, now it's the new forty apparently, at least I hope so as I turn sixty this year."

"Sixty? I would have said you were forty at the oldest."

"Ah, that's kind. I think it's not having kids that keeps you looking young. Plenty of sleep is the key. Hasn't stopped me going grey, though."

"Are you married?"

"Oh no, I never fancied it. I've had a few long-term partners, but I don't want to be tied down, you know?"

Kate didn't know. All she wanted was to be tied down, a couple of kids getting under her feet. She'd take all the good bits from her mum and not repeat any of the mistakes. "I've always wanted a big family. I'm not sure it will happen now."

"How old are you?"

"Thirty."

"But that's so young! You've got plenty of child-bearing years ahead of you."

"Not if I can't hold on to or find the right man."

"You don't need a man to have kids these days."

"Technically, you do."

"Yes, but not one you're attached to."

"True, but I don't want to be a single mum. Not that there's anything wrong with that. I just want the kind of family I never had."

"There's more than one way of having a family. Good friends, for starters."

Kate thought of Joy and her relationship with Moira.

"I blame books and films," said Gloria, on a roll and her second glass of wine. "They make us think we need the perfect man, two point four kids, blah blah blah. What we really need is to make our own happiness, not rely on some chap to provide it. You said something about hanging on to the right man. Is there someone in the picture?"

"Urgh, I'm not sure. I met someone at uni, and we'd been together ever since. Then about a year ago we finally moved in together and it didn't work at all. I don't know what I did wrong, but six months into it, he needed space and I had to move out. I'm not sure where we stand now. He's sent weekly texts since I moved down here but just *Hi, hope you're well* sort of messages, nothing that lets me know where I stand. Plus, he's involved with someone else now, though he says it's nothing serious."

"Hold on a second, you're telling me he a) kicked you out b) sends a text once a week and c) has another woman. And you think he's the right man for you?"

Kate suddenly felt foolish, and more than a bit narked at Gloria's plain speaking. "It's more complicated than that. He was there for me when Mum died. I've needed a lot of support since then and he's been the one to give it. I owe him big time."

"You seem pretty self sufficient to me."

"Looks can be deceptive. I'm a crumbling mess behind closed doors."

"Really?" It was a statement, not a question, and Gloria scrutinised Kate with narrowed eyes and pursed lips.

"Yeah, you know, it's not like I've done much with my life. I can barely hold down a minimum wage job."

"But you went to uni?"

"Yeah, but I dropped out when Mum died, just before finals. No qualifications to my name, so minimum wage it is."

"Well, if you got into uni you must have A levels. And setting up a business on your own takes guts. You clearly have a creative streak, the house looks beautiful, and I can tell it's recently redecorated, which I'm assuming was your handy work. If you ask me, you're selling yourself short."

"Thanks," said Kate, telling herself Gloria was a stranger and didn't know the first thing about her life. "I'd better be getting back."

Chapter 17

"Hi, are you ready? I'm parked outside, but there's a parking attendant hanging round, so I don't want to risk a ticket."

"Sure, no problem, I'll be out in a tick." Kate put the phone down and gathered up her bag.

Saturday had rolled round unsurprisingly slowly, given how little Kate had to do. Cleaning the room after Gloria left had only taken a couple of hours, and she'd spent a day and a half wandering aimlessly around the house, hoping Joy might call again, which she didn't. By Friday evening Kate was feeling so sorry for herself she called Alex. He hadn't appreciated her disturbing his Friday evening lads-night and fobbed her off with the promise to call back over the weekend. A call to Maddie had been even more unsuccessful, her phone having been switched off all evening. Kate didn't bother trying Flo, knowing she was on a late shift at The Sunbeam.

Bob had promised to continue his local tour that morning. All Kate knew was that she needed to dress sporty and in layers. Kate left the house to find two bikes attached to the back of Bob's car. She got in and looked at him quizzically.

"No," he said, clocking her expression. "You'll find out where we're going soon enough."

"Hmm, well, I thought this was supposed to be a local

tour. How come we're taking the car?"

"I'm easing you in," Bob laughed. "We can go by bike if you want, I just wasn't sure if your legs were used to hills."

"Um, how many hills are we talking?"

"Look, let me drive, then next time we can cycle if you're up for it."

"Deal," said Kate. Bob turned to smile at her and Kate gasped. "What on earth's happened to your face?"

Bob's right eye was puffy, the surrounding skin varying shades of purple.

"Got hit in the eye with a squash ball."

"Shit, that must have hurt like hell. When did it happen? It looks pretty recent?"

"Oh yeah, the evening before last."

"I didn't know you were a fan of squash."

"I'm full of surprises me."

"Who do you play with?"

"Look, can you stop with all the questions?" snapped Bob, making Kate jump.

Kate considered getting out of the car there and then. The angry side of Bob was back, and she didn't like it one bit. "I'm not sure this is a good idea. Perhaps we should leave it for this week."

"I'm so sorry, Kate, I don't know what's been getting into me lately. Just, got a lot on my plate."

"And ferrying me around the place is adding to it."

"I didn't mean that. This is a pleasure, not a chore. It gives me a break from home."

"Home?"

"Oh, you know, my laptop, files piling up."

"You work too hard Bob Carter."

"Then let's redress the balance with a bit of fun," he said, starting the engine.

*

Bob pulled the car into a National Trust car park. "Oooh, Larnidrock, this sounds posh," said Kate.

Bob stared at her in disgust. “Crikey, I can see my work to turn you into a local is a long way from done. It’s Lanhydrock, there’s a *hi* in the middle.”

“OK, sorry. Hey, maybe next weekend you can take me to Polzeeeth.”

“It’s Polzeath, as in *eth* not... oh, you’re joking.”

“Got ya,” said Kate, grabbing her bag from the back seat.

Bob got out of the car and began unloading the bikes from the rack.

“Whose bike is that?” asked Kate, crossing her fingers it hadn’t belonged to his wife. For some reason, the thought of riding a dead woman’s bicycle gave her the shivers.

“It’s Mum’s. She’s fine with you borrowing it, she doesn’t use it these days. You can keep it till you’ve decided if you want to get one of your own.”

“That’s very kind of her, but I have a bike already.”

“That folding thing? You need a proper bike for where we’re going, trust me.”

Bob handed Kate a helmet and put one on himself. His large head looked ridiculous in the helmet, but Kate could tell he was feeling self-conscious and fought the urge to tease. He wheeled his bike through the car park and Kate followed. It was busy, men unloading muddy mountain bikes from trailers, kids whizzing round on balance bikes.

“We’ll start you off on the skills trail and see how you get on.”

Kate wasn’t sure whether to be touched or insulted by Bob’s show of masculine concern. She decided actions would speak louder than words, and jumped on her bike.

“Hey, wait for me,” called Bob as Kate flew round a corner, getting some air as she sped over a ramp. Kate waved her hand in the air, enjoying Bob’s shouts of protest as he raced to catch her up. Despite the odd patch of rust, her borrowed bike was an expensive make and Kate felt it’s value beneath her feet as she guided it over jumps and sent gravel spraying in her wake on the bends. The feeling of speed was a therapy in itself and she relished the air that rushed through her hair, *blowing out the cobwebs* her mum would've said.

On the fifth go round the skills track, Kate realised Bob was nowhere to be seen. She jumped off her bike and wandered through the woods until she found him sitting at a picnic bench sipping water from a flask. His face was beetroot, his thick greying hair wet with perspiration.

"Where did you learn to ride like that?" he asked, eyes wide.

"I was a bit of a tear-away as a kid. Mum wasn't often around, and when she was, she was usually pissed. We didn't have the money for a TV license or computer games, so I spent most of my free time on my bike. She got me an old BMX for my tenth birthday and I got pretty good at tricks and stuff."

"This feels a bit like teaching Granny to suck eggs," said Bob, looking deflated.

"Not at all. I never knew about this place. I love it, thanks so much for bringing me here." Kate reached across and squeezed Bob's shoulder. He flushed and jumped off the bench to pick up his bike.

"Want to try one of the harder trails?"

"Sure, lead the way," said Kate. She'd made her point. There was no need to go speeding off again. Bob pedalled deeper into the woods until they reached a clearing with signposts pointing in all directions.

"You pick which route you fancy. There's a map there that shows them all."

Kate free-wheeled over to the map and picked the blue route. Not too easy, not too difficult. "Let's have a go at this one," she said.

"I thought you'd go for red. You're not going easy on me, are you?" Bob asked, frowning.

"No, it's for my sake, not yours. It's been years since I

rode on tracks, or hills for that matter. I'm done in after the skills section. I can feel muscles in my legs I'd forgotten existed."

"I believe you, thousands wouldn't," said Bob, wiping his brow with a hanky and getting back on his bike.

As they were setting off, Kate's mobile rang. "Hold on a sec," she called to Bob. "I'll just answer this."

He gave her a thumbs up as she retrieved her phone from the bottom of her bag. Alex's face was lighting up the screen.

"Hi, Alex. Sorry, I can't really talk right now. Can I call you back in a couple of hours?"

"What are you doing?"

Kate was tempted to answer *none of your business* but remembered it was she who called him on Friday, so she didn't have the right to be rude. "I'm out on a bike ride, actually. A friend brought me to some bike trails nearby. They're really..."

"Who's the friend?"

Kate had forgotten his habit of interrupting her half way through a sentence. Why hadn't it ever bothered her before? "I'm with my mate Bob. You know, the solicitor I told you about?"

"Oh, him. Haven't you met anyone else yet?"

"I've spent a bit of time with my guests and this lady Joy who..."

"You called me, remember? I thought you wanted to speak to me, but if you can't be bothered, don't worry about it."

"No, no, I did want to speak to you. I mean, I do. It's just I'm in the middle of a wood, covered in mud with bad signal. Can I call you back in a couple of hours? We can catch up properly then."

"I'm busy later, I'll call you another time."

Alex hung up and Kate stared at her phone, wondering what exactly she'd done wrong this time. She looked over at Bob, who was studying his own phone screen, a murderous look on his face. She free-wheeled over to him.

"Everything alright?"

Bob jumped, startled, and put the phone back in his pocket. "Yes, everything's fine, why?"

"Oh, nothing. No reason. Shall we get going?"

"Catch me if you can," said Bob, setting off with a skid down a dirt track.

Kate kept Bob in her sights, making sure to stay a little way behind, even though she knew she had it in her to catch him if she wanted. Something was up with him, and she got the feeling he could do with a boost to his pride.

Kate wished she'd been looking at the track rather than Bob's back. If she was, she would have seen the stick in the middle of the path. The stick caught between the spokes of her wheels and sent her flying over the handlebars. She felt skin tearing from her leg as she landed, her hands burning as they planted palm down into a patch of nettles. Like a wounded animal, Kate crawled further into the undergrowth, pulling her bike out of the path of oncoming cyclists.

"Kate? Kate!" Bob had heard the scream as she fell and came racing the wrong way down the track towards her. "What's happened? Are you OK?"

"I'm fine, just a bit battered and bruised. It was a rooky error and I should have known better. I wasn't watching the track, and a stick got wedged in my wheel."

"Where does it hurt?"

"Everywhere." Kate managed a little chuckle, and Bob looked relieved.

"Do you think anything's broken?"

"No," said Kate, unconsciously running her hands around her body to check for unexpected pain. "I think I've cut my leg, though."

"Let me take a look at that."

Kate winced as Bob rolled up her leggings, revealing a

nasty graze on her right knee. “Ouch,” he said, “you’ve taken a fair bit of skin off. I don’t think there’s any dirt in it, but I’d better give it a rinse, just in case.” He pulled his water bottle from his bag and Kate winced again as the water hit, digging her fingers into his arm as the stinging intensified. “Well at least it’s clean. Let’s see what I’ve got in here.” Bob rifled through his bag and eventually pulled out a spray can of Savlon and a roll of fabric plasters.

“Were you a boy scout or something?”

Bob grinned. “How did you guess?” He sprayed Savlon onto the wound, causing Kate to yelp in pain, then pulled out a Swiss army knife from his pocket, cutting a large square of plaster and delicately covering Kate’s knee. “The best thing would be to let the air get to it, but you should keep it covered while we’re in the woods. Do you think you can walk?”

Kate stood and pain shot through her ankle. She fell back to the ground with a thud. Bob knelt beside her.

“Do you mind if I take a look?”

Kate shook her head and Bob began feeling around her ankle for any signs of a break. His fingers were soft, and he used the lightest of touches. Kate felt herself relaxing with every stroke of his thumb.

“Hmm, it doesn’t feel like anything is broken, but it’s probably best we get it checked out at minor injuries. Are your arms OK?”

“Yes, fine.”

“Good, put them round my neck and hold on tight.”

Kate giggled as she wrapped her arms around Bob’s neck and he got unsteadily back on his feet. “Please don’t drop me, I’ve got enough injuries already.”

“It would be a damn sight easier if you stopped giggling,” he laughed. “And can you stop hanging there like a sack of spuds? Put your legs around my waist if you’re able, it would make this much easier for me.”

Kate did as she was told and somehow, Bob managed to

pick up a bike in each hand and push them, with Kate on his back, through the wood. Passers-by gave them strange looks, the big man giving the tiny blood covered woman a piggy back.

"Giddy up horsey," said Kate, bursting into another fit of giggles.

"You owe me big time for this," said Bob, trying to sound grumpy but failing to hide the smile in his voice.

Kate decided she should give walking a try, despite how comfortable she felt pressed into Bob's warm back. He was surprisingly strong for someone she had assumed to be out of shape. "Hey, can you let me down for a minute? I think I should try putting some weight on the ankle and see how I get on."

"You sure?"

"Yep."

Bob bent his knees and Kate allowed her feet to hit the floor. The ankle hurt like crazy, but she found herself able to walk on it, using her bike as support. When they reached the car, Bob tried to insist on a visit to the hospital, but Kate matched him in stubbornness and persuaded him to drop her at home instead.

"Thanks for today. You've been my hero."

"Ha, I'm pleased I could help. You're just a bit rusty on the bike, that's all."

"Hey!" said Kate, ready to protest, but looking over at him, she saw his eyes creasing in a smile. "Bastard," she said, smiling back. "I dread to think what you've got planned for me next weekend."

Chapter 18

"You did what?" Maddie was hooting with laughter on the other end of the phone.

"Stop it. It was so embarrassing, especially after I'd been boasting about my cycling skills. That will teach me."

"And... and... he had to... carry you?" Maddie struggled to get the words out between giggles.

"He was super kind actually. My knee still hurts like hell. Mind you, so does the rest of my body. I'm so out of shape."

"Yeah, you must be if you're still aching four days later. How's your week going?"

"Oh, so-so. I'm getting a bit bored, to be honest. I've got more guests arriving on Saturday, but I think I need to get myself another job, or maybe do some volunteering till I figure out what I really want to do."

"You're regretting the move?"

"No, not really. I guess I just haven't found my purpose yet. It's bound to take a while to settle in."

"Yeah, of course. Hey, I'm not sure you want to hear this, but I saw Alex the other day."

"Saw? Saw how?"

"Bumped into him in Co-Op. He didn't look too good."

"What's happened?" Kate, who had been lounging on her bed, sat up straight, pressing the phone hard to her ear.

"Is he OK?"

"Oh, he's fine, it's only his pride that's wounded. Jess finished with him."

"Finished with him? But why?"

"No idea. He didn't say she'd dumped him in so many words, it was more what he didn't say that gave it away. I actually felt a bit sorry for him."

"Do you think I should call him?"

"No! Why would you do that?"

"Because it sounds like he's hurting and could do with a friend."

"Friend my arse. Don't you be going down that road again. Promise me you won't. You've only just started standing on your own two feet. I like this new version of my best friend and don't want to lose her again to Alex's evil clutches."

Kate laughed. "You're so over-dramatic, I think you missed your calling as an actress. Anyway, I've always been independent."

"Bollocks have you. I can't remember the last time you made a decision without checking it with him first, or me, for that matter."

"That's not true. And anyway, I decided to come down here, didn't I? Maybe I'm not as hopeless as you think."

"Maybe." Maddie didn't sound convinced. "Anyway, have you thought about Christmas yet? It's only a few weeks away. You can come up here and spend it at my parents' if you like? You know they'd love to see you."

Kate smiled. Ever since her mum died, Christmas at Maddie's childhood home had become a tradition. Alex had always been too busy with his own family, but Maddie's parents welcomed her with open arms.

"I've not really thought about it, to be honest. You know I'd love to come to yours, but part of me wonders if it might be nice to spend it here, you know, first Christmas in the house and all that."

"Well, if you won't come to me, I'll come to you."

"But what about your parents? They'd be devastated!"

"Not on Christmas Day, you idiot. I could drive down early on Boxing Day. It could be fun."

"That sounds brilliant. I'd love for you to come. I was going to invite Bob round on Boxing Day, too."

"Ah, the lovely Bob, it would be great to see him again. How are you two getting on?"

"Yeah, good. Obviously, he's my hero after the cycling incident, but he goes a bit weird sometimes."

"Weird how?"

"Like moody, snappy. And he had a black eye last time I saw him that he said was from a squash ball, but something didn't add up. Oh, and there's the phone calls and messages. He gets them a lot, won't tell me who's contacting him, but he gets a face like thunder every time they do."

"Probably woman trouble."

"Maybe." Kate didn't like that thought, but struggled to pinpoint why.

"Oh shit, I just realised the time. My lunch break ended twenty minutes ago and I'm due in court at two. Speak soon, love you."

"Love you too," said Kate, but Maddie had already hung up.

Kate decided not to intrude on Alex's space and instead sent him a text. *Maddie said you and Jess have split. Sorry to hear that. Hope you're OK xx* Kate winced at the white lie. She wasn't sorry at all. In fact, as much as she hated to admit it, she hoped Jess was suffering as much as she had. Kate's phone pinged.

I'm fine. The Jess stuff was a massive mistake. I think I was trying to fill the gap left by you. Can we talk sometime? Xxx

Kate frowned at the screen. From what she remembered, her leaving had been at Alex's insistence, but here he seemed to be implying it was by choice. What did he want to talk about? Did he want her back? Kate's stomach fluttered at the thought. Looking round her bedroom, she tried to picture Alex here with her, but couldn't. If they got back together, would she have to give up the house? She hoped not.

A tapping on Kate's bedroom window made her jump. She leaped up and saw Joy's nose pressed to the glass, hands shading her eyes as she squinted into the room. She spotted Kate and gave her a wave. Kate walked through to the kitchen and opened the back door.

"You scared me half to death, Joy. What are you doing in the garden?"

"Oh, I was doing my visits at the old folks' home and remembered you had a back gate. Seemed silly to waste my legs walking round when I could slip in that way."

"I have a gate in the garden?"

"Of course, dear. Hadn't you noticed? Well, I suppose it is a bit overgrown up there." Joy pulled an ivy leaf from her hair to emphasise the point. "Now, I seem to remember you promising something stronger than tea last time I was here?"

Kate laughed. "Wine or beer?"

"Whisky?"

"Sorry, I don't have any, but I will get some in."

"All right then, dear. How about we take the civilised option and go for wine? I hope it's chilled."

"Yes, madam, it's chilled. Now would you like to come in to drink it or stay standing on the doormat?"

"I'll stay out here if that's OK. But a blanket would be nice."

"And I thought my B&B guests were demanding," Kate muttered under her breath.

Kate took the wine and blanket out to Joy, who was puffing her way through a Silk Cut. "You know smoking will kill you, don't you?"

"Don't you start on that, dear. At my age, anything could kill you. May as well have some fun while you can." Joy gave Kate a wicked grin and blew a perfect smoke ring her way.

"You said you were up at the old people's home?"

Joy let out a throaty bark. "I know what you're thinking, you think I should be in there myself. Well, let me tell you, age is all in the mind. My body may have shrivelled up like a rotten walnut, but inside I'm still twenty-one. No, scrap that, thirty-one, at twenty-one I was still a shy little mouse who wouldn't say boo to a goose."

Kate couldn't imagine Joy ever being described as shy. "What do you do up there?"

"Oh, you know, natter away, sing a few songs."

"You're a singer?"

"Only an amateur. My Fred used to say I had the voice of an angel. He was a piano player, you know, used to accompany me while I belted out the old classics. It was our party trick. Every birthday and Christmas, we'd get round that piano and take a trip down memory lane."

"Do you have children? Grandchildren?"

"One son. He lives in Australia, so may as well be dead the amount I get to see him. No grandchildren. He's a confirmed bachelor, if you know what I mean..." Joy tapped the side of her nose knowingly.

"Have you been out there to visit him?"

"Several times, but not for years now. My blood pressure's not too good. My doc reckons I'd cark it if I got on a plane. Could be a fun way to go." There was that wicked grin again. "He hasn't been over here in six years. Too busy with work, apparently. My mother had a saying about children- *A daughter's a daughter for life. A son's a son till he finds a wife*. My Malcolm doesn't have a wife, so I've no idea what his excuse can be."

"I'm sorry to hear that."

"Oh, don't be. It's not like I'm lonely."

"What are your plans for Christmas?"

"I'll be spending Christmas Day with some friends from the WI. We're all widows. The only rule we have is that none of us are allowed to cook."

"What do you have for your lunch? Sandwiches?"

"Not on Christmas Day!" Joy seemed genuinely affronted at the thought. "No, we have an Indian takeaway. You know, the one down the road? Have you tried it yet? Won lots of awards, you know."

"Oh, I've sampled it a few too many times. I've had to ration myself or I'll end up the size of a house."

"Ha! Not likely. You've got your grandmother's figure, skinny as a needle."

"Thanks, I think. Do you fancy coming round here for lunch on Boxing Day? Only if you don't have any other plans, of course."

Joy reached over and clasped Kate's hands. "That would be wonderful, dear. I can't remember the last time someone invited me round for lunch."

"Oh, but I thought..."

"Usually I invite myself. I was planning to do the same with you, but you beat me to it." Joy let out another throaty laugh. "Top me up, girl."

Kate topped up both their glasses. "Could you tell me a bit about my Nan? I really didn't know anything about her."

"Let's start at the very beginning, a very good place to start..." sang Joy, in a clear, powerful voice.

"Sounds good," said Kate, tucking her own blanket around her knees and taking a sip of wine.

"As I told you, I was a bit of a mouse when I was younger. Moira was the opposite. Her parents doted on her. Nowadays, you'd probably say she was spoilt. Anyway, doted, spoilt, whatever it was, it gave Moira confidence that the rest of us girls envied. She took me under her wing on the first day of school and I never left it until the day she died. She was a bright spark. The teachers hated her as she'd often correct them. She had scars on the back of her legs from the amount of beatings she got, but it never seemed to bother her. I think she was actually rather proud of her 'battle scars', as she called them."

"Sounds brutal."

"They were different times back then. Anyway, in those days, there was no prospect of university. We left school at sixteen and Moira got a job as a typist. Got me a job there too shortly after. That's where she met her Philip. Love at first sight it was. They'd only been courting two weeks before he asked her to marry him. Her father was furious, but she was bloody headstrong and only went and eloped. It caused quite a scandal. Word was that Philip had got her up the duff, but that turned out not to be true. They were married five years before they had your dad. It was a difficult birth. We all came close to losing her that day, but she battled through in that headstrong way of hers. They were the perfect family, from the outside, but I think Philip and your dad clashed a fair bit. Too similar, Moira used to say. Your dad became a bit rebellious, stealing from the local newsagent, drinking, fighting, the usual stuff. It was when Philip died that things really started to go wrong for them."

"How old was my dad when he lost his father?"

"Thirteen. Such an important age for youngsters. Moira couldn't cope at all. She shut everyone out, even me. She admitted later she'd had a nervous breakdown. Philip was the love of her life. She was never quite the same after that. Anyway, Philip's death sent your dad spinning off even further down the wrong path. By the time Moira had pulled herself together, your dad was in with a bad crowd and there was little she could do about it."

Tears filled Joy's eyes and Kate offered her a tissue.

"Thank you, dear. I think perhaps we should leave it there for now. I could bring some photographs with me next time I come round, if you'd like that?"

"Yes, I'd love that, thank you."

"Well, I'll let myself out. See you soon, dear."

"Bye." Kate downed the last of the wine and went inside to warm up.

Chapter 19

Kate woke up to one of those winter days that come so rarely they take your breath away. The grass outside glistened with frost, the bright morning sun not yet warm enough to melt it away. She wrapped up in two jumpers and her fluffy dressing gown and took her morning coffee outside. The cold air nipped at her fingers and she curled them tighter around her mug. This brief spell of good weather brought with it an optimism she hadn't felt for a while. Between Joy and Bob, she had begun to feel settled, like she was putting down roots, small as they might be.

Bob had a walk planned for that morning, and Kate was looking forward to seeing more of the local sights. Her *Guest Information Book* was filling up nicely. It occupied many long winter evenings as she'd filled it with some of the house's quirks (let the shower run for two minutes before you get in, don't turn the radiator to five unless you want to sleep in a furnace, don't put anything other than loo roll and human waste down the toilet…) and other useful information (Wi-Fi code, where to leave rubbish, nearest shops). The *activities* section was still a bit bare, but with Bob's help and a trip to the local Tourist Information office, it wasn't as sparse as it might otherwise have been.

Kate shivered and headed back to the warmth of the kitchen. What she'd really love was a bath, but she'd cleaned the upstairs bathroom the day before and couldn't face doing it again. Two more guests were due to arrive that evening, six p.m. they'd said, which should give her plenty of time to have a walk and make up the beds before they appeared.

In the hallway mirror, Kate checked her hair. It could go another day before needing a meeting with the shampoo bottle, she decided. And the only people she'd be seeing that day were Bob, and two strangers, so there was no need to make much effort.

At ten o'clock, Bob appeared at the front door, looking hot and bothered. "Are you all right?" asked Kate as he pulled a hanky from his pocket and wiped his brow.

"Yes fine, I thought I'd cycle over this morning rather than bring the car."

Kate leaned out of the doorway and saw his bike and helmet propped against the door. "Was it a long way? You look knackered."

"No, only a mile or so. It's those bloody hills that killed me. I decided after last weekend I needed to get a bit fitter so I can keep up with you next time we're on the trails."

Kate grinned and moved aside so he could bring his bike in. He wheeled it through to the back door and locked it up against a drain pipe.

"So, where are we off to today?"

"I thought I'd show you my favourite walk."

"Does it involve any driving? You know I've not got round to getting a car yet?"

"No, no need for the car. Are you ready to set off?"

"Yep, I'll just grab some water and snacks."

"Great, I'll wait out the front, I need to cool off."

"There'll be no problem cooling off. It's freezing out there."

Moments later, they were walking down a steep road towards the imposing jail. When they reached the bottom of the hill, Bob veered off to the right, and began climbing the lane which passed the entrance to the museum.

"What goes down has to come up," he said.

Kate groaned. "You've got that the wrong way round, you know?"

Bob winked and pressed ahead.

"Hey, slow down a bit will you, my legs aren't as long as yours."

Bob waited by the jail entrance. "I'll take you there soon. It's probably best to go at this time of year when it's less busy. Actually, I meant to ask you, our office are having our Christmas bash there. I don't suppose you fancy coming along?"

"Really? Won't that be a bit awkward? I mean, you're the only one I know. They may view me as an intruder."

Bob laughed. "Not at all. You'd be doing me a massive favour. Everyone is bringing a plus-one. It's a rule I hate. Morag from accounts brings her sister every year in the hope of setting me up with her. Her sister's into snakes." Bob shuddered.

"Snakes? What do you mean, like *snake* snakes?"

"Are there any other kind? She has a house full of them, apparently. It's all she talks about. Last year I was worried she had one in her handbag."

"You're not scared of snakes, are you?"

"Too right I am, and heights, in case you were wondering. Sensible phobias they are too, so no laughing."

"I wasn't going to laugh. But I'm not sure the prospect of snake-woman is making this Christmas party very appealing."

"Hmm, no. Maybe I should've kept that quiet. What do you think, anyway?"

"When is it?"

"Next Saturday."

"I'd better check my diary."

"Yes, of course."

"Bob, I'm joking. Of course I don't have anything in my

diary. Plus, I'm intrigued to meet your scaly admirer."

Bob huffed and pressed on up the hill. Soon the houses thinned out, and the road narrowed, becoming little more than a track, with grass poking through the tarmac in the middle. The few houses they passed were a mix of large new-builds and traditional cottages.

"I can't believe we're in the countryside, so close to the town."

"Lovely, isn't it?"

Kate nodded and followed Bob as he turned down yet another tiny road.

"Just stop here a minute and look at that."

Kate turned around and gasped at the view. The whole town lay spread before her, sparkling in the winter sun. It looked beautifully quaint, and very different to the slightly depressing place of empty shops and daytime drunks she'd witnessed so far.

"What's that up there?" she asked, pointing to a large monument above the town.

Bob looked at her with surprise. "It's the beacon. Don't tell me you've not noticed it yet?"

"Um, no."

Bob slapped his hand to his forehead and let out a theatrical sigh. "I've really got my work cut out with you, haven't I? It's a nature reserve, Kate. A bloody great nature reserve practically right behind your house. Well, a five-minute walk more like, but not more than five minutes. What on earth have you been doing with yourself all this time?"

"Hey, it's not even two months since I moved in, and I've been so busy with the house..."

Bob wasn't buying her excuses. "Right, well, consider this homework from your tour guide. By the time I see you next weekend, I want you to have explored up there. Deal?"

"Deal."

They turned off the road and onto a track that wove between two enormous fields filled with solar panels. The track led them into a forest, majestic conifers towering above their heads.

"Wow, this is so Christmassy. I feel like I'm in Scandinavia."

"I know a great spot. Come on."

They walked through the forest, Kate feeling like she'd been transported to Narnia, just without the snow. Near the bottom of the hill, Bob stopped and pushed through wide pine-covered branches, indicating that Kate should follow. He led her into a moss-carpeted clearing, their feet sinking into the soft ground, trees looming over them, blocking the sky.

"Oh my God, this is beautiful."

"Yeah, it is. Me and Dad used to camp out here when I was younger. Looks like people still do," said Bob, kicking the remains of a fire. "He'd insist on us building our own shelter, then he'd help me make a fire and we'd toast marshmallows and tell ghost stories. Scared me so much I'd be pinned to him all night."

"He sounds like such a cool dad. I'd like to meet him sometime."

"Did you say you brought snacks?"

"Um, yes," said Kate, digging a box of flapjack out of her bag and wondering why he'd avoided her suggestion of meeting his parents. Was he embarrassed by her? Or them? Maybe they weren't as good friends as she thought. They sat in silence, eating the sticky flapjack and sharing coffee from her flask. Kate felt a pang of sadness at all the opportunities missed with her own dad. Had he enjoyed camping? He probably did if it involved drugs or booze. She pushed the thought away.

"Want to see the place me and Dad called our bathroom?"

"You mean the place you went to the loo?"

"God no, that was anywhere a shovel would sink into the ground. No, I mean the place we washed." He used his fingers to air quote the word *washed* and Kate wondered where on earth they were going.

They left the clearing and re-joined the path. A couple of mountain bikers whizzed past them and Kate made a mental note to return here with her borrowed bike. Before long, she heard the sound of running water and glimpsed a river through the trees.

"Is this the place?" she asked, but Bob shook his head and walked on.

"Here we are," he said, stopping at a stone sign with instructions for anglers carved into it. He scrambled down a muddy embankment and Kate followed. Kate lost her footing and stumbled into Bob, who was standing on a beach of sorts, made from earth rather than sand. Bare tree branches hung over the wide river, tickling the water like fingers. The bank on the opposite side was grassy, jutting out into the water like a pontoon.

"That's a great spot for jumping in," said Bob, pointing to the bank. "The river over that side's deeper than it looks. I'll bring you here in summer if you like. It's a great spot for a picnic and swim, and best of all, none of the tourists know about it. They squish like sardines onto the north coast beaches, while we have our own empty beach right here."

Kate looked dubiously at the brown swirling water. "And you say this is where you washed?"

Bob laughed. "Yeah, Mum would be mad when we got home stinking of river, mud sticking to God knows where. She'd hold her nose and send us straight for a shower."

"She didn't come with you on your expeditions?"

"No, those were boys' trips. She would sometimes bring a picnic down and meet us by the river." Bob looked wistful, as though caught up in memories. "It's been a long time since I've been here. Last time it was for Dad's sixtieth, Ellie was with us then. She loved it here, not that I could ever persuade her into the water. That was a step too far for my city girl." A sad smile played on Bob's lips, his eyes glistening.

"You must miss her."

"I miss them all."

"All?"

"Oh, ignore me, I'm being a sentimental old fool. Come on, we'd better get going. It's a fair old way back."

Bob was quiet on the walk back. Kate left him to his thoughts, focusing instead on moving her tired legs forward. They can't have walked more than five miles, but with all the hills, her legs were really feeling it. The worst hill was the one leading back to the house. She was relieved when Bob had to stop halfway, allowing both of them to catch their breath. When they reached the top, both were red in the face, too out of breath to hold a conversation.

The thought of a refreshing cup of tea drove them forward the final few hundred meters. As they turned the corner onto Kate's road, she gripped Bob's arm and pulled him to an abrupt stop.

"Oh no."

"What's the matter?"

"Look." Kate pointed to her house, where two men were sitting on the doorstep, hiking back packs lying on the ground beside them.

"Who are they?"

"Well, I really hope I'm wrong. But I think they're my next guests." Kate checked her watch. "If it is them, they're four hours early, and I'm in no way, shape or form ready for them."

Chapter 20

Despite her leg muscles screaming in complaint, Kate ran the final hundred metres to her house. On reaching it, she leaned against the wall, waving her hand frantically in a greeting, whilst trying to get enough breath to speak.

"Hi... I'm...Kate. Are you... Nicholas?"

"Yes, I am. Pleased to meet you. This is Ryan, my son."

Kate gave them both a wave and took a few deep breaths. "I'm so sorry. Have you been waiting long? I wasn't expecting you till six."

"Really? I'm sorry, I thought I'd said two in our messages, but I'm not great with computers, so it could easily be my mistake." Kate saw the teenager roll his eyes and glare at his father before putting his head down to stare at his phone.

"Look, I'm really sorry, but I'm not quite ready for you. Are you OK to sit in the living room with a cuppa while I get the last few bits sorted?"

"I can do better than that," said Bob, appearing by Kate's side with a clinking carrier bag. Kate looked at him in astonishment. He gave her a grin and mouthed, *nipped to the shop*.

"This is my friend Bob," said Kate, unlocking the door. "I'm guessing there are some beers in that bag of his, so make yourselves comfortable while I sort out your rooms."

Kate showed them into the living room and settled them on the purple sofas. Bob followed her through to the kitchen to get a bottle opener.

"Are you OK? Is there anything I can do to help?"

"Entertaining them while I get their bedding ironed would be a massive help."

"Ironing? Seriously, Kate, I don't think they care if their duvet covers are ironed. I'll check."

"Bob, no," Kate hissed, but he already had his head around the living room door.

"No need to bother with the iron, Kate," he called back, getting a glare in return.

Kate gathered up the un-ironed bedding and ran up the stairs. It was typical she had two beds to make, she thought, pulling out the sofa bed for the young lad to sleep on. She whipped a duster around both rooms, checked the coffee, tea, and biscuits were well stocked, then gave both wooden floors a final sweep. She ran back down the stairs, pushing away the hair that had stuck to her forehead as she raced around.

"I'm so sorry about the wait," she said as she joined the three men in the living room.

"Honestly, it's no problem at all. Bob here's been keeping us company, telling us all the things we can do in the town."

Kate noticed the teenage boy give Bob a shy smile. Wow, he must have done a good job of entertaining if he'd even won the sullen Ryan round.

"So, what are your plans while you're here?" asked Kate, more out of politeness than interest.

"We thought we'd head to the north coast and try out a bit of surfing tomorrow. Ryan's always wanted to have a go."

"Yeah, like, when I was five," Ryan muttered, loud enough for them all to hear. Nicholas gave a nervous laugh.

"I'm sure you'll enjoy it when you get there," said Kate.

"Do you surf?" Nicholas asked her.

"No, I don't. I've not long moved to the area actually and that's one thing I definitely want to try."

"Don't worry, it's on the list," said Bob, grinning up at her.

"List?" asked Nicholas, confused.

"Oh, it's just this silly thing me and Bob are doing. He's taken on the role of tour guide and week by week he's showing me all the things on offer locally." Kate flushed at her unintended innuendo. "We've not made it as far as the coast yet, we've stuck to Bodmin so far."

Ryan gave a snort, making it clear he didn't expect there'd be much to do in the town. Kate felt her hackles rise.

"What have you done so far?" asked Nicholas, making up for his son's rudeness.

"Mostly walking, biking and touring local pubs." Kate grinned at him.

"Sounds good to me. I wish we were staying longer so I could join in."

Ryan recoiled in embarrassment at his father's friendly banter.

"Actually, Ryan might enjoy the Lanhydrock trails."

Ryan looked up from his phone. "What are they?"

"Mountain bike trails."

"Didn't bring our bikes," he said, returning to his phone.

"You can hire them there. I think they're open till 5 so you've got plenty of time if you fancy it this afternoon."

"Can you come with us?"

Bob looked at Ryan in surprise. "Me? I'm not sure you'd want me there. Kate's the cyclist round here. I'm a bit too out of shape but I'm working on it," he said, patting his belly.

"You don't want to come, I get it," growled Ryan,

blushing.

"No, it's not that at all."

Bob looked at Nicholas who shrugged and said, "It's fine by me if you want to come."

"Great, count me in. What about you, Kate?"

"No, you're alright. My legs are still aching from all the walking. How about I show you to your rooms before you go?"

"Sure, lead the way," said Nicholas, getting up and indicating that Ryan should do the same.

Kate was relieved to find they were both extremely happy with the accommodation, neither noticing the crumpled bed linen, or if they did, showing no sign they cared. Twenty minutes later she was waving the unlikely trio off, praying Bob's hostess with the mostess routine would win her a five-star review.

*

"How was it?" Kate asked Bob. They were sitting on her bed, finishing up the Indian takeaway she'd brought him as a thank you.

"It was good fun, but a little awkward."

"Really, how?"

"Well, I got the impression Ryan only wanted me there so he wouldn't have to be alone with his dad. I'd even go as far as saying he invited me with the express intention of pissing Nick off."

"Oh dear. That's pretty cruel."

"Yeah, I felt awful for Nick. He kept trying to engage the lad but was either ignored or scoffed at. I know teenagers can be difficult, but I don't ever remember being like that with my dad."

"Maybe there's more to their relationship that we know. You can never tell what goes on behind closed doors."

"Yeah, I don't get the impression Nick is around much. He told me he'd booked this trip as a bonding exercise. Not sure how that's going to turn out. Don't get me wrong, Ryan's a great kid, but he doesn't seem to have much respect for his father. Let's hope the next day or so helps rectify that."

"How old is he?"

"Fifteen."

Kate grimaced. "That's an evil age to be."

"Really?" asked Bob, his voice full of surprise. "I loved being that age. How come you hated it so much?"

"I think maybe it's different for girls. I hated the way I looked; too skinny, too short, too spotty. It didn't help that Mum did bugger all around the house so I was constantly trying to find something clean to wear. Even once I'd figured out the washing machine, most of my clothes were ill fitting or had holes. I became pretty adept at accessorising to hide holes. I was quite handy with a needle and thread too."

"That sounds rotten. I think that's the best thing about aging, feeling more comfortable in your own skin."

"I'm not sure I'll ever get to that point."

"Really? But I can only see one... two... three...four spots on your face these days."

Kate leaped up and studied herself in the mirror.

"Kate, I was joking. You really have nothing to worry about. You're so pretty."

Both Kate and Bob flushed at the compliment. "Um, thanks," she said. "Well maybe my thirties will be the decade I finally get some self-confidence."

"Let's hope so. It's all downhill from forty so you don't have that much time."

Kate frowned at him, but saw he was joking and chucked the corner of her Naan bread his way. "Do you fancy watching a film or do you have to get back?"

"A film sounds good, as long as it's not too girly."

"Too girly?"

"Yeah, you know, romantic, full of hot guys wooing hot

girls."

Kate laughed. "I'm not sure anyone uses the word *wooing* these days. You choose the film. Just make sure it's nothing too *manly*."

Bob grinned and began scrolling through Netflix. In the end they chose to watch *Little Miss Sunshine* after Kate discovered to her horror Bob had never seen it before. They propped themselves up against the headboard, Kate's laptop forming a natural barrier between them. The film was only half an hour in when she heard a snorting sound and turned to see Bob slumped against the pillows, snoring away. *All that walking and cycling has caught up with him*, she thought, pausing the film to save it for another day.

Kate grabbed a blanket from the armchair beside her and spread it over Bob. He looked like an overgrown child, mouth open, snoring away. He stirred and curled up on his side, his messy hair falling across his forehead. Kate smiled, grateful that she had made such a good friend so soon after moving to the town.

Kate picked up the book from her bedside table, and had read half a page when her phone buzzed. She grabbed it quickly so as not to disturb Bob and saw a message pop up from Alex. He'd started messaging her several times a day. Nothing of any consequence, just a series of YouTube videos that she either didn't understand or didn't find funny. Needless to say, she always responded with a laughing emoji, reluctant to show her ignorance. She tried sending a few conversational texts *How are you? Good day at work?* But as the only replies she received were in the form of cat videos, she'd stopped trying. It was enough that he was in contact with her in the first place.

Kate threw her book down in surprise as Bob began flailing his arms, mumbling in his sleep. It was hard to make out what he was saying, but she picked out the phrases *I can't. I've tried everything. I don't know what to do*. The next thing she knew, Bob was whimpering beside her, actual tears streaming down his face. She wasn't sure what you're supposed to do with someone having nightmares, but decided it was better to wake him than let him be tortured any longer.

A gentle tapping on the arm achieved nothing. Bob flailed his arms all the harder and Kate had to duck to avoid a flying fist. Next, she tried saying his name. "Bob, Bob," she whispered. Nothing. Kate said his name as loud as she dared for fear of waking the guests. She tapped his arm harder until it verged on a slap. Eventually Bob's eyelids flickered and he turned his head towards her.

"Where am I?" His voice was groggy with sleep, and Kate wondered if she'd done the right thing in waking him.

"You're at my house. We were watching a film, remember? You fell asleep and had a bad dream."

Bob wiped his mouth against his sleeve and rubbed his palms against his eyes.

"Sorry about that. What time is it?"

Kate checked her watch. "It's nine o'clock."

Bob leaped out of the bed, running his hands frantically through his hair. "No, no, no. Are you sure? Nine o'clock?" Kate nodded. "Argh," he wailed, bashing his palm against his forehead. He turned to Kate his face like thunder. "Why didn't you wake me sooner?" His tone was accusatory, as if she'd done something terribly wrong.

"Sorry, I..."

"Oh no, oh no, this can't be happening. I have to go, I have to..."

Before Kate could ask what he had to do, and where exactly he needed to be, Bob ran out of the room and slammed his way out of the front door. Kate looked at the empty takeaway cartons and faces frozen mid-sentence on the laptop screen. What the hell had just happened?

Chapter 21

Nicholas had read his newspaper from cover to cover by nine-thirty, and decided he couldn't leave Ryan to sleep any longer. The surf lesson was booked for twelve, and he needed to find the beach, somewhere to park and the wetsuit hire before then. He folded the paper and threw it on the nearest table before padding through to Ryan's room. Nicholas gave a tentative knock but there was no answer. He tried again. Nothing.

"Ryan?" No answer. "Ryan?"

"Fuck off," came a voice from behind the door.

Nicholas recoiled, feeling simultaneously hurt and angered by the way his son spoke to him.

"Not a morning person then?" he called back cheerfully.

He heard Ryan groan, and guessed his son had put his head under a pillow. Nicholas opened the door to find Ryan had done just that. He walked into the room and sat on the edge of the sofa bed, which squeaked in protest at his weight.

"Look mate, I'm sorry to wake you, but we need to get going if we're to make it to the surf lesson in time."

"I'm not your mate and I don't want to go surfing."

Nicholas shoved his fist in his mouth to stop him saying something he'd regret, and took five deep breaths as his meditation teacher had taught him. What he'd give to be back in his Hong Kong office right now.

"I'm afraid you don't have a choice," Nicholas said, sounding calmer than he felt. "You need to get up now or it will be the cold-water treatment for you."

Ryan couldn't help removing his head from under the pillow. "Cold water treatment?"

"A trick my dad used on me when I was your age. Trust me, you don't want to find out how it works. I suggest you get up before I'm forced to use it."

Ryan threw his pillow on the floor and moved to the edge of the bed. "Aren't you going to give me some privacy while I get changed?"

"No problem. I can wait downstairs if you want to use the bathroom in peace too."

Ryan nodded, so Nicholas gathered up his stuff and headed down into the living room. Moments later, his host wandered in, watering can in hand. "Morning," she said, clearly surprised to find him in her sitting room.

"Oh hi. Sorry, I know this isn't part of the guest accommodation, but I have a teenage boy upstairs who's like a bear with a sore head, and I was worried what he'd do if I didn't get out of his way."

Kate laughed. "That bad?"

Nicholas nodded and smiled a sad smile.

"It's tough being a teenager. I remember it too well," said Kate, pouring water into the base of a large Aloe Vera.

"Yeah, I'm older than you and don't remember much about my youth. And I have zero experience of teenagers so I'm really out of my depth here."

Kate paused her watering and looked at Nicholas with curiosity.

"I've not been around for my son. Not through choice, but the truth is I don't know him at all. I wish we could've reconnected when he was a bit younger. Might have been easier then. I'm worried now it's too late."

"Well, I lost my dad a long time ago, and I can tell you that I'd give anything to be able to spend more time with him. Ryan may not appreciate the effort your making right now, but give him time."

"Thanks," said Nicholas, blushing slightly as his son shuffled into the room.

*

Nicholas took the roads at a snail's pace, aware that there was precious cargo on board. Ryan meanwhile, tapped his fingers against the passenger side window and sighed each time Nicholas hit the break.

"Sorry, mate, I have to be gentle with the hire car. It will cost a fortune if I take it back scratched."

"Whatever," said Ryan, sneering as he turned his face back to the window.

Nicholas had travelled to all corners of the world, but he wasn't sure he'd ever encountered roads as narrow as those he was now driving on. If he met another vehicle he'd have to reverse miles, as there was no way he was getting too close to the stone-filled Cornish hedges. His hands gripped the wheel so tight he had to keep rubbing their sweat away on his jeans. He could have cried when he finally caught sight of the sea. It must be a glorious view on a warm sunny day. Unfortunately, drizzle had set in shortly after they left Bodmin, and the sea resembled a sheet of steel rather than the cerulean promised in his guide book.

Parking the car proved no problem, as few other souls were tempted by the freezing temperatures, brisk wind and drizzle. Plus, it was a Monday. All the locals would either be at work or school. The car pulled up onto tightly-packed sand and Nicholas fought against the breeze to pay for a ticket.

"It's a bit blowy out here," he said, leaning into the car. Ryan was scrolling through Instagram and didn't even bother to look up.

"This is such a shit plan, Dad."

Nicholas' heart squeezed and tears welled in his eyes. *Dad*. Forty-seven years on the planet and that was the first time anyone had used that word to describe him. He pulled himself together and zipped his raincoat tighter around his chin.

"Come on, Ryan, the surf school's just over there. Let's go."

Ryan got himself out of the vehicle at the speed of a sloth and with the enthusiasm of a pig on its way to the abattoir. His thin, brand name jacket was no protection from the elements and Nicholas could see how uncomfortable he was.

"Do you want to borrow my coat? Might keep you warmer?"

Ryan looked his father up and down with disgust, before slouching off in the direction of the only surf school still open this late in the year. Nicholas jogged to catch up with his son. A tanned young man with long beard and even longer bleach-blond hair sat doing a crossword in a surfboard filled van. He looked up as father and son approached.

"Hi, welcome you nutters." The man held up a fist and Nicholas and Ryan each gave it a self-conscious bump. "As you can see, we've got the beach to ourselves."

The man laughed, showing a perfect set of pearly whites. In that moment Nicholas hated their instructor. He'd felt his masculinity being torn away shred by shred ever since they'd left the comfort of London. First, he'd been shown up on the bike trails, not just by lack of skill but in Ryan's clear preference of the random bloke who'd tagged along. Now here he was stood next to a hairy bronzed Adonis, his own few remaining wisps of hair being torn off by the wind. Not only that, he was about to squeeze his middle-aged spread into the surfing equivalent of a condom. Great.

Ryan, on the other hand, seemed completely taken by the surfer dude, laughing at his crappy jokes and listening intently as he ran through a safety briefing. All Nicholas had picked up was *try not to drown, there's no lifeguards on the beach at this time of year.*

Ryan slipped on his wetsuit with the ease of someone who had done it a thousand times before. Nicholas, who had tried surfing in Hawaii, Brazil and Australia, fell over twice, and in the end had to concede defeat and get the instructor to yank the thing on for him. He caught Ryan's eye and noticed a smirk as Adonis heaved a wetsuit leg over Nicholas' foot. At least he'd made his son laugh, even if it was at him not with him.

"Hey guys, you got phones, want me to take a photo?"

"Yeah, cool," said Ryan who looked both handsome and ninja like in head to toe black.

They stood side by side, Nicholas sucking his gut in, feeling like a pregnant penguin while Adonis snapped away. With the photoshoot over, Adonis lay three surfboards out on the sand and gave them a lesson on how to jump up to standing. It was reassuringly straightforward on dry land, but Nicholas knew with a sinking heart it wouldn't be such an easy feat out on the water.

Adonis slipped a board under his arm as though it weighed nothing, while Nicholas and Ryan struggled to coordinate themselves with their boards. They'd been instructed to work as a team, one at the front, the other at the back, *sharing the weight*, Adonis informed them. Nicholas wanted to point out they were total strangers, so teamwork may not be their forte, but Adonis was already striding off towards the sea.

By the time they caught their instructor up on the shoreline, both Ryan and Nicholas were sweating profusely and seriously pissed off. Adonis appeared not to notice the tension, running them through the basics once more before launching himself into the crashing waves.

As he stepped into the sea, Nicholas felt ice-cold water travel up both legs. His genitals shrivelled and his heart pounded so hard he wondered if he'd die right there and then. Weren't wetsuits supposed to keep you warm? The water around them was angry, churning up seaweed as foaming white horses crashed against the sand. Adonis shouted instructions, but they were carried away on the wind, father and son following blindly, as the water deepened and the cold reached their bones.

Nicholas should never have mentioned he'd surfed before. The result of boasting was being left entirely alone to fend for himself, while Adonis focused all his attention on Ryan. He gave up trying to get on his own board and watched in awe as Ryan began paddling ahead of a wave, jumping up as it pushed him on, and standing up, arms flailing for a precious three seconds before falling flat on his face into the water.

"Woohoo!" came Ryan's scream as his head surfaced from beneath a wave. "Did you see that, Dad? I did it!"

Nicholas gave a thumbs up, unable to shout congratulations due to the lump blocking his throat. He paddled further out, the salt water washing away the salt water streaming from his eyes. As he lay on his board, buffeted by wave after wave he wondered what it would have been like when Ryan was younger. He could've bought him to the beach, played cricket with him, built sandcastles. He could've done all the things with his son that his own dad did with him.

A black clad figure broke into Nicholas' thoughts as Adonis slid through the water like a seal. "Your boy's doing great," he shouted. "How about you give it a try?"

Nicholas was happy lying splayed out on top of his board, but his pride accepted the challenge and he maneuvered the board around, looking over his shoulder as a large, angry wave headed his way.

"Remember what I told you," yelled Adonis. "This is a big one so be careful. Ready? PADDLE!"

Nicholas began paddling furiously. He felt the wave hit the back of the board, lifting him higher and higher. His mind went blank of all technique he'd been shown and he tried to scramble first to his knees then to his feet. The board wobbled precariously beneath him and the world went into slow motion as his feet left the solid board and his head cut into the wave.

Nicholas had felt fear many times in his life, but nothing compared to the sensation of being pulled under the black water, tossed around like a rag doll, not knowing which direction to swim to reach the precious air his lungs craved. Time stood still as his senses dimmed. After what felt like a lifetime his head made contact with the sky, and he took deep choking breaths. Adonis and Ryan appeared beside him, each grabbing him under an arm, dragging him through the water towards the shoreline.

Back on firm ground, Nicholas threw up a stomach full of seawater and held his head in his hands trying to get his breath. Ryan sat next to him, stroking his back and telling him- *Everything's alright now, Dad. Just take deep, slow breaths. That's it, you're doing really well.*

Nicholas took his head from his hands and looked into his son's eyes. They shared the same green eyes, but Ryan's were all the more startling thanks to the thick lashes he'd inherited from his mother. Relations between the parents had been formal at best, strained at worst. Nicholas admired Karen's wariness to his new role in Ryan's life. It was a sign of her protectiveness as a mother. It had taken a lot of persuading before she'd allowed him to bring Ryan away for a couple of days, even more so as it involved time off school. Hearing Ryan's compassion, Nicholas felt immense gratitude to the woman who had single-handedly raised his son. The grumpy teenage act was just that, an act, he now realised. A method of self-preservation against being let down again. Nicholas grabbed Ryan's hand and squeezed it. To his surprise, Ryan pulled it away, but only so he could reposition it across his father's shoulders.

"I think my surfing days are over, mate. But you carry on. I'll watch you from here."

"Are you sure? I won't leave you if you're still feeling

shit."

"I'm fine, honest. Off you go."

Ryan grinned and ran back into the waves, jumping on his board and paddling out into the sea.

Chapter 22

Kate stepped outside carrying a full bin bag and narrowly missed tripping over the boy on her front step.

"Ryan? What are you doing out here?"

Ryan tried to blow smoke out from the corner of his mouth, but ended up choking and needing a few back slaps from Kate before he could catch his breath.

"Does your dad know you're out here smoking?"

"Yeah, none of his business though."

"Fair enough. I don't suppose you can spare one of those?"

"I've only got rollies."

"Even better," said Kate, taking a pinch of tobacco from the offered tin and expertly twisting the thin paper into a tube. Ryan offered her a light, and she sat beside him on the step, taking a deep drag and trying not to cough.

"You don't look like a smoker."

"I'm not really. Gave up a few years ago, but the odd one now and then can be very tempting. Anyway, I thought all young people were into vaping these days?"

"Yeah, most are."

"But not you?"

"I like to be different." He smiled at her, the first open, warm smile she'd seen from him since he arrived.

"How did you get on today with the surfing?"

"Good yeah, I stood up a few times. Dad properly stacked it, thought he was going to need CPR." He laughed and took a puff of his rollie.

"I'm glad you guys are having a good time."

"Yeah, I didn't want to come if I'm honest, but it's not been as bad as I thought it would."

"Why didn't you want to come?"

Ryan looked at his feet.

"Sorry, you don't have to answer that if it's too personal a question."

"No, it's fine. I don't really know my dad. I only met him a couple of months ago."

"Wow."

"Yeah, mad isn't it? He didn't abandon me if that's what you're thinking. Him and Mum lost touch, and by the time she knew she was pregnant she had no way of contacting him."

"That must have been so hard for her."

"It was. I've always hated him for leaving her, but he didn't really, did he?"

"So how did you get in touch with him after all this time?"

"Mum found him on Facebook after I started hassling her about tracking him down. Knowing how old he was, Facebook was the obvious place to start the search." Kate winced, wondering if her own Facebook account put her in the *old* category. "They didn't have Facebook back when they got together, or she could've found him sooner. It was only a one-night thing between them, so she didn't know where he lived or anything like that."

"How do they get on now?"

"It's a bit frosty. I think Mum feels he owes her big time for all the years she's spent looking after me by herself."

"That's understandable. So, this was a getting to know you sort of trip?"

"Yeah, that's right. I'm still not sure I like him, I mean,

he's well embarrassing. But he's sort of growing on me, you know?"

"He seems a decent bloke from the little time I've spent with him. Will you spend more time together when you go home?"

"He lives in Hong Kong, but he's promised to come and visit again this year, and says I can go and stay with him. I've told him I'll think about it."

"I doubt you're looking for advice, but I'll give it anyway," said Kate, stubbing her cigarette out beneath her shoe. "My dad died when I was really young. I never got the chance to know him properly. The cruellest thing is I still miss him, I mean, how crazy is that, missing someone you barely knew?"

"I get it," said Ryan, looking at Kate intently. "I've missed my dad for years, and I didn't even know who my dad was."

"Then all the more reason to spend as much time with him as you can. I wish I'd had that chance. There's so much I want to know about Dad that I'll never find out. If yours is offering to fly you out to Hong Kong, grab the opportunity. I'm sure you won't regret it."

"Thanks. You're pretty cool for an old bird, you know."

Kate looked at him in horror, but his mouth was curled up slightly at the sides and she could tell he was joking. "Well, you're pretty cool for a yoof. Now, instead of nattering away to me, why don't you go back inside and spend some time with your dad."

"May as well," said Ryan. "I'm freezing my tits off out here."

Kate shuffled over to let him pass and sat staring out onto the street. Had her dad rode up and down here on his bike? Had he smoked cigarettes where she sat now? Was he sullen like the Ryan she'd met yesterday, or thoughtful and sensitive like the Ryan she'd spoken to this evening? Hopefully Joy would be able to shed some light onto her dad's character next time she came over.

With a blanket covering the bin bags to deter the gulls, Kate headed back inside to warm up. She made herself a cup of tea and checked her phone for the thousandth time that day. There had been no word from Bob since he'd shouted at her the previous night, and she wasn't prepared to be the one to break the stalemate. It wasn't just Bob who'd gone dark on her, there were no messages from anyone. Kate wondered if her absence from Bath had resulted in out of sight and out of mind. There hadn't been a single cat video from Alex that day.

Kate wondered if Bob still wanted her to go to the office party at the weekend. She wasn't sure she wanted to anymore, not until he apologised anyway. At that moment her phone buzzed with a message from Bob, in that spooky, *your phone is reading your mind* way it did sometimes.

Hi, really sorry about last night. I shouldn't have spoken to you the way I did. I was a shit, and understand if you don't want to come on Saturday.

Kate considered waiting to reply, but leaving people hanging wasn't really her style.

Thanks for saying sorry, and yes, you were totally out of order. It wasn't my fault you fell asleep. I'll still come on Saturday as long as you leave shouty Bob at home... and buy ALL the drinks. What's the dress code?

Bob's reply came in a matter of seconds. *Shirt, jacket and trousers.*

Haha. So formal, proper dress kind of thing?

Yes, sounds about right? Just your usual Christmas party stuff.

Usual Christmas party? Kate couldn't bear to admit she'd never been to one. In all the years she'd been with Alex he never once invited her to his office party. Not that she'd minded, she'd accepted his explanation that it was a chance to press the flesh with the right people, do some deals etcetera. But still, she would have liked to go, just once to see what all the fuss was about. The Sunbeam didn't do staff parties, unless you count Angie's leaving do when they went bowling and were banned for life after Flo threw up and did a moonie at the same time.

Kate put her phone down and scoured her wardrobe for anything party suitable. She found bugger all and was beginning to think she'd need to make an emergency dash to the charity shop when she remembered the dress belonging to her grandmother. Kate pulled out the box she'd stored it in and took off layers of tissue paper. Aside from the musty smell, the dress was as good as new.

With the bedroom door locked, Kate took off her leggings and hoodie and slipped the dress over her head. She moved over to the mirror and scrutinized the fit. It was too big on the bodice but that was easily rectified. The hemline skimmed the floor, heels would be needed unless she wanted to spend the entire night tripping up. Kate turned around and grimaced at the sight of her greying bra straps. Either she'd have to fork out on a fancy low-backed bra, or go without. She pulled the dress down to her waist and took off her bra. Pinching the fabric at the sides Kate assessed whether she could get away with the lack of underwear. Just about, she decided, but if it was cold in the jail she'd need a shawl to cover her modesty.

Kate pulled the dress back over her head and put her old, comfortable clothes back on. She grabbed her battered old sewing box from a cupboard and took out some pins. Her hand stroked the magazine clippings glued to the top of what was really an ice cream tub. There were several faded boy band members staring up at her, partly covered by flowers and butterflies. The sewing box had been her one slice of girly girlness. The walls of her bedroom had been too damp to hold posters, her clothes too stained and shabby to be considered pretty. But she'd spent quiet hours making friendship bracelets for the friends she'd one day have, or sewing patches onto clothes with scraps of fabric found in charity shops.

The sewing box transported her back to her old bedroom, a place she'd long since tucked firmly in her memory. Her mum was humming in the kitchen, radio on too loud. She'd been well and truly back on the booze when they lived in that flat. Kate thought of all the times she'd topped the vodka bottle up with water, but somehow Mum still managed to get pissed.

Her bedroom door back then had a hole in it, where one of Mum's boyfriends had kicked it during a fight. There had been a conveyor belt of men over the years. Kate never bothered to get to know them, knowing they'd only be in Mum's life for a month at best. She retreated to her room when they came around, some of them probably hadn't even realised there was a child in the house.

Kate opened her eyes and looked around her bedroom. It couldn't be further from her past. Clean, fresh damp-free walls, crisp, ironed M&S bedding, fairy lights around the window. Perhaps one of the reasons she started the Airbnb was that she didn't know what to do with all the space. Her bedroom and kitchen were more than enough for her, after years living in poky hovels, the thought of spare rooms felt extravagant.

Kate turned her attention to the teal dress in front of her. She slipped it on inside out to pin it, and searched for a matching thread. The tasks would be easier with a sewing machine, silk was notoriously tricky, you only had to watch Sewing Bee to know that. Still, sewing up the dress would take all her concentration, a welcome distraction from the past occupying her thoughts. Kate threaded a needle, pushed thoughts of her childhood aside, and set to work.

Chapter 23

One thing Kate always found puzzling, was people's attitude to charity shops. Since arriving in Bodmin she'd heard plenty of sniffy comments about how the town was *all charity shops these days.* Kate thought it was one of the best things about the town. They were an Aladdin's cave of goodies, full of the surprising, quaint, quirky, and best of all, random. Kate felt a thrill searching through the rails and shelves looking for bargains. It seemed stupid buying new clothes when you could pick up quality second hand for a fraction of the price.

Kate whiled away many hours that week in the vast array of charity shops in town. Her mission had been to find a pair of heeled black ankle boots. In doing so she had broken her golden charity shop rule- *never go with something specific in mind.* Do that, and you'd be guaranteed not to find what you were looking for. No, the best approach was an open mind. Having searched for black boots and drawn a blank, Kate walked down to the bottom of the town to begin her trawl again.

It was fortunate she was size five, and four at a squeeze as there was no shortage of footwear in her size. In the first shop she tried on a pair of fake snake-skin stilettos. They looked good, but there was no chance she could walk in them. Her attempt at doing so resulted in a rail of jumpers being pulled to the floor and an annoyed shopkeeper.

In the second shop she found a pair of silver sequined platform shoes. There was no way they'd go with the dress but Kate was so tempted by their sparkle she paid the £2.99 for them and put them in her bag. She couldn't imagine ever needing them in Bodmin, but life was full of surprises so best to be prepared. Kate sent a picture of them to Flo, who sent back a dancing gif, followed by a photo of her cleaning bucket and a message *chat after work*.

Kate found nothing suitable in shops three or four, but in shop five she struck gold. In her focus for black she'd overlooked the crimson suede ankle boots sitting at the back of the shelf. Crimson and teal, could she get away with it? It would be a big departure from her usual monochrome, but maybe her wardrobe needed a shake up, and where better to start than a Christmas party?

Kate slipped on the boots, feeling like Cinderella about to go to the ball. They had enough of a heel to be considered *dressy,* but it was low enough that she could still walk, even dance if the mood took her. She checked the price on the label, £3.99. Just what she wanted, and a bargain at that.

Opposite the charity shop was a gift shop selling trinkets, jewellery and clothes. Kate nipped across the narrow road and the door pinged as she let herself inside. She scoured the cabinets before settling on just what she wanted. The assistant wandered over to unlock the cabinet and handed Kate the large hoop earrings, crimson and teal beads jangling from the silver. It really was her lucky day.

On her way home, Kate passed a smart menswear shop. She noticed a familiar figure in the middle of the shop and stopped just out of sight to look in. Bob was staring into a mirror, a willing shop assistant holding up a selection of ties and bow-ties. Bob held each one up in turn, squinting at his own reflection before trying another. Kate's stomach fluttered at the sight of him, *must be excitement about the party*, she told herself before moving on.

Back at home, Kate laid her haul on the bed. It was a bold combination of colours, but Kate pushed away the nagging insecurities in her head and booked herself a hair appointment for Saturday morning. *Why are you making such an effort? You can't polish a turd. It's only a local Christmas do.*

Shut up, Kate said to herself, determined for once to override the negative thoughts in her brain. When was the last time she properly dressed up? It must have been while she was at uni, a full ten years earlier. What the hell had happened to her life that she shuffled around in black, grey and navy? Her mum, that was what had happened. But that was ten years ago, and the excuse for not living to the full was wearing thin.

*

Saturday morning dawned and Kate woke to butterflies in her stomach, wishing she'd opted for a simple black shift dress instead of her colourful ensemble. It wasn't the outfit that was bothering her though, or the fact she'd not spoken properly to Bob since his hasty retreat the previous weekend. It was the thought of sitting on a table of strangers, pretending to be interesting. She had nothing interesting to say. If they asked about her career, she had nothing. If they asked about her family, what could she tell them? That her father was a drug addict and her mother an alcoholic? That was a party pooping tale for sure.

As she walked through town towards the hairdressers, Kate tried to think of anecdotes she could pull out later. Could she make up some story about a glittering career? Could she pretend she was married with kids? No, too risky. Everyone there was bound to know about her situation, they'd dealt with Moira's Will after all. Perhaps she could practice her conversation skills on the hairdresser. But chatting to a stranger while trusting them with your locks was frightening, and the reason it was three years since her last visit.

Kate walked into the hairdressing shop and was hit by

the scent of flowers and hairspray. A young girl with bleach blonde curls greeted her at the reception desk, offering her a chair and a glass of Prosecco. This was a step up from the ten-pound trim she'd had last time. Back then, she'd only been offered an over-brewed cuppa which she drank out of politeness rather than enjoyment. Kate declined the Prosecco in favour of coffee. It was only eleven o'clock and the alcohol would go straight to her head. Risky when someone was holding sharp scissors an inch from your scalp.

A heavily made up, willowy brunette appeared beside her, carrying an americano with shortbread biscuit on the side.

"Kate? I'm Simone. Come on through."

Kate followed the woman through to the main salon, thinking how plush it was in comparison to the cheap and cheerful place she'd used in Bath. The stylist asked what she would like doing, and Kate instructed her she only wanted a trim and blow dry.

"Do you have somewhere special to go later?"

Kate told her about the Christmas party. The hairdresser's eyes widened when she heard the name of the solicitors' firm. Kate needn't have worried about talking, for the next forty minutes were taken up with tales of a recent divorce. Apparently, Bob handled the legal side of what sounded like a very acrimonious split. Somewhere in the middle of her monologue, the hairdresser persuaded Kate to get a choppy fringe, though she'd stood her ground on the suggestion of *adding a little colour*. Kate knew from Maddie's intensive grooming it was code for *adding a hundred pounds to the bill.*

Two hours and sixty pounds later, Kate emerged onto the street, holding a bag above her head to protect her hair from the pouring rain. She prayed the stylist's handiwork would survive the short walk home, for despite herself, Kate had been pleasantly surprised when she looked in the mirror. Her hair was shorter, bobbed neatly to just above her chin, and hung in loose 'natural' waves that had taken half a bottle of hairspray to achieve. The fringe looked OK, though the jury was out on how long it would be before she grew it out again.

Kate ran up the high street, attracting looks from passers-by, not because of her smart haircut, but due to the bag she held above it. She made it to her front door and rushed inside to check her appearance in the mirror. Apart from a little extra frizz, the waves were still intact and would be good enough for a small local party.

Half way through applying her makeup Kate's phone buzzed with an incoming FaceTime from Maddie.

"Hi," said Kate, waving at the screen.

"My God, you look amazing. What's happened to your hair?"

"I went to the hairdressers, that's what."

"You? But you hate getting your hair cut."

"I know, but needs must. I'm going to a party tonight."

"Oooh, tell me more."

"Oh, it's nothing special just Bob's office Christmas do."

"Wow, so are you and Bob..."

"God no! I'm going as a friend, to save him from a snake lady."

"A what?"

"Doesn't matter. Anyway, you're looking really glam yourself. Going somewhere nice?"

Maddie pursed her bright red lips into a kiss and blew it at the screen. "You always know how to make me feel good about myself you know."

"Shush you, you always feel good about yourself. Come on, tell me where you're off to."

"Same as you, office Christmas party. It's at some fancy hotel out of town so I've had to book a room for an extortionate price. To be honest I'm not looking forward to it all that much. There's lots of other companies going so it could get a bit rowdy."

"Oh, don't give me that. You'll be the first on the dance-floor and will drink everyone under the table knowing you."

Maddie laughed. "So anyway, are you going to show me the dress you've got to go with those awesome boots?"

Kate walked over to the door where Moira's dress was hanging.

"Wow Kate, that's gorgeous. You'll have men queuing round the block for you in that."

"I don't want men queuing round the block!"

"Don't tell me you're still hung up on arse face."

"At least you've moved on from arse wipe. I'm not sure what our situation is to be honest, but I'd feel disloyal dating anyone else until I know where I stand with Alex."

"Have you even spoken to him in the last few months?"

"Not really, but he's been sending me loads of funny memes and videos."

"What, like you're still at school? Come on Kate, you deserve better than that."

"Can we change the subject? When are you coming down over Christmas?"

"Early boxing day."

"Early? Are you sure?"

"Oh yeah, I'll be out on Christmas eve so won't be able to face booze by Christmas Day and will be sober as a judge by Boxing Day morning."

"OK, well it will be great to see you."

"Is it just me and you or are your waifs and strays coming too?"

"If you mean Joy and Bob, then yes they are. But they're not coming over till lunchtime so we'll have plenty of time to catch up before they arrive."

"Good. I really miss you. It will be nice to have you to myself for a while. Anyway, I'd better get going, I've got a spray tan booked in half an hour."

"OK, see you soon. Love you."

"Love you too."

Chapter 24

At half past six, Kate opened the door to a suited and booted Bob.

"Wow... you look... um... different."

"You think it's too much?" said Kate, anxiety prickling her skin. "I knew I'd gone over the top, it was so stupid of me. I got over excited at the thought of going out. Should have opted for something low key. I..."

"Kate." Bob grabbed her flailing hands and looked deep into her eyes. "What I should have said is you look beautiful. Not overdressed, not different, beautiful."

Kate pulled her hands from his grasp and ran one through her hair. Her fingers stuck against the bucket of hairspray and she turned away from Bob to discretely untangle them. "Thank you. You look very smart yourself."

"Just another day at the office," laughed Bob, looking down at his typical work day outfit. "I did buy a new shirt though."

"Well I'm glad you made an effort. You really don't think I'm overdressed?"

"Just wait till you see what the other women put on. In previous years I've not known where to look. I have no doubt you'll be the most elegant woman there."

"Elegant as in...overdressed?"

"Shut up and get a glass of wine down you. Here," said

Bob, handing her a bottle he'd brought with him. "I expected you'd be nervous so thought it may be a good idea to have a pre-party drink to calm your nerves."

"Is it that obvious how out of practice I am at socialising?"

"No, but you do yourself down constantly so I saw no reason tonight would be any different. You really have nothing to worry about."

"Yes, but everyone from your office will be super clever and successful. I've spent the past ten years cleaning up manky bedrooms after stags and hens."

"And I bet you've got some good stories to tell from it."

"Yes, but it hardly screams success, does it?"

"Then talk about setting up your Airbnb business."

"Bob, I've only had three sets of guests."

"No need to include that detail. It's early days. And trust me, most of the people you'll meet tonight are more likely to bore you to death than make you feel inadequate. Now come on, I'll pour us that drink."

*

Two glasses of wine later, it was a relaxed Bob and Kate who headed into the night. By some Christmas miracle, the rain had stopped and Kate didn't need to bother with her unsightly raincoat. As they wandered down the steep hill to the jail, Kate was grateful for the relatively sensible boots. It would feel a long walk uphill on the way home, she was certain.

Her nerves began to jangle as they walked through into the Jail courtyard, but Bob gave her a reassuring squeeze on the shoulder and took charge, leading her towards the main entrance. The courtyard glowed with thousands of fairy lights, soft jazz piped out from a hidden speaker. Several groups were huddled together, drinking champagne and smoking cigarettes.

"This way," said Bob, leading her inside towards the bar. "The others should be around here somewhere, but let's get some drinks in before we find them, you'll probably need one." He grinned at Kate, and she felt herself relax a little.

"Bob!" A scantily clad woman screeched his name from across the room. Bob groaned and gave her a wave.

"Get ready for the onslaught. That's Mildred, the snake lady."

"Mildred? Is she some character from Harry Potter? Surely it's not her real name?"

"No, it's not. Morag told me once her real name's Amelia, Millie for short, but when she was 16 she changed it by deed-poll to Mildred."

"Why would anyone do that?"

"Not a clue."

The woman pushed through the crowd towards them. Her black sequined dress was more like a napkin, barely covering her bum and hanging low at the front to reveal two large breasts. Her eyes were thickly kohled, her lips painted deep purple. She reminded Kate of a vampire.

"Bob, my sweetheart. How the hell have you been? I can't believe it's a whole year since I've seen you. Come here." She dragged Bob into a tight embrace, and when he extricated himself, Kate noticed a smudge of purple lipstick staining his new shirt. She'd keep quiet about that, for now.

"Hi, Mildred, good to see you. This is my friend Kate," he said.

"Hi," said Mildred, not taking her eyes off Bob. She linked her arm into his, pulling him away into the crowd. "Now, I need to tell you all about my new babies. There's a corn snake called Nathaniel, a Python called Micky..."

Help, Bob mouthed over his shoulder. Kate shrugged to show she was powerless against Mildred's charms. He stuck his middle finger up in reply, and Kate grinned back. She gathered their drinks from the bar and followed Bob to where he now stood, surrounded by a large group of people. It was strange, seeing him central to the throng of colleagues. The women flicked their hair and giggled when he spoke. The men let out hearty laughs and clapped him on the back.

Kate hung back from the group, feeling more of an outsider than ever. Did these people know what troubled Bob? Did they know what caused him to switch suddenly from happiness to anger? Did they know whose messages and calls could prompt him to disappear at a moment's notice? Around these people, he became so animated. It was as though he were the conductor and everyone else in his orchestra.

Bob looked beyond the group to where Kate stood, two drinks in hand. He signalled for her to join him and she pushed her way through the tightly-packed bodies. As she reached him, he took his beer from her and pulled her close with his spare hand.

"Everyone, this is my friend Kate. She's fairly new in town, so please make her welcome."

Glasses were raised in acknowledgment of Bob's request, though the women looked less thrilled about the prospect of entertaining Kate than the men. Snake loving Mildred wheedled her way between Kate and Bob, and Kate found herself pressed up against a sweating middle-aged man who introduced himself as Trevor.

"Do you work with these guys?" Kate asked, shouting to make herself heard above the roar of voices.

"Christ no. I'm here with my wife, her plus one as she likes to say."

"Oh, I see. Do you know everyone well?"

"No, not really. I only ever see them at the Christmas do, and there's often new partners each year. I have to be careful, I got in trouble last year when I engaged Sally's husband Mark in conversation about his plumbing business, only to discover I was talking to her new partner Chris who worked in insurance. It's a minefield I can tell you. The worst part is I don't think anyone even likes bringing their partners along. It's just one of those traditions no one thinks to change. Anyway, enough about me. How do you know Bob?"

"Oh, we met through the solicitors. He's been helping me deal with my grandmother's will, and through that we've become good friends."

"Just good friends? I've heard that before," said Trevor with a wink.

"Honestly it's nothing like that. We really are just friends."

"Well there's a few women here who'll be glad to hear that."

"Really?" said Kate, struggling to mask her surprise at Bob being considered desirable by the fairer sex.

"Oh yes. It's an office sport, fighting to win the heart of Bob. I think it's a combination of kindness, manly charm and complete disinterest in any romantic attachments that keeps them all hooked."

Kate laughed, deciding she could have ended up with company far worse than Trevor's. Unfortunately, just at that moment another man joined them, thin as a rake, holding a whiskey in one hand and champagne flute in the other.

"Mind if I join you? I'm Archie," he said giving Kate a smile that showed several gold teeth.

"I'm Kate, pleased to meet you."

As soon as he let go of her hand, Kate wiped it discretely on her pashmina, praying he didn't notice. Not only was his handshake limp as a dead fish, his skin felt like he'd recently dipped it in a bottle of olive oil.

"Nice to see you Archie, it's been a while." Kate was grateful to have Trevor by her side.

"Good to see you too, mate, business going well?"

"Good as can be expected."

"What is it you do?" Kate asked Trevor, but was drowned out as Archie began a lengthy monologue about his used car business. Kate had a passing interest in cars, but none that could sustain her interest in the ins and outs of Archie's business for longer than a minute. It didn't help that she could only catch his every other word above the din. She hoped she was nodding and smiling in the right places.

The sound of a gong broke through the chatter, and everyone began scrambling towards the door.

"Time for dinner," called Trevor over his shoulder. "Have to hurry if you want a good seat."

Before she could move, Kate was pushed out of the way by a large lady in a very small dress. Kate pressed herself against the wall, watching the hoards as they rushed towards their roast turkey. She'd be too late for a good seat by now, so may as well wait till the danger of being crushed passed. It was amusing to watch the women tottering along on ridiculous heels and Kate felt reassured that she was in no way overdressed. Well, only in the sense that unlike ninety percent of the female attendants, she didn't have her boobs or bum on show.

"Madam, could you please take your seat in the dining hall," asked a harassed looking waiter as he swept past carrying a tray of champagne flutes.

"Yes, sure, I was just waiting for the scrum to die down."

The waiter nodded politely and Kate made her way out of the bar. Despite the waiter's wishes, she took a moment to step outside. The cold air hit with a welcome force, the quiet night reviving after the deafening noise inside. Perhaps she hadn't been missing anything all these years after all. What a lot of effort it was to spend an evening with strangers, drinking cheap booze and eating dry turkey.

Kate took one last, long breath of fresh air before heading towards the dining hall. She walked into a wall of noise and heat, her nose filling with cheap aftershave, sweat, and an undertone of perfume. Despite her reservations, the hall was magnificent. A double height room built of solid stone, the walls were decorated with greenery, fairy lights peeking out of twisting ivy, glass jars glowing with tea lights. It was a breath-taking sight, made all the more impressive by the amount of people they'd managed to cram into it.

Walking through the rows of long tables was something of an assault course. By the time Kate found her table, she'd tripped over a chair leg, had a glass of champagne tipped down her front, and been trodden on by a stray stiletto. Her heart sank as she saw the only chair free on Bob's table was next to her new friend Archie. Bob was in the centre of the table. He looked up as Kate approached, cocked his head to the two women on either side of him, and grimaced. Kate tipped her head towards the only free chair and met his grimace with one of her own. She wandered to the end of the table and slid back the chair beside Archie, who began engaging her in his used car spiel before she'd had the chance to sit down. It looked as though it was going to be a long night.

Chapter 25

On the bright side, thought Kate, the food was delicious. It was a shame everything else about the evening was like pulling teeth. It took an age for the waiters to serve hundreds of guests, meaning Kate drank far more than she usually would on an empty stomach. Rather than getting her into the party spirit, the alcohol made her sleepy.

As Archie droned on, Kate tried every trick in the book to stay awake. She checked her watch under the table, pinching the skin on her hand as she went. Good, that little jolt would keep her eyes open a while longer. Twenty minutes. That was how long Archie had been running through his company finances with her. There must be some people who could make accounts sound interesting, but Archie's voice was as boring as his subject matter. He spoke in a high-pitched monotone, and sounded like he either had a cold, or a peg attached to his nose.

"You know, Kate, the thing about profit margins is..."

Kate dug the heel of her right foot into the shin of her left leg, the jolt of pain buying her a few more minutes of consciousness.

"And as I tell me customers..."

With Archie distracted by the spreadsheet he was drawing on a napkin, Kate took a piece of ice from her glass and held it to her neck. Her skin pricked with goose bumps and she calculated the cold spell should keep her awake for a good five minutes.

"It really is a car eat car world out there, Kate."

Kate threw her head back and let out a raucous laugh. It made Archie jump, but it bought her another few minutes and he seemed grateful she found him funny.

"Finally," she muttered as the waiters reached her table with desserts.

"I see you went for the warm chocolate brownie," said Archie, leaning over her pudding and giving it a sniff. "Safe choice. Very safe choice."

"Um, OK. And how about you?"

At that moment, a waiter laid a delicate pot of creme brulee in front of Archie. "As you can see, Kate, my tastes are more exotic." To emphasise this, his eyebrows wiggled in her direction. "Yes, *acrema bruleya* as they say in Italy. Classic Italian dish this. I should know. Did I tell you my great grandfather was Italian?"

Yes, thought Kate, *you did*. She refrained from pointing out the dish he was eating was a French classic. "So, have you visited Italy much?"

"No, but I've seen lots of photos."

"Oh, that's a shame," said Kate. "Do you have any plans to go out there?"

"Crikey, not likely, all that funny food. Plus, there's no way I could leave my business in the hands of my employees. It takes a special skill set to run a business like mine. Last week, this chap brought his old Ford Fiesta in for part exchange and..."

Beneath the table, Kate sent a message to Flo complaining about Archie, followed by sleeping emojis. Flo replied straight away, with a photo of her in The Sunbeam's waitress uniform, a grimace on her face and a packed room of office workers behind her. *Could be worse*, thought Kate, slipping the phone back into her bag.

"Sorry to interrupt you, Archie." Kate could've kissed Bob as he appeared at her shoulder. "I don't suppose you'd mind if I steal Kate away for a while? I've not had the chance to chat to her all evening."

"Well, actually, I was about to tell her about the Ford Fiesta..."

"Good chap," said Bob, cutting Archie off and taking Kate's arm so she couldn't get drawn back into conversation.

"You owe me a warm chocolate brownie with fudge sauce," said Kate as they made their way out into the courtyard.

"I'm sorry, you're more than welcome to head back in and finish it if you want to?"

"And get my ear bent about used cars for another two hours? No thanks." Kate noticed a smirk playing at the edges of Bob's mouth. "Oh yeah, have a good laugh. You wouldn't find it so funny if it had been you sitting there. There was no one to talk to on my left, the woman on my right was engrossed in a different conversation, and the man diagonally opposite me wouldn't catch my eye."

"Can you blame him? He's probably been caught by Archie before."

"Who is Archie anyway? He didn't pause for breath long enough for me to ask who he was with."

"He's Morag's husband. I don't know why she brings him along, she'll spend all night ignoring him. Anyway, I'm sorry I didn't come and rescue you earlier."

"Yeah, well, you had your harem to keep you busy."

Bob tipped his head back and laughed till he had tears in his eyes. "My harem? Are you serious?"

"Damn right I am, they've been pawing at you all evening. No wonder I was left with only Archie for company."

"Dear me, Miss Trenain, you're beginning to sound like you're jealous."

"Jealous? In your dreams. I just don't appreciate being left on my own all evening, that's all."

Kate was pleased it was dimly lit in the courtyard for her face was hot despite Bob's words holding no truth at all. Anyway, so what if she was jealous, it's not against the law to want to spend time with a friend.

"Look, I really am sorry for abandoning you. I got pulled along in the crowd when the gong sounded and found myself trapped in that spot. I tried saving a place for you, but Mildred's a force to be reckoned with."

"Don't worry, you can make up for it by getting me another drink. Though I should probably have lemonade as I've had too much wine already."

"Lemonade, are you sure? This is a Christmas party."

"Go on then, I'll have a white wine, but don't let me have another and you have to promise to help me back up the hill later."

"I will, as long as Mildred hasn't persuaded me to go home with her."

Kate looked at him open-mouthed, then realising he was joking, sent him on his way with a grin.

"Thanks," said Kate, as Bob returned with their drinks. "You know, I'm seeing a very different side to you tonight."

"Really? In what way?"

"I don't know, you're very popular for starters. You're like the popular kid at school, you know, the one all the girls want to be with and all the boys want to be."

"Wow, how many glasses of wine have you had?"

"Learn to take a compliment when it's given, Mr Carter."

"Ha, alright then, but I have to disagree with your character assessment. The main reason they're all being so nice to me is I hold the power to hire and fire. They want to stay on my good side, that's all. Plus, I don't think any of the popular kids at school had a beer belly and modelled their hair cuts on a bird's nest."

Kate laughed. "Well whatever their motivation, it's nice to see you're appreciated. I appreciate you too you know.

Not many people would've given up so much of their time to welcome a stranger to the town."

"You're forgetting I know what it's like to start over. I was lucky enough to have a few familiar faces around to help me settle in. You had no one. It's a bloody brave thing you did, moving here and starting over."

"I've never been called brave before."

"I think you're one of the bravest people I know. All you've been through, and you just keep going. By the way, I've been meaning to apologise for the times I've been snappy. There's stuff going on that I've tried to deal with alone, but I'm not doing a great job of it. To be honest..."

They were interrupted by a frazzled looking Trevor making his way unsteadily into the courtyard. Kate liked him, but his timing was crap, just when Bob was about to open up to her. She'd have to try and raise the subject later.

"I can't take much more of that Archie chap," said Trevor, perching himself on the edge of a table and running his hands through his thinning hair.

"He collared you too?"

"Yeah, made a beeline for me as soon as you left. I hoped the wife would help me out but she's too busy getting pissed with her mates to notice. He doesn't half go on."

"You're a trooper Trevor, so's Kate, she had him bending his ear throughout the meal."

Trevor gave Kate a sympathetic smile. "I reckon he's lonely, poor chap. Anyway, I thought I'd let you know the dancing's just getting going. They'll be a riot if you don't show up on the dance floor."

Bob stretched his arms, linked his fingers together, cracking them as he did and announced "Got to give the ladies what they're after. Come on Kate, you're coming too."

"What's going on?" said Kate looking to Trevor for

answers.

"Oh, your friend Bob is Bodmin's answer to John Travolta. Come on, you've got to see this."

*

On the peripheries of the dance floor, Kate stood open-mouthed as Bob took centre stage, surrounded by a drunk, clapping crowd as he attempted a few break dance moves. She clapped her hands over her eyes as he attempted a headstand, peeking through her fingers just in time to see him stopped from falling by a buxom older woman who grabbed his ankles and rubbed his feet against her chest. This sent the crowd into raptures, with several other red-faced men joining Bob. Oh no, was he? Were they? Yep, they were twerking alright. Kate felt she was watching a complete stranger. This was sensible, reliable, middle-aged Bob. The man in front of her was unrecognisable.

Kate gasped in horror as he threw an imaginary lasso her way and began jumping towards her, reeling her in.

"What the hell?" shouted Kate above the racket, but Bob grabbed her wrist and pulled her onto the dance floor. A cheer went up from the crowd. "I can't dance," she screamed at Bob.

"Neither can I," he screamed back.

"That's not what it looks like."

"You just have to lose your inhibitions, then it will be fine."

A woman's voice belted "What you want?" from the speakers and a sea of arms flew up in the air, everyone taking on dramatic freeze frames between beats. Kate attempted a side step, shuffling move, arms clasped firmly by her sides. Bob danced over to her and took her hands in his. For the next two minutes she was twirled, flung, wiggled and shoved so much she stopped caring what anyone thought and let herself relax into the music.

The lift caught her unawares. Kate screamed as Bob lifted her above his shoulders and straightened his arms.

Perched on his palms, Kate lay rigid with terror as the room began to spin, slowly at first, but as Aretha demanded *sock it to me sock it to me* over and over the spinning grew faster and faster until her hair flew out around her and the ceiling lights became a blur.

Bob pulled his arms down and held Kate close to him before setting her feet gently back on the dance floor.

"Sorry," he shouted, "I couldn't resist. Are you OK?"

"Fine," Kate shouted back, knocking into two women as dizziness took hold of her legs. "Your arms must be killing you," she said, lurching back towards him.

Bob laughed, posing like a bodybuilder before taking out a hanky and wiping his brow. *Ah, there's the Bob I know,* thought Kate, wondering if she knew anyone else that still used hankies these days.

"Do you want another drink?"

"Yes, I'll come with you. I need a rest."

Bob followed her over to the bar and leaned against it, getting his breath back. "That was fun," he said, grinning at her.

"You're full of surprises," said Kate, shaking her head in disbelief.

"I don't often get the chance to let my hair down. Have to make the most of it while I can."

"So I see."

Kate turned to the barman and gave her order, wondering what other surprises Bob was keeping up his sleeve.

Chapter 26

A buzzing beside Kate's head stirred her out of deep sleep. She grabbed her phone and squinted at the screen. A FaceTime call from Alex? Wow, his timing was impeccable. She let the call ring out, doing the same again for his second and third attempt. Kate pulled herself up against her headboard, catching her reflection in the mirror and groaning. Her hair was sticking up in all directions. The remains of yesterday's makeup lay smudged across her face, and although she'd removed the dress, her feet were covered by crimson suede.

She kicked the boots off and downed the pint of water beside her bed. Every detail of the previous night lay fresh in her memory, so she couldn't have drunk that much. It had been three a.m. before she and Bob had dragged themselves back up the hill. What time was it now? Eight. Oh well, Kate thought, five hours' sleep is better than no sleep.

Wrapped in her cosy dressing gown, Kate padded through to the kitchen to make a pot of coffee. Bob would be grateful for it, she was certain. He'd drunk far more than she had, although he was still acting pretty sober by the end of the evening. He must have sweated all the booze out of his system with all that dancing. Kate smiled at the thought, making a mental note to check Facebook for video evidence of his impressive moves.

Coffee in hand, Kate wandered upstairs to the guest room. The door was ajar, and poking her head round she could see the bed made and no sign that anyone had slept in it. Kate was certain Bob stayed last night. It had been far too late for him to go home. She wandered into the bedroom and picked up a note from the bed.

Thanks so much for last night. Had to leave early. See you on Boxing Day! x

Kate lay the coffees on the bedside table and slumped down onto the pillows. She had hoped they'd be able to talk today. He'd been so close to opening up to her. Plus, she wanted to put her mind at rest that there was no atmosphere between them.

Eyes closed, the memory of *that* dance played in her mind. It had all been so fun up till then. Bloody Ed Sheeran and his soppy bloody pop songs. They'd been having a laugh on the dance floor when the DJ announced it was the last dance. Most people had gone home by then and the few stragglers coupled up, leaving Bob and Kate awkwardly facing each other. He'd given her a shrug of resignation, before taking her in his arms.

It was fine, she told herself. *Just a friendly dance between friends*. But the churning in her stomach screamed *it was more than that*. She'd had her hands against his back, damp from all the energetic dancing, but warm and comforting at the same time. He held her so lightly it was as though he was scared she'd break. Kate remembered laying her head on his chest and his arms closing in around her. She felt so safe in his arms she'd stopped dancing and just breathed him in. Her stomach did somersaults at the thought. *Don't be stupid* she told herself. *It's just the booze making everything feel soppy*. But she hadn't imagined the look they'd shared, as she'd lifted her head and his had bent down closer to hers. His eyes had drilled into hers, but without warning, something had changed. He'd taken her hands and spun her around in one of the jokey dance moves he'd been pulling all evening.

Kate shook her head to rid the thoughts. He'd made it clear in that moment they were just friends, which was exactly as she wanted it to be. Besides, in the light of day, she would have seen him as he really was, a middle-aged man with a beer belly who was a wonderful friend but nothing more. Her romantic interests lay elsewhere, and it was about time she took some action to move things forward.

Back in her bedroom, Kate found Alex's number on her phone and dialled it. He answered on the second ring.

"Kate, I've been trying to get hold of you all morning. Where have you been?"

"I slept in. I was at a Christmas party last night and it was a bit of a late one."

"Who were you with?"

"Just Bob and his workmates."

"I see."

"Yeah, so I'm feeling a bit rough this morning, not through booze, but lack of sleep."

"Is Bob there with you? Is that why you didn't want to face time?"

"No, of course not. I'm here by myself, as usual." *Why don't you tell him Bob stayed the night if you're just friends?* "Anyway, how are you?"

"Fine. Had a small Christmas bash myself last night. Lots of fun with the lads, as usual. What are your Christmas plans?"

"Nothing much really, just a quiet one on Christmas day, then a few friends are coming over on Boxing day."

"Will Bob be there?"

"Yes, and Maddie and my friend Joy."

"The old lady?"

"Yes, that's right," said Kate, wondering how Alex knew about her. She must have told him and forgotten. "How about you? What are you up to over Christmas?"

"Oh, the usual, spending it at Mum and Dad's. You

know what they're like, making Christmas into such a big deal."

Actually, thought Kate, *I don't know because you never invited me*. "That sounds nice."

"Yeah. Hey, I was thinking, it would be cool to catch up in the New Year. I miss you. It's about time we got things sorted between us, don't you think?"

"Um, yes, I s'pose?" Did he mean sorted as in officially break up, or sorted as in get back together?

"Great. Well how about I give you a bell after Christmas is out of the way and we can fix something up."

"Sure, sounds great."

"OK, well I'd better get on, lots to do. Thanks for calling, it was good to catch up. See you."

"Bye."

Kate hung up the phone and stared at it in her hand. What the hell was that all about? Alex was a master at being vague, yet something told her he'd called to check up on her. Maybe she was just paranoid. Either way, it would be good to see him again and get some answers about where she stood. Kate had been happy waiting on the sidelines in Bath, but now she'd started her new life, she needed answers. She'd love nothing more than for them to be a proper couple again, but even if that wasn't possible, the thought of being able to move on brought its own sense of relief.

*

Kate was forcing down a piece of buttered toast when Joy appeared at the kitchen window holding a tin in her arms. Unlocking the back door, Kate stepped aside as the old lady bustled her way in.

"It's freezing out there today. Damp too. No good for my old bones. I should've moved to the Costa del Sol years ago."

Kate smiled. "It's warm in here. Do you fancy a tea or coffee?"

"No ta, dear, this is only a flying visit. I just wanted to bring you this." Joy lay the tin down on the kitchen counter, "and this." Next to the tin was a fat brown envelope.

"Thanks," said Kate, "but what are they?"

"There's a Christmas cake in that tin. Should be a good one, I've been feeding it since August, and in that envelope are photos of your grandmother, and a few I found of your dad. I don't have time to go through them with you now, but if you have any questions about who's who I can sit down with you on Boxing Day. That's if I'm still invited."

"Of course you are. Thanks so much for bringing these round. I promise not to eat all the cake before you get here on Boxing Day."

"I'd prefer it if you do. I've got a whole cake for myself at home. It should last me a year if I'm careful."

"OK, well thanks. I really appreciate it. Where are you off to now?"

"I've got a couple more cakes to deliver, then my Christmas presents to buy. I can't believe Christmas is only a week away, it sneaks up on me every year."

"Yes, time flies when you're having fun."

"And it travels at the speed of light when you reach my age. Every year I think it will be my last Christmas, then every year I stick around for the next. Part of me wants to join my chums in the sky. I bet they're all having a right laugh up there at this time of year. Anyway, dear, I'd better be off. See you next week."

"Bye," said Kate, closing the door behind Joy and carrying the envelope through to the living room.

Kate stacked the pile of photos on the table and began looking through them one by one. There was no rhyme or reason to their order. In some, Moira was a young brunette, with unlined skin and made-up face. In others she appeared much older, white hair fixed in a perm, a smattering of lipstick the only trace of makeup. Kate began sorting the photographs into piles, judging the decades by the changing hairstyles of the women.

The Christmas theme ran through the photographs, with the Christmas pile twice the size of all the others. In most of the photographs Moira had either a cocktail or sherry in her hand. In one picture she had both. There were several photographs of couples gathered around a dining table in what was now Kate's bedroom. The only faces she recognised were Moira's and Joy's, so she stuck a post it note to the back as a reminder to ask Joy about it.

Kate's breath caught at a series of photos showing a small boy opening a present. The boy grinned up at the camera, holding his new train set aloft. She recognised the boy as her father, and wondered whether her own boys would look like him, if she ever got around to having children of her own.

Another pile contained photos of Moira and Joy on what looked like a cruise ship. Another set showed various days out to the beach, two small boys building sandcastles while the two women sunbathed on towels. There were several photos taken in the room where Kate sat, and she felt a strange colliding of lives as fading faces peered out at her. Kate sat back in the chair and looked at the piles of memories scattered over the table. She knew exactly what to get Joy for Christmas now. She collected her laptop and phone from her bedroom and set to work.

Chapter 27

The last-minute booking came through late the previous evening. When Kate read the message accompanying the booking request, it had taken all of one second to accept it. *Coming back to where my husband lived as a little boy... his last Christmas... making memories...*

As it was so close to Christmas, and given the couple's circumstances, it felt right to go the extra mile. Kate nipped into town first thing and bought all she needed. A bottle of wine stood beside the usual tea and coffee, two slices of Joy's Christmas cake sealed in a mason jar beside it. Despite being so close to the day itself, Kate managed to pick up a small artificial Christmas tree in the charity shop and it stood, all winking fairy lights and tinsel in pride of place in the guest living room. The final touch had been a small gift, a book she'd found full of old photographs of the town. She lay the wrapped book on the bed.

Kate worried how her guests would fare with the stairs. After hearing about the husband's condition, she'd made it clear that all guest facilities were on the first floor, but the woman had assured her it wouldn't be a problem. Kate had her doubts, but hoped they proved unfounded.

The guests arrived at ten. As it was such a quiet time of year for bookings, Kate felt no qualms about offering an early check in. On the dot of the hour, she opened the door to a smart, middle-aged couple.

"Good morning, are you Kate?"

"Yes, I am, pleased to meet you." Kate held out her hand, and the woman shook it. Kate warmed to her wide smile and kind eyes immediately.

"I'm Rissa, and this is Jeff."

The man reached forward and shook Kate's hand. If she hadn't been warned, Kate would never have guessed he was ill. The only clue was how thin he was, but for all she knew he was like that before. His skin was tanned and his sky-blue eyes twinkled when he smiled.

"Come in," said Kate, stepping aside to let them pass. "I hear you're originally from Bodmin?"

"Yes, I was born three doors that way," said Jeff, pointing in the direction of his old house. His voice was soft, with a hint of a rasp.

"This will be a real trip down memory lane for you, then."

"Yes, I couldn't believe it when I saw your listing. It's exactly where we wanted to be. Thank you for accommodating us at such short notice." Rissa's voice was deeper than her husband's and had a singsong lilt hinting at a long buried Indian accent. Her thick glossy hair sat pinned against the back of her head and a trace of red accentuated her smiling mouth.

"To be honest, it's such a quiet time of year there was no problem fitting you in. I'm pleased the rooms are being used. I still can't get used to having all this space to myself."

"You've not been here long?"

"A few months. My grandmother lived here before me."

"What was her name?" asked Jeff.

"Moira Trenain, did you know her?"

"Not that I recall, but I was only nine when we moved away. I'll ask Mum and Dad when I next speak to them."

"Great. Why don't I show you to your rooms?"

"Thank you."

Kate needn't have worried about the stairs, as Jeff took them with the nimbleness of a much younger man. Rissa took their bags, though, and Kate noticed Jeff didn't put up a fight. As she led them upstairs, she found herself offering them the use of the kitchen and her living room. It wasn't what she'd usually do, but something about this couple put her at ease, and if anything, she'd like to spend some time with them.

"This is all so wonderful. Thank you," said Rissa, after Kate gave them the tour.

"I'm glad you like it. I'll leave you to settle in, and if you need anything, I'll be downstairs."

*

As soon as their host left the room, Jeff flopped down onto the bed. Rissa understood his need to keep up appearances. It was a matter of pride, but she also knew how much the pretence exhausted him. She fetched him a glass of water and propped some cushions behind his back.

"There, feeling better?"

Jeff gripped his wife's hand and looked at her with his beautiful eyes. "I'm sorry I've become such a burden to you lately."

"You will never be a burden, my love. *In sickness and in health*, those were our vows."

Jeff leaned forward and kissed his wife. They'd been kissing more since he'd been ill than they ever had before. It was as if he needed to make up for the years he was too distracted by work to give her the attention she deserved.

"I don't want to leave you."

"I know, but remember what we said? Live for the moment. At this moment we are together, that's what matters."

"I love you."

"I love you too. Now do you want to rest, or take a stroll into the town?"

"I can rest when I'm dead," said Jeff, his eyes twinkling mischievously.

Rissa sighed and gave him a tap on the arm. He'd always been one for joking, but she didn't approve of his recent subject matter. "How about I fix us a coffee first?"

"Make it a strong one. I'll need a good dose of caffeine to propel me along."

*

"Excuse me?"

Kate opened her bedroom door to Rissa, holding two mugs from upstairs.

"Hi, is everything OK?"

"Oh yes, wonderful thank you. I don't want to be cheeky, but as you offered the use of your kitchen, I wondered if I could heat up some milk for coffee?"

"Yes, of course. I'll show you where the pans are."

"Goodness me, what a wonderful kitchen," said Rissa as she followed Kate in.

"Thank you, it was one of the few things in the house I didn't change. I know it's a bit marmite, but I love it."

"Me too. Your grandmother obviously had good taste in choosing it, and keeping it all those years. Were the two of you close?"

"No, not at all. I hardly knew her. I didn't even know she had died till I was contacted about the house. I feel closer to her now I'm living here than I ever did when she was alive."

"It's such a shame you were estranged. Sorry, it's really none of my business."

"Don't worry, my family history is something of a muddle. After my parents died, I should have made contact with her. It's something I'll always regret, but I spent years trying to move on from my childhood and she was part of that."

"And have you? Moved on I mean?"

"Who knows," laughed Kate. "I've moved here, but

that's about the only brave thing I've done. I've not exactly made a success of my life."

"I don't know about that. You've set up a wonderful business here and you're a charming host. That's an achievement in itself."

"Thank you, that's very kind of you to say."

"It's not kind, it's true. Don't do your achievements down."

"I'm not sure my twenty-year-old self would be very impressed by my achievements."

"Really? And what were your ambitions back then?"

"Well, I was the first person in my family to go to University. I thought I'd leave and become a teacher. Instead I left without finishing my degree and ended up working in a downmarket hotel as a cleaner. Not exactly the stuff of dreams." Kate smiled at a thoughtful looking Rissa.

"You know," Rissa said, "it's never too late to finish a degree. If you want to, of course."

"I've never really thought about it. I guess I gave up on that dream a long time ago."

"Well it's your life, but it might be worth thinking about."

"I will," said Kate. "Anyway, enough about me. What are your plans while you're here?"

"We don't have much planned at all. Coming back to Bodmin was something Jeff felt he needed to do, but we hadn't thought much beyond that. He says he'd like to walk around the town, but I bet by the time I take the coffee up he's fast asleep. He does a lot of sleeping these days."

"That must be hard for both of you."

"Yes, it is. The worst thing is he feels bad for what he's putting me and our daughters through, when all we want to do is be there for him."

"How old are your daughters?"

"They're all grown up now. My three older girls have

children, so it's the youngest who's been helping out the most. It's been pretty hard on her."

"I bet."

"Well, we're into the final stage now, so it will all be over soon. I don't know if that's a good or a bad thing. I'll be grateful when Jeff's suffering is over, but as for the rest of us..."

"I suppose it will be like losing half of yourself."

"Hmm, that's not really how I see it. I mean, of course, my heart will splinter into tiny pieces, I know that already... but at least I've always been independent. I know I'll cope, it's just that life will have less shine, less fun. Jeff and I have talked a lot about my life after he's gone. He's made me promise to have adventures." Rissa gave a sad smile and Kate wanted to wrap her arms around her and tell her everything will be alright.

"Do you know what any of those adventures might be?"

"Well, as soon as I know my daughters are all right, I'll be getting on a plane to India. It's been a couple of years since I've visited family over there and I'm longing to get back."

"You must be very brave, travelling by yourself."

Rissa laughed, and looked at Kate. "You're not serious, are you?"

"Yes, I mean, I'm not sure I'd be brave enough to travel the world alone."

"Goodness me, you don't know what you're missing. Jeff and I have taken many holidays apart over the years. His work schedule made it tricky to go together. There's a lot to be said for holidaying alone. You can do exactly what you want to do, lie in bed all day, get up at four a.m. to watch a sunrise. It's exquisitely self-indulgent."

"Maybe I should try it sometime..."

"You really should. Do you have a man in your life?"

"Sort of. He needed some space, so we're technically not together at the moment."

"In my experience, it's perfectly possible to have space and still be in a relationship."

"Hmm, maybe...I guess I was a bit too needy."

"You don't strike me as needy in the slightest."

Kate laughed. "That's because you're not going out with me."

"Perhaps, but if you don't mind me saying, you have quite a tendency to do yourself down. Life's too short to be too self-critical. Trust me, it's important to make every moment count, and self-loathing is a pointless waste of time. If you don't like something about yourself, change it. But only change yourself for you, not for anybody else. Goodness me, I'm rather droning on a bit, aren't I? It's a professional hazard. I'm a trained counsellor you see. But today I'm on holiday, and shouldn't take up any more of your time."

Kate smiled and poured hot milk into the two cups. "I've enjoyed chatting to you. You've given me a lot to think about. In fact, I probably owe you for your professional opinion."

Rissa laughed and took the cups from Kate. "In all seriousness, it sounds like you've had quite a lot to deal with in your past and present. I'll be out of action for a few months, but if you did ever want to talk to someone, in a professional capacity, I'd be very happy for you to get in touch. And I'm not haggling for business, or trying to be pushy. I'd give you some counselling for free, but only if you ever felt you needed it."

"Thanks," said Kate. She should probably be offended that a stranger had suggested she need counselling. But there was something so genuine about Rissa, that it sounded like a very good idea. An idea Kate would happily tuck away in case she ever needed it.

Chapter 28

When Rissa appeared upstairs with the coffee, she was surprised to find Jeff sitting up in bed reading.

"You took your time," he said, grinning at her.

"I thought you'd be asleep, so didn't rush."

"I've had enough of sleeping. We're on holiday, I need to make the most of it."

Rissa handed him his mug. "I was chatting to our host Kate. She's a lovely woman, but very lacking in confidence."

"Oh God, you didn't offer her counselling, did you?"

"So what if I did? Everyone should have counselling at least once in their life."

"Yes, but not many people appreciate that suggestion."

"Oh no, you don't think I've offended her, do you? I was only trying to help."

"I'm sure she's fine. It's hard for anyone to be offended by you."

Jeff pulled Rissa close, and she leaned her head against his chest. She could feel the rapid beating of his heart, and breathed in his scent, storing it safely in the box of memories in her mind.

"We should call the girls and let them know we got here safely."

"The girls can wait. Let's get out before my energy fails

me."

"Alright. You'll need to wrap up warm, it's very cold out."

"Rissa, please stop fussing. I'm not a child."

"Sorry," she said, but threw a hat and scarf his way anyway. He sighed, but put them on to please her.

*

"Right, let's go," said Jeff, stepping out onto the street. His pace didn't match his enthusiasm, and Rissa supported his arm as he took slow, deliberate steps.

"Do you remember much about the town?"

"No, but I don't get the impression it's changed all that much. A few less shops than I remember, but that's the case wherever you go. It's nice to see they've made an effort with the Christmas lights."

They wandered down the main shopping street, stopping at a clock tower at the far end. "It looks very quaint down there," said Jeff. "You can't go wrong with a street named Honey."

"Come on then, let's see what's down there."

They passed a gaming cafe full of excitable children, a classy restaurant and a cosy pub. "Oh now you're talking," said Jeff, stopping outside an antiques shop.

Rissa groaned. "Please, not more junk. The house is groaning with stuff already, in fact, I might set up my own antiques shop once you're gone."

Jeff looked horrified. "Tell me you're not going to get rid of my treasures as soon as I snuff it?"

Rissa laughed. "Don't worry, I'll honour your wishes. I'm sure the children will be thrilled to have the random sideboards, chests and knicknacks passed down to them."

"Don't be cheeky," said Jeff, digging his wife in the ribs.

"Fine, but please remember it's me who will have to carry whatever you buy back up the hill to the car."

"Point taken," said Jeff, disappearing into the quirky shop. "Come on then," he called, beckoning her to join him.

Rissa sighed and prepared for the musty smell to hit. The aroma, as Jeff called it, was one of his favourite things about these types of shops. The only effect it had on Rissa was to make her sneeze. Jeff pointed to a large ornate mirror, swirling vines twisting around its glass. A raised eyebrow from Rissa was enough to make him move on.

"What do you think of this?" he asked her, pointing to a yellowing map on the wall. "It's an old map of Bodmin, great, isn't it?"

"You've got me with this one, it's not like I can claim I can't carry it, and it will help me remember our trip."

Jeff handed over a couple of bank notes, and left the shop a happy man. He would have been happier with two hours browsing and a van to pack with all the items that caught his eye, but no one can have everything.

"How about a drink? Do you fancy a trad pub or posh bistro?"

"Let's splurge on the bistro. I saw a sign saying they do cocktails."

They found themselves a comfortable sofa in the window and settled down to study the drinks menu. Rissa picked a Chilli Margarita, while Jeff stuck with a Nojito. It surprised Rissa how easily he'd adapted to his no alcohol lifestyle. Not that he had much choice given the number of pills he was on, but as a lifelong beer lover, his dedication to quitting booze impressed her.

"I'm going to miss this."

"Drinking mocktails?"

"No, people watching. I don't miss work at all, which is strange considering how much it dominated my life. What I'll miss are the incidental moments, watching TV with you and the girls, sitting in a cafe guessing the lives of passers-by."

"Don't worry, darling, I'm sure wherever you're going will have all those things and more."

"But it won't have you."

Jeff gazed at his wife and shared a moment of deep sadness, only broken by the waitress coming to take their order.

"You might have me sooner than you think if I die of a broken heart," said Rissa once they were alone again.

Jeff laughed. "You're the strongest woman I've ever met. I'm glad it's me going first, as I could never cope the way I know you will."

"I'm not as strong as you think," said Rissa, twirling the ring on her left hand. Jeff cupped a hand beneath her chin and pulled her face up to his.

"You are a remarkable woman and don't you ever forget that. The girls will be there for you, and your friends. Please don't stop living because of me."

"I've already booked my flight to India," said Rissa, trying desperately to lighten the mood.

"You haven't?"

"No, of course not. How heartless do you think I am! But please don't worry about me. Now, can we move on to a cheerier subject?"

They talked about their daughters, their granddaughters, politics, house prices, all the usual things middle-aged couples discuss over drinks. Reality sat between them like an unacknowledged stranger, but they had given enough time to reality, and Rissa couldn't face going over it all again. Jeff hadn't been able to detach himself completely from his management history, planning his funeral in precise detail, right down to the dress code. Rissa would appreciate his organisation when the time came, but it was hard hearing about his plans when he was living, breathing right beside her.

Rissa watched her husband wave his arms around in animation as he listed all the politicians he felt should go. She committed every movement, every inflection of his voice to memory. Her mind drifted back over thirty years of marriage. It hadn't always been easy, but they'd stuck it out. She met so many couples these days who just gave up, like marriage was something to be thrown away and replaced like a broken iPhone. Jeff had never cheated in the conventional sense of the word, but for years his work had been his mistress, as had the children to her, and that had led to a gaping chasm between them they'd only just began addressing before he got his diagnosis. If anything, Rissa was more angry than sad. They were just entering a new phase in life, planning adventures, finding ways to reconnect, and that future had been stolen by one lousy set of test results.

"Don't tell me you like him?"

"Sorry, who?"

"Aren't you listening to me? I've just been doing a comprehensive character assassination of Boris. I thought you were listening, I'm not going to have to go over it all again am I?" Jeff grinned at her and rested his hand on hers.

"I was away with the fairies, sorry."

"Come on Mrs, it might never happen." He winked at his wife, and she smiled back, feeling another corner crumbling away from her heart. It would happen, and it would happen soon, too soon. She felt the weight of her best friend's hand on hers, swallowed down the tears in her throat, and ordered another drink.

Chapter 29

Kate woke early on Christmas morning. The day held mixed feelings for her, on the one hand the excitement of a young child, on the other the disappointment of knowing the day never lived up to expectations.

When she still lived with her mum, the day would follow the same pattern every year. Her mum claimed Christmas day as her favourite, probably because everyone else in the country was getting pissed and for that one day she wasn't alone.

Mother and daughter would be up by eight, a Christmas miracle in itself given how much Mum would've drunk the night before. They'd open presents, snuggle under a duvet and Kate would watch Christmas TV while Mum snored beside her. At lunchtime, they'd walk around the block, peeking in at all the happy families, gazing enviously at their large spreads of food and enormous piles of presents. Back at home, they would pull crackers over whatever food Mum picked up on the reduced aisle, then sit down again for more TV. The Queen's speech was a must, Mum was a royalist through and through and made Kate stand every time they heard the national anthem. By early evening Mum would be well on the way to sloshed. Kate knew the signs well, retreating to her bedroom to play with whatever new toy she got that year.

The build-up to the day was always better than the

event itself. Kate's favourite part was watching the light switch on in town. It was free, so they went every year, revelling in the mass excitement and festive cheer, despite the lights being turned on in November, so a little premature. As she got older, Kate would be given a fiver to buy presents. There weren't many to buy, but even back then, a fiver wasn't a lot, and Kate had to find ingenious ways to make it stretch.

Christmas presents were always bought at the charity shop. Mum said it was because they were Eco Warriors, and Kate liked the sound of that, despite knowing deep down the real reason was they were poor. None of Kate's handful of school friends were rich, but they always had more to spend at Christmas than she did. It was a point of pride for her, beating the odds and choosing the best gifts.

One year she'd found a Gucci top for a friend. It had had a stain running down one side, so Kate plaited pieces of ribbon together and sewed them on. It only cost £1, probably because the label had been cut out, but Kate had seen a celeb wearing it in one of the tacky magazines in the doctor's surgery, so was sure it was the real thing.

Another time she picked up a photo frame for fifty pence, and filled it with magazine cut outs of Ronan Keating for her super fan friend Annie. She screamed when she opened it, which Kate had taken as a positive reaction.

Despite their relative poverty, not a year went by without Kate getting a present from her mum. She never asked how she got the money, or where she found the toys, but every Christmas morning there was a present under the tree, along with a stocking filled with her favourite packets of crisps and sweets. Kate smiled at the memory. The situation with her mum had been made all the harder by the fact she wasn't a monster. It was tricky to feel angry when you knew someone was trying their best. During her teenage years she'd struggled to keep her frustrations quiet, but their confrontations always ended with Kate consoling her remorseful parent.

Kate pushed thoughts of her past to the back of her mind and made herself a coffee. As it was Christmas and she had nowhere to go, she carried her laptop and blanket into the living room and laid herself out on the sofa, ready to scour Netflix for Christmas movies. The soppier and more predictable the better.

The opening scenes of a snow-covered pine forest were appearing on the screen when a knock came at the door. Kate wrapped her blanket around her shoulders and went to open it.

"Joy? What are you doing here?"

"Merry Christmas to you too," said Joy, holding out a Christmas card. "Sorry the card is late, but it would have been worse to give it to you tomorrow."

"Oh, thanks. Are you off to the WI lunch?"

"Oh no, not for another few hours. I'm on my way to Church. I wondered if you'd like to join me?"

"At Church?"

"Goodness me, dear, you do know today's a Christian festival? The clue's in the name."

"Of course I do, I'm just not really a church goer."

"Neither are ninety percent of the people who fill the pews. It's not like they'll turf you out or check your credentials. To be honest, I could do with the company. There's something a bit pathetic about going to church by yourself on Christmas day."

Not as pathetic as spending the whole day on Netflix, thought Kate. "What time does the service start?"

"Half an hour. It takes me a while to walk there these days so I leave in plenty of time."

"Alright, I can be ready in five. Why don't you come and wait inside?"

Joy settled herself down on the purple sofa and Kate rushed through to the bedroom. What did people wear to church these days?

"Joy? What should I wear?"

"Clothes?"

"Helpful, thanks."

Kate heard Joy chuckling away. She flung on a pair of jeans and fluffy jumper. To add a Christmassy touch, she slipped on her new crimson boots and slid a layer of red across her lips.

"Perfect," said Joy as Kate joined her in the living room. "You might want to bring some gloves with you though, it's bloody cold in that church."

Kate grabbed gloves, scarf, a duffle coat and followed Joy outside. The town was quiet as they walked along the high street, but the few people they passed wished them a Merry Christmas, and both Joy and Kate returned the sentiment. Joy leaned heavily on Kate's arm. For the first time Kate noticed how frail she was. When she was in the house, or puffing away in the garden Kate saw her as a force of nature. Negotiating the hills in town, Joy seemed to shrink to a little old lady, all alone on Christmas day.

"Thanks, dear," said Joy as Kate helped her step down from the curb. "It's no fun getting older. Your grandmother felt the same. All we wanted to do was go out dancing, but getting to the butchers was like climbing Everest."

"Did my Nan come to church with you at Christmas?"

"Oh yes, and Easter. We used to go out for a roast dinner after the Easter service."

"Well perhaps you and I could continue that tradition."

"That would be marvellous," said Joy, squeezing Kate's arm. "Have you been into the church yet?"

"No, I haven't thought to go down there. I didn't even realise it was open to visitors."

"It's open every day. They have all sorts going on during the week. But I'm glad you've not been before, trust me, this is the time of year to go. If it doesn't take your breath away, you've got no heart."

"Um, OK," said Kate, doubting the church would be any

different from others dotted around the country.

Joy took the steps up to the church slowly, greeting several people who rushed ahead of her. They stepped into the lobby and through a heavy oak door. The first thing to hit Kate was the smell. Pine. Not the kind found in crappy air fresheners but real, fresh pine needles.

"Wow."

"Has it taken your breath away?" Joy asked, studying Kate's face for a reaction.

Kate nodded and moved further into the church. It was an enormous space, stone walls sweeping up to high arches holding a wooden ceiling. Colourful stained-glass windows turned the weak, wintry sun into a rainbow streaming in. There were the usual decorations, candles lit, nativity scene at the front. What took Kate's breath away were the trees. Christmas trees lined each side of the church as far as her eye could see.

"They have the Christmas tree festival here every year," said Joy. "Schools, community groups, businesses, you name it they're here. Come on, we've got time to have a look."

Joy led Kate along the side of the church. Each tree held decorations unique to the group who had decorated it. Kate's favourite were the children's efforts. Imperfect, covered in glitter and exuding all she loved about Christmas. Every tree held a story of the group it belonged to, and spoke of a town brimming with community spirit and kindness.

"Come on, dear, we'd better find ourselves a perch."

Kate followed Joy as she shuffled into a pew. The church was fit to bursting, noisy with the chatter of old friends, and whoops of delight as children showed off their new toys. Quiet descended as the vicar appeared in her finery, the only sound the odd gurgle from a baby, and whispered chatter from toddlers.

Perhaps magical was the wrong word to describe a

Christian service, but to Kate that was how it felt. She helped Joy up as they sung through the carols Kate remembered from her childhood, and squeezed Joy's hand as she shed happy tears at the sight of children walking to the front to display their presents to the congregation.

Joy's hearty voice carried above those around her as she sang *Hark the Herald Angels*, softening to a velvet vibrato filled croon during *Silent Night*. Kate felt proud to be standing by her side. As Joy sang, the years fell away to reveal the young woman beneath the wrinkles and arthritis.

The vicar stood to send her congregation away with a blessing, but her words drowned beneath a commotion at the back of the church.

"Get your hands off me. Who are you? I'm calling the police!"

Necks craned to see where the sound was coming from, but with the pews packed, it was impossible to tell. Unfazed, the vicar raised her voice, drawing people's gaze back to the front of the church, as if nothing were going on.

Occasional shouts from the back punctuated the vicar's prayer, but with her head bent, Kate had no idea who the culprit was. The blessing ended and people rose from their seats, some staying to chat, others desperate to get back to a glass of Port and roast turkey. A scream pierced through the hubbub and Kate turned to see a figure being dragged out of the door by someone who looked just like Bob.

"Was that Bob?" Kate asked, spinning round to face Joy.

"I don't know what you mean," said Joy, shuffling her feet, refusing to look Kate in the eye.

"The men who just left the church, I'm sure one of them was Bob."

"Sorry, dear, my eyesight's not what it was. I'm sure it wouldn't have been Bob, though. Come on, let's grab ourselves a mince pie."

Kate looked on as Joy made her way unsteadily along the pew. Her friend knew more about the scuffle than she was letting on, but Kate let the matter drop.

Chapter 30

Kate screamed as she opened the door to her best friend and drew her into a tight hug.

"You're crushing me," said Maddie, laughing as Kate squeezed even tighter.

"Sorry, I've just missed you so much! Come in, come in."

Maddie dropped her bags onto the living room floor and flopped onto a sofa.

"Are you OK?" Kate asked. "You look awful."

"Thanks," said Maddie, managing a small smile. "I'm just tired after the festivities, that's all."

"OK, well, let me get you a drink. Tea? Coffee?"

"Hmm, much as I'd love some caffeine, I'm not sure I could face it right now. Do you have any lemonade?"

"Oh. No, sorry I don't. Would tonic water do? I've got fresh lemons I can add to it?"

"That sounds great, but don't go to too much trouble. As long as it's fizzy, it's all good."

"Bad hangover?"

"Yeah, something like that."

Kate left Maddie slumped on the sofa and went through to the kitchen to fix Maddie's drink. Despite saying it as a joke, Maddie looked awful. Her glossy blonde hair was dull and greasy, her chin dotted with spots, and her face had grown rounder, like she'd been hitting the beer too hard. Did Maddie have an alcohol problem? The thought had niggled Kate on and off since she'd known Maddie. If anyone could recognise the signs, it should be Kate, yet Maddie held down a stressful job and was bloody good at it, too. But from experience, Kate knew alcoholics were adept in hiding the problem. Maddie was too fragile right now to broach the subject, but Kate would keep a close eye on her. Sometimes being a good friend meant giving a few home truths, something Kate had never been very good at.

"Here you go," Kate said, grabbing a coaster.

"This place is looking so homely. You even use coasters now."

"I'm all grown up," Kate laughed. "Anyway, how was Christmas?"

"Same as ever. Brothers rowing, parents not speaking, everyone boozing too much."

"You didn't enjoy it then?"

"I loved every second. There's nothing like the comfort of dysfunctional family dynamics that never change. Oh, sorry, I didn't mean to..."

"Don't worry about it," said Kate. "I love hearing about your family. I'm sorry I didn't visit this year. You know what it's like though, first Christmas in a new place."

"Yeah, but I know it must have been tough, and I do realise how lucky I am."

"It wasn't as tough as I expected. I spent some time thinking about Mum, went to church with Joy..."

"Hang on, you went to church?"

"Yes, and I loved it."

"Wow, you've changed."

"I'll have to take you down there sometime. They've got this amazing Christmas tree festival, but I'm not sure how long they'll be up for."

"Sounds... fun...?"

"Don't be like that. It's actually pretty magical. Joy said

they do it every year."

"You're turning into a proper small-town girl."

Kate smiled, but noticed the edge to Maddie's voice. Was she trying to put her down? It must be the hangover making her grumpy, Kate decided.

"So how was the Christmas do you were heading to when we last spoke?"

"Oh, just your average office bullshit. Nothing special. Shall we watch a movie?"

Kate felt a tug of disappointment. This was supposed to be their time to catch up, but Maddie wanted to watch TV? Something was up with her friend, but Kate couldn't put her finger on what... yet.

Maddie fell asleep five minutes into the film. Kate studied her pale face and the purple rings around her eyes. She looked across at the Christmas tree. Maddie hadn't even mentioned it. Kate had spent Christmas afternoon adding fairy lights and handmade decorations she'd picked up at a Christmas market a few years ago. It would have been the first thing Maddie noticed usually. Nor had she commented on the greenery decorating the house.

After getting back from the church with Joy, Kate had heated up a microwave lasagne, poured a glass of Prosecco, and raised a toast to absent family. She doubted Moira would have approved of her lonely Christmas dinner. It wasn't exactly *filling the house with love and laughter*, but Kate had Boxing Day to do that, and there was something liberating about spending the day alone. Not that she was truly alone, Flo had joined her for a FaceTime lunch during her break at The Sunbeam. As well as enjoying the comfort of friendship, seeing Flo sitting in the grotty Sunbeam staffroom on Christmas Day confirmed to Kate she had made the right decision to leave.

With lunch cleared away, she had strolled up to the nature reserve behind her house and filled a basket with holly and ivy, singing the aforementioned carol as she went. Back at home, she'd tied greenery around the house, before settling down to the Queen's speech with a glass of wine. It was the no pressure, relaxed day she had been hoping for.

Maddie let out a snore, and Kate retreated from the room so as not to disturb her. She used the opportunity of a spare couple of hours to begin the food prep, wishing she'd opted for a takeaway. Cooking wasn't a skill she was known for, and she crossed her fingers that the old Delia Smith book found among her grandmother's stuff would be a reliable guide.

An hour later and the potatoes and carrots were peeled, sprouts prepared, lamb in the oven on a low heat and everything that couldn't be cooked in advance laid out ready on the kitchen counter. Kate ducked her head around the door to check on Maddie, who lay on her back, dead to the world. Her phone had fallen from her hand. Kate picked it up and placed it on the table. The phone buzzed and Kate stared at the screen. Alex's name flashed up with the message: *We need to talk.*

Kate retreated to the kitchen, leaning over the kitchen sink and splashing water over her face. What did Alex and Maddie have to talk about? It had to be about her, but why go behind her back? This wasn't school. She was big enough to have a conversation herself without needing an intermediary. There was no point asking Maddie about it yet. Kate would have to wait until Maddie was a) awake and b) not hungover.

Kate's own phone flashed with a message from Bob- *I'm here early, but can head off for a walk if you fancy some time alone with Maddie?* Kate smiled at the thoughtfulness of his message and tapped out a reply- *Maddie's asleep so fine to come in now, but can you come around the back so we don't wake her?* Seconds later Bob replied with a simple- *No probs x*

"Merry Christmas," said Kate, opening the door and giving Bob a brief hug.

"Ouch," he said, clutching his side.

"Are you OK?"

"Yeah, sorry, I just hit my side against a metal railing yesterday."

"Let me see."

Before he could protest, Kate had taken his jacket and lifted his shirt. "Bob, that looks terrible! Have you had it checked out by a doctor?"

"No, I might have broken a rib or two, but they can't do anything about those."

"Sit down and put this on it," said Kate, pulling a bag of petits pois from the freezer.

"Ever think of training as a nurse?" asked Bob, wincing as the cold stung his skin.

"No chance. I had enough practice cleaning wounds when Mum was alive to last me a lifetime."

"Fair enough. I don't suppose you have anything to take the edge off the pain?"

"Yes, sure," said Kate, searching through a drawer and pulling out two packets of pills. "Ibuprofen or paracetamol?"

"I was thinking wine or beer?"

Kate laughed. "There's no shortage of either of those. What's your preference?"

"Maybe a beer for starters, then I'll move on to wine at lunch."

"Wow, you're going for it today. How was yesterday?"

"Um, OK," said Bob, offering up no further information. "How about you?"

"It was a surprisingly lovely day in the end. Joy dragged me along to church, then I had lunch with Flo on FaceTime, went for a walk, and did a bit of decorating."

"You were at St Petroc's church?" asked Bob, colour draining from his face.

"Yes, why? Were you there too?"

"No, no, I wasn't," said Bob, refusing to catch her eye.

He was lying. Kate's shoulders slumped. First Maddie had been acting weird, now Bob. She'd been so looking forward to this day, and so far, it wasn't going the way she had hoped.

"Cooee," came a voice from the garden.

"Joy," said Bob and Kate simultaneously, smiling at each other.

Bob moved his chair away from the door and Joy joined them in the already squished galley kitchen.

"Blimey this is a squeeze," said Joy, laying down a clinking bag on the kitchen counter.

"It sounds like you've brought an entire brewery with you," said Bob, peering into the bag.

"Just all the booze I could find in my pantry. Some of it's been there years, so best check the labels before tucking in. I don't want to poison anyone."

"Well it's a lovely thought," said Kate, inspecting a bottle claiming to be orange and peach liquor.

"Mind if we sit outside for a bit?" asked Joy, pulling a packet of cigarettes from her bag.

"Not at all, probably better if we do actually. Maddie's asleep," said Kate, nodding her head towards the living room.

"Over done the celebrations hey?" asked Joy. "Oh, to be young again."

Bob grabbed his beer and the two glasses of wine Kate poured and followed Joy to the garden table.

"Fancy lighting the fire pit for me?"

"I'd love to. Nothing makes a man feel manlier than fire."

"You're a good chap, Bob. Kate's lucky to have you."

Joy's words caused them both to blush, but at least Bob could disguise his redness as he turned to gather up some logs.

"So, Bob," said Joy as sat back at the table. "How are your parents doing?"

Joy fixed Bob with an intense look, one he met with a rising blush across his face. "Same as ever."

"I'm sorry to hear that. dear. Tell your mum she can call me any time she needs a chat."

"Thanks, Joy, I will do."

"She's been missed down the WI. Everyone's asking about her. She's a strong woman to keep pushing through all that nonsense. You're a good boy to be helping her with it all."

"Thanks, I try my best."

"I know you do, and it can't be easy for you. Just remember there are plenty of people happy to help out if you need it."

"Thanks, but I'm managing fine at the moment." The muscles in Bob's face tensed and he took a long swig of his beer.

Kate looked between her two friends, wondering what on earth was going on. She was about to ask for clarification when a disheveled-looking Maddie wandered out into the garden, yawning loudly.

"I see you've got the party started without me," she said, giving Bob a lazy smile before leaning over to kiss his cheek.

"Good to see you, Maddie, you're looking well."

Another lie.

"Ha, always the gentleman. Don't worry, Kate's already told me I look like shit."

"I was joking," said Kate, holding her hands up in protest.

"Yeah, whatever. Anyway, I thought I should let you know I can smell burning in the house?"

"What?" said Kate, pushing her chair back so hard it fell to the ground, and racing into the kitchen.

She dropped to her knees beside the oven, smoke pouring from it, the meat inside turning crispy and black.

"Looks like you could do with a hand," said Bob,

peering over her shoulder. “Don’t worry, we’ll have this sorted in no time.”

Chapter 31

Despite Kate's protests, Bob insisted on taking over in the kitchen. "Don't worry," he said. "I'm not going to take the credit, you've done all the hard work already. Think of me as your sous chef."

"You're sure you don't mind?"

"How many times do I have to say it? No, I don't mind. Now get lost and drink wine with the girls."

Kate smiled at his referring to Joy as a girl. She'd been doing a sterling job of entertaining a sullen Maddie while Bob and Kate were distracted in the kitchen. Kate even heard Maddie laugh a few times, which looking at the state of her, was another Christmas miracle.

Kate carried a bottle of white wine through to the living room, where Maddie and Joy had decamped. She filled her and Joy's glasses, but when she went to top up Maddie's, Joy put her hand over it and gave Kate a shake of the head. Maddie, distracted by her phone hadn't noticed the exchange, so Kate put the bottle down on the table. She wasn't going to stop Maddie drinking on Boxing Day, but it was probably best not to encourage it either.

"How was the WI lunch?"

Joy launched into a tale of the ins and outs of the meal, what they'd eaten, who had said what to annoy who. "Of course, it was over pudding that the real scandal broke."

"And what was that?" asked Kate, engrossed by Joy's lively story telling.

"Well..." Joy paused for dramatic effect. "Maureen has only been seeing Maurice behind Charlotte's back."

"Are Maurice and Charlotte married?"

"No, but they've been stepping out since our pensioners Harvest Festival lunch so he was officially off the market. I'm pleased it came out. I haven't met the man often, but I wouldn't trust him as far as I could throw him. A right scoundrel he is. There were plenty of tears running into the Christmas pudding I can tell you, and both women have sworn off men for life."

"I'm going for a lie down."

Maddie cut through the conversation like a knife, stomping out of the room like a grumpy teenager, phone clamped to her hand.

"That girl's got a bee in her bonnet about something," said Joy, as Kate stared at the door in surprise.

"I don't know what's got into her. I know she's hungover but Maddie's been rude ever since she arrived. I've been looking forward to her coming for ages, now I'm looking forward to when she goes."

"How long is she staying with you, dear?"

"Only a couple of days."

"Let's hope she feels better after a lie down. A spot of lunch should do her good."

Bob popped his head round the door to inform them lunch would be half an hour. Once again, he insisted he didn't need help, so Kate began setting up the table. Technically, it was a child's table tennis court, but it was the perfect size for a makeshift dining table. Even better, she could keep it stored flat in the under stairs cupboard when not in use.

Joy hooted with laughter on seeing the table. "You are resourceful dear, just like your grandmother. She would have loved this."

"Thanks, I hope it's strong enough for all that food."

"We'll find out soon enough. Now, do you need any help laying the table?"

"If you could grab the cutlery that would be great."

Joy bustled through to the kitchen and Kate pulled out the tablecloth she had bought. It cost more than the table, but laying white lace across the chipped, faded games table, she decided it had been worth every penny. By the time Joy returned, Kate had an impressive candle display in the centre, holly and ivy leaves trailing round an elaborate candelabra.

"This is what I imagine Michelin star restaurants look like," said Joy, laying out the knives and forks. Kate smiled, pleased she approved. "Did you get any crackers, dear?"

"Tada," said Kate, pulling them from the cupboard. "Are you OK if we do presents after dinner?"

"Of course. That sounds very civilized."

"Grubs up," Bob shouted from the kitchen.

"I'll go and wake Maddie," said Kate. "Grab yourself a chair, I'll be back in a minute."

Kate ran upstairs and knocked on the bedroom door. Maddie didn't answer, so Kate pushed the door open and called out her name. When Maddie didn't respond, Kate tiptoed towards the bed, assuming she must still be asleep. The bed was empty, but from the bathroom came the sound of Maddie throwing up. Kate wondered how many bottles of wine Maddie had got through the day before. Unable to stop herself, Kate picked up Maddie's phone from the bedside cabinet. On the screen was another message from Alex - *?*

What the hell did a single question mark mean? The sound of the toilet flushing caused Kate to drop the phone back where she found it.

"Are you OK in there?"

"Yeah, fine, coming out now."

Maddie appeared, looking better than when she

arrived. She'd washed her face and her cheeks were regaining their pinkness.

"Maddie, how much did you have last night?"

Maddie smiled weakly and pulled on an old cardigan. "Are you OK for lunch? I can bring some up to you if you'd rather eat up here?"

"No, it's fine, I'll come down. You've gone to so much trouble. I'm sorry I've been a pain. I feel much better now I've got that out of my system."

"OK, but don't feel you have to stuff yourself on my account. I'm sure Bob will be happy to polish off anything you can't manage."

Maddie smiled and pulled Kate into a hug. "I'm sorry I've been such a crap friend."

"Don't be daft, I'd hardly call a minor grump being a bad friend. Let's get downstairs before lunch gets cold."

By the time they reached the living room, the table was groaning with food. The lamb looked delicious, and if Kate hadn't watched him do it, she would never have guessed Bob had cut a thick layer of charcoal from it.

Chapter 32

They had just pulled their crackers and propped bright paper hats on their heads when a knock came on the door.

"Are you expecting anyone?" asked Joy, as Kate squeezed around the table to reach the door.

"No, no one."

Intrigued, plates of food lay untouched as Kate opened the door.

"Merry Christmas!" yelled Alex, holding aloft two bottles of champagne.

"Alex? What are you doing here?"

"Aren't I allowed to surprise my girl on Boxing Day? Come here." Alex placed the champagne down beside him and drew Kate into a hug. His girl? She had assumed all property rights ended with him kicking her out of his house. Alex nuzzled his face into her neck, pushing away hair with his nose and kissing her skin. Kate felt a shiver of excitement despite herself. She pushed him away, aware three sets of eyes were on her.

"Come in. It's a bit of a squeeze." She picked up Alex's leather overnight bag and slung it on a sofa. "Everyone, this is Alex. A surprise visitor."

Mutters of *welcome* and *hello* resounded round the room, none filled with much enthusiasm. Maddie's eyes were wide open as she stared at the approaching figure of

Alex. Joy had hers narrowed, assessing him and by the looks of things, finding him wanting. Bob had his gaze fixed firmly on the tablecloth.

"Let me take your coat," said Kate. Alex handed it to her and she flung it on the sofa beside his bag.

"Kate, do you mind hanging that up? It's a wool cashmere mix."

"Oh, yes, sorry."

"I'll take it," said Bob, looking up for the first time.

"And you are?"

"Sorry, I forgot introductions are needed," said Kate, blustering over Alex's rudeness. "This is my friend Bob, and my friend Joy. You know Maddie of course."

"Hi Maddie," said Alex, but Maddie looked away. "Good to meet you Bob, and you too Joy. So, where can I sit? Looks like I arrived just in time for food."

"Hand me your coat," said Bob, "and I'll grab an extra plate while I'm there."

"You're not going to hang it in the kitchen, are you?" asked Alex, looking horrified. "Sorry mate, you probably think I'm a right old fusspot, but if I get food smells into the wool, I'll never get them out."

Bob threw Alex a brisk nod and disappeared off with the overpriced jacket. By the time he got back, Alex had settled himself into Bob's seat. Bob filled Alex's plate with food and perched himself on the sofa arm, looking less than thrilled about it. Kate dug a cracker out of the cupboard and passed it to Alex. If he also had a paper hat on his head, she'd feel less tense with him around. Alex pulled the cracker, holding Kate's eye as he did. Rather than place the hat on his carefully coiffured hair, he scrunched it in a ball and dropped it onto the table.

"So, Alex, how was your Christmas?"

Kate threw a smile of thanks Joy's way. With Maddie and Bob sitting in sullen silence, she was grateful for the effort the old girl was making.

"Same as ever. Mum and Dad bicker over who will cut the turkey, we all get pissed on champagne then move onto Dad's latest purchase of vintage whiskey. Once the whiskey comes out the day goes by in something of a blur."

"Oh, right. And do you go to church?"

"Fuck no. Does anyone these days?" Alex chuckled, glancing round the table for support. Bob gave a tight-lipped smile back and Joy suddenly found her sprouts very interesting.

"Actually, I went to church with Joy yesterday," said Kate. "It was wonderful."

"Fuck me, my Kate in a church. Has the world gone mad?" Alex laughed again, before filling his face with brussel sprouts. He chewed thoughtfully, pricking one with his fork and holding it up to study it. "These are really good. I didn't think you could even boil an egg Kate. What did you cook them in?"

Kate looked at Bob, and he mouthed the ingredients at her. "Honey and bacon," she said with conviction.

"Wow. All that slop you used to cook for me and all the while you could make food like this."

"Actually, Bob did most of the cooking."

It was the first time Maddie had spoken since Alex's arrival, and all eyes turned to her. Kate felt a stab of betrayal. Shouldn't Maddie be on her side?

"All I did were a few finishing touches. Kate did most of the cooking."

"From what I saw, you spent a lot longer in the kitchen than she did," said Maddie.

"Well, dear, from what *I* saw, you were sleeping off a bad hangover upstairs. I shouldn't think you have the first idea who prepared the meal that's in front of you."

Beneath the table, Joy reached for Kate's hand and squeezed it. Alex found the whole interlude hilarious, holding a hand up to a bemused Joy for a high five. The rest of the meal passed in tense small talk, punctuated by periods of awkward silence. Kate felt immense relief when the last mouthful was eaten and she could escape the room on the pretext of clearing dishes. Joy and Bob offered to help, but Kate insisted she could manage herself. Both looked disappointed.

"I'm stuffed," said Bob. "How about we do presents before pudding?"

"That sounds a wonderful idea," said Joy, clapping her hands together in glee.

"Sounds good to me," said Kate. "Just let me clear away these things. I'll be back in a minute."

Despite the change in atmosphere brought on by Alex's arrival, Kate felt excited to be giving her friends gifts, and hoped that she had chosen wisely. She lay the plates on the kitchen worktop and gathered up the bag of gifts from her room. She had posted Alex's gift, (a set of beautiful cuff links from the gentlemen's shop in town) before Christmas, and hoped he wouldn't feel too left out without a gift to open.

"Does anyone need another drink before we open presents?" Kate asked, laying her gifts down on the table.

"I wouldn't mind a tea," said Bob, "but I'll make it. You relax."

"Tea?" scoffed Alex. "I'll have a beer, please."

"Sure thing. Anyone else?" Bob had taken on the role of host and looked at Joy and Maddie.

"I'm good with my wine, thanks," said Maddie.

"I'd have a tea if you're making one," said Joy. Kate wondered if she really wanted a cuppa or if it were a show of solidarity with Bob.

Kate wandered into the kitchen to see if Bob needed a hand. "Are you OK in here?"

"I thought I told you to relax," said Bob, smiling at her.

"It's more relaxing in here," said Kate. "I really don't know what's got into Maddie, and as for Alex..."

"So, it wasn't a good surprise, him showing up, I

mean?"

"I don't know. I mean, I'm pleased to see him, but I have no idea where I stand anymore."

"It sounds like you two need to have a good talk about things. But, Kate?"

"Yes?"

"Don't be pushed into anything. You've changed so much since you've been here. Just remember how capable you are. You don't *need* a man. If you want one, fine, but please know you don't need one."

"Thanks."

When Kate and Bob returned to the living room, they found Alex and Maddie staring at phone screens and Joy drumming her fingers on the table. Kate wished they'd make more of an effort with her. If they took the time to talk to her, they'd realise what a remarkable woman she was. At that moment, Kate felt ashamed on Alex and Maddie's behalf.

"Right, as host, I feel I should be able to give my presents first."

"Yes, Ma'am," said Bob, giving a mock salute.

"Right, Maddie first." Maddie continued to scroll through her phone. "Maddie? Maddie?"

"Sorry, what?"

"Here's your Christmas present," said Kate, handing over a large squishy parcel. Kate felt her excitement drawn out of her like a deflating balloon as Maddie opened the parcel with no reaction at all. It had taken weeks to find the perfect outfit from the various charity shops, and Kate had been certain Maddie would love it. Instead of delight, Maddie thanked her with a small smile and Kate could have sworn she looked sad. Confidence dimmed, Kate pulled a box shaped parcel from her bag and handed it to Bob.

Bob unwrapped the paper carefully, eyes wide as he took in the shoe box, collaged with photographs from around Bodmin.

"Wow, I love it, thank you."

Kate laughed. "The box isn't the present, you idiot. Look inside."

On the inside of the lid she had written *Tour Guide's Survival Kit.* Bob reached inside the box and pulled out Kendal mint cake, a swiss army knife, compass, bike lights, town map, thick woollen socks, hand gel, and a mini first aid kit. He looked up at Kate and she was surprised to see tears in his eyes.

"Thank you," he said, voice choking as he spoke. "This is the most thoughtful gift I've had in a long time."

"You're welcome," said Kate, reaching across and squeezing his hand.

"Thank God you bought me cuff links," said Alex. "I'd hate to be lugging all that crap back with me."

Bob shot Alex a glare across the table.

"Your turn, Joy," said Kate, moving swiftly on from Alex's comment. She passed a large square box across the table. "The present is inside."

Joy lifted the lid, her hands shaking, and set the lid down on the floor beside her. Several hard-backed books lay inside the box, and Joy gasped as she began flicking through them. "But, how did you? These are..."

"They're your photos," Kate said, smiling.

"But how did you get them into these books?"

"I scanned them onto my laptop. It was easier than I expected. I thought this way you could have them on a shelf and look at them whenever you like, rather than having to sift through piles. I've tried to sort them by date or location, but I might have muddled some up."

"I... I..." Tears began streaming down Joy's cheeks and Kate rushed round the table to hug her friend.

"Are you OK?"

"I'm just being a daft old bat. I love them, I love them so, so much. Thank you, dear."

"The pressure's really on now," said Bob, smiling

across at the two emotional women.

"Come on then," said Joy, dabbing her eyes with a napkin. "Your turn, Mr Carter."

"Right, OK. I just need to nip out to my car."

Bob appeared moments later, hidden behind a large rectangular box and holding a bag for life. He propped the box against the wall and handed Kate the bag. Inside were several large presents and at the bottom, one tiny one.

"I hope these are the right size," he said, looking flustered as Kate began unwrapping the packages. She opened the first one and laughed.

"These are so perfect for Cornwall," she said, holding up a pair of waterproof trousers for the others to see.

"Wow, stylish," said Maddie, but her tone was softer than it had been previously.

The next parcel contained a fancy waterproof jacket. Kate protested about the amount Bob must have spent, but he insisted it was second hand so she let it drop with a thank you. Also in the bag were a pair of bright red wellies, "To match your duffle coat," Bob explained.

"How did you know my shoe size?" Kate asked. Bob tapped his nose, and threw a grin over to Maddie.

At the very bottom of the bag lay a small package. "As I'd gone practical for the other gifts, I thought I should end on a frivolous note," said Bob.

Kate tore off the wrapping paper, finding leaf-shaped silver earrings hanging from a piece of cardboard. "I love them. Thank you," she said.

"Well, you know what they say; *There's no such thing as bad weather, only bad clothing*. But no one said you can't add a bit of bling into the sensible outfit."

Alex muttered something into his drink, but Kate ignored him, mouthing a *Thank you* across the table to her kind, thoughtful friend.

"Right, Joy, it's your turn," said Bob, carrying the large box over to her.

"What on earth can this be? It's enormous!"

"This is a present from Mum, too. She says she misses you and hopes to come around and see you using it before long."

Joy slowly peeled back the wrapping paper, folding it on the table for reuse at a later date. "Oh, my dear. But this is too much."

"Bloody hell, I wish you women would just be grateful and not force me to admit when my presents are second hand." Bob grinned, and helped Joy pull a keyboard from the box. "Mum was remembering how you used to sing all the time. Her hands are too arthritic to play these days, so we thought you could make better use of it. Fancy singing us a few carols after lunch?"

Joy's eyes lit up at the thought. Everyone ignored the groan which escaped Alex's lips.

"Right, my turn," said Joy, digging into her handbag and pulling out three presents. "I'm sorry dear," she said to Alex. "If I knew you were coming I would've got you a little something."

"No problem, Joy," said Alex, giving her one of his winning smiles. His smile could melt any woman's heart, except Joy's apparently, as she nodded and moved on.

"Maddie, I wasn't sure what you liked, so this is just a little something." Joy handed Maddie a small gift. On finding a bag of clotted cream fudge inside, Maddie gave Joy her widest grin of the morning.

"Now, Kate. This one is for you."

Kate unwrapped a rectangular package. Beneath a layer of bubble wrap, sat a framed photograph of Moira. She was wearing the green dress Kate wore to the Christmas do, her head was tipped back in laughter, as if someone had told the funniest joke in the world. Kate's own eyes filled with tears. "That's how I always remember her," said Joy. "The life and soul of any party, big hearted, funny and gregarious."

“Thank you so much, Joy. I’ll put it in pride of place on the windowsill.”

“Now for you, young man,” said Joy, holding out a similar shaped package to Bob. “I found this when I was sorting through my old photos to give to Kate. It was taken years ago during a Church day out at the beach.”

Bob unwrapped his present and made a strange noise, somewhere between a choke and a gasp. Kate looked over his shoulder at the photograph he was holding. A couple sat close together on a beach, their hands entwined, gazing into each other’s eyes. The woman was beautiful, thick hair caught by the breeze, long legs kicked out in front of her. The man was the spitting image of Bob. Tall, broad, with a thick head of hair. The only difference was the thick-rimmed glasses that perched on his nose.

“Joy... thank... thank you,” said Bob, before pushing back his chair and hurrying from the room.

Chapter 33

With lunch over and stomachs full, Alex went for a nap in Kate's room and Bob accompanied Joy outside when she went for a smoke. Maddie offered to help pack up the table, and Kate hoped she could use the opportunity to get to the bottom of what was troubling her friend.

"Maddie, be honest with me. Have I done something to piss you off?"

Maddie's eyes filled with tears and she looked at the floor. "You hate your present."

"No, of course I don't hate it. It was very generous of you." Kate was telling the truth, but what she didn't add was that the expensive set of shower gels were a far cry from the thoughtful gifts Maddie had presented in the past. "This isn't about presents Maddie, it's about you. You've been weird ever since you arrived, and I get the feeling I've done something wrong."

"What could you have possibly done wrong?" Maddie snapped, as a single tear dangled perilously from her nose. "Sorry. Seriously though, this isn't about you. I'm just going through some shit right now and I'm not the best company. I almost cancelled, but hoped a change of scene might do me good."

"What's wrong?"

"Oh, just the usual. Work is crazy at the moment and

I'm working on a case that's really getting to me."

"You're sure it's just work?"

"*Just* work? Do you have any clue what I have to deal with? No, of course you don't, you're just playing at running a B&B whilst living off your inheritance." Maddie's words stung like a slap in the face. "Sorry, Kate, I didn't mean that. I'm just jealous I guess."

"Jealous of me? As you implied, I'm a nobody, living in a small town contributing nothing to society. You're the hot shot lawyer."

"Don't be like that, it doesn't suit you."

Kate bit her tongue. So, it was alright for Maddie to be moody and snappy, but not Kate? What the hell had happened to her friend. "Are you sure this doesn't have anything to do with a man?"

Maddie stopped folding the table cloth and stared at Kate. She seemed on the verge of saying something as Alex walked in, hair scruffy from lying down.

"Sorry to interrupt, but you don't have any feather pillows, do you? You know I can't sleep properly on synthetic fibres."

"Sorry I don't. It wasn't like I was expecting you."

"Woah, no need to be like that," said Alex, shaking his head and retreating back to the bedroom.

"What the hell's going on with you two?" asked Maddie.

"I've got no idea. I've spent months hoping he'd want me back, praying he'd turn up at my door, but now he's here..."

"The reality doesn't live up to the fantasy?"

"Exactly."

"Well I think you should just sort things out one way or the other. It's getting painful watching the constant back and forth, on, off, on, off. Frankly it's boring."

"Right, well thanks for the advice. Look, why don't you go and have a lie down. It will take Joy a while to get set up for carols."

"Sure. Can't wait," said Maddie, in a tone that suggested she really could.

*

In the end, it took even longer to get Joy set up behind the piano than Kate had predicted. She'd insisted on going home for her sheet music, and Bob and Kate walked her home, worried she might fall after all the booze she'd consumed. When they finally made it back to Kate's, the house was quiet, with no sign of either Alex or Maddie. Kate peeked into her bedroom but the bed was empty, duvet and sheets crumpled and messy. She walked upstairs to Maddie's room and opened the door.

"What the hell is going on here?"

Maddie was propped up against the headboard, Alex sat cross legged facing her on the bed. They were holding hands, and Maddie's face was red and puffy as if she'd been crying.

"I heard Maddie crying," said Alex, as if that were explanation enough.

"Right, and you decided you'd be her shoulder to cry on?"

"Yes, exactly. You don't have a problem with that, do you?"

Kate did, but could give no rational explanation for why her stomach was churning as if something was very, very wrong with the scene in front of her. "No, of course not. Is there anything I can do to help, Maddie?"

"I'm all good, thanks. Is Joy ready to serenade us?"

"Yes, she's all set up. Are you coming?"

"Yes sure," they both said. A look passed between them and Kate felt her stomach knot up once more.

"Ah, here you are," said Joy as the three of them walked into the living room. "Now, I should tell you, I'm very rusty..."

"Great," muttered Alex, and Kate dug him in the ribs with her elbow.

"So, I'd love it if you could join in."

Maddie gave a snort and Kate turned to look at her. *I'm not singing* mouthed Maddie. Kate chose to ignore her.

"I'm happy to join in," said Bob.

"Me too," said Kate, smiling at him.

"Right, well this isn't a carol, but it is my favourite Christmas song of all time."

Joy's fingers hovered above the keys and she began to play. Given the stiffness of her aging joints, Joy played with the nimbleness of someone far younger. Her voice joined the piano notes as she struck up a version of *White Christmas.* Her voice was smooth and strong, vibrato filling the long notes, a wispy breathiness adding texture to certain phrases.

"Your turn Bob," said Joy, as her fingers tapped out an instrumental section.

Bob stood up, coughed and took the next few lines. Kate stared at him open-mouthed. His baritone voice rang out deep and luxurious. He had his eyes closed, lost in the music. Kate closed her own eyes, letting herself be carried away on the sweet sentimental melody. This was the kind of day she had imagined, not the sniping awkwardness of earlier. She opened her eyes and turned to Maddie and Alex. Both seemed unmoved by the music, and as Joy called out *Everybody join in!* they made no move to open their mouths. Kate felt self-concious as she let her own voice quietly join that of her friends.

As the song drew to an end, Kate's rapturous applause were drowned out by Joy hammering the keys and launching into a jaunty version of Jingle Bells. Joy played through all the carols and Christmas songs Kate had grown up with, before declaring herself exhausted and in need of a drink.

"I'll play one more song, but Kate and Bob, you need to come up here and join in. Maddie and Alex are welcome too of course."

Kate turned to Maddie and Alex, both were scrolling through their phones and neither seemed to have heard Joy's invitation. Bob joined Joy beside the piano and Kate followed his lead. As Joy's fingers ran gently down the piano keys, Kate studied her face. Sat behind the piano, it was as though the lines on her skin faded, and the young woman she had once been shone through.

Silent night, Holy night...

Was she having a religious epiphany, wondered Kate, as tingles ran through her limbs and the light in the room softened. Bob joined the singing, adding a harmony below Joy's melody. Kate struggled to break any sound through her emotion, but added a quiet echo to Joy's clear alto. As the carol ended, the three singers stood motionless, smiling at each other in recognition of the moment they had shared.

"Anyone for another drink?" Alex's voice shattered the atmosphere and Joy began packing up her music.

"Not for me thanks, dear. I think it's time I headed home."

"Bob?"

"No thanks, Alex. I should probably make a move too."

"Looks like it's a party of three then. Kate? Maddie?"

Each accepted the offer of a top up and Alex went through to the kitchen to fetch the wine bottle. Kate said goodbye to her friends, promising to drop the keyboard round to Joy in the morning.

"Thank you so much dear, I've had a wonderful day. I shall spend this evening looking through those photo books." Joy kissed Kate on both cheeks and took her hands. "You take care of yourself, won't you, dear. I'd hate to think of anyone messing you about."

"I can look after myself, don't worry," said Kate, letting go of Joy's hands and turning to Bob. "Thank you so much for your help today. See you at the weekend?"

"Yes, I'll expect you fully waterproofed and ready to

face the weather."

"Yes, sir!"

Bob leaned in closer and in a quiet voice mirrored Joy's sentiment. "Remember what I said earlier. You're much stronger than you think."

"Thank you," said Kate, giving him a quick hug and opening the door for her friends. "See you soon," she called, waving till they were out of sight.

Alex appeared with a bottle of wine in one hand, a beer in the other. "Have they gone?" he asked. Kate nodded. "Thank God, I thought the old dear would never stop singing." Maddie laughed, and Kate flopped down onto the sofa, feeling a stranger in her own home.

"Shall we watch some TV?" asked Maddie.

"Sounds good to me," said Alex. "Got any popcorn, Kate?"

"Seriously? You want popcorn after all that food we've just eaten?"

"Yep, do you have any?"

"No, no I don't."

"Any shops open round here?"

"There's a garage at the bottom of the hill. Shall I go and have a look?"

"No, I'll go."

"Me too," said Maddie. "I could do with some fresh air."

"OK, I wouldn't mind a stroll either. Just let me clear up a bit first."

"How about Maddie and I go while you clear up? That way we'll all be ready to sit down by the time we get back?"

"Fine," said Kate, thinking it would have been a greater help to have a hand with the dishes.

Forty minutes later and Alex and Maddie still weren't back. Kate walked through to the living room to see if she could spot them. Surely, they would have called if they'd got lost? Muffled shouting reached her, and she peered through the net curtain. Alex and Maddie were outside on the pavement. Their arms were flailing around in what could only be an argument. Bloody double glazing, thought Kate, wishing she could hear whatever it was they were saying. She noticed them moving towards the house and jumped onto a sofa, picking up a magazine in an effort to look as though she'd been sat there for ages.

"Everything alright?" Kate asked as they stepped through the door.

"Yeah fine, why do you ask?" said Maddie.

"It's just you've been a while so I wondered if you'd got lost."

"Oh, yeah, we did a bit, but we found the garage in the end."

"Here you go," said Alex, throwing a packet of popcorn at her. "Do you have some bowls to put that in?"

Kate inwardly groaned at the thought of more washing up. "Yep, I'll grab some."

Chapter 34

"So, what are your plans, long term I mean?"

Kate was lying beside Alex on the bed, her morning coffee growing cold on the table beside her. It had been an awkward evening with Alex and Maddie for company, and bedtime had been no better. Alex climbed into her bed without discussion but made no moves to do anything other than a quick peck on the cheek before saying goodnight. Kate woke early and put a bit of makeup on, but despite a quick squeeze of her hand, Alex showed no affection.

"What do you mean long term?" asked Kate, leaning on her elbow to look at Alex.

"You know, job, house, what city you live in?"

"I kind of assumed I'd be staying put for a while."

"And I don't get any say in the matter?"

"Look Alex, I'm really struggling to know what's going on here. I mean, you asked me to move out, claimed you needed space, took up with some busty blond, dumped said blond, started texting me again, then turned up on my doorstep out of the blue. What exactly do you want from me?"

"I don't know Kate, I guess I miss having you around."

"Yes, but around in what sense? Around as one half of a couple, or around the corner bumping into you in the supermarket from time to time?"

"It's hard for me you know. I was independent for so long. I want to be in a relationship with you, I'm just not sure I can do the whole living together thing."

"But where does that leave me? Does that mean we go back to dating like we're in our early twenties? What about starting a family?"

Alex visibly winced at the mention of family. "Woah, girl, you're getting a bit ahead of yourself there. You know I love you, always have, always will. I'm just not sure I see myself as a family man. But I do want a relationship with you, so I wouldn't write it off in the future."

"This is all so confusing," said Kate, putting her head in her hands.

"Hey," said Alex, taking her hand and putting her fingers to his lips. "You need me, you know you do. And I need you. We're a team."

"It hasn't felt like that recently."

"It was you who moved away."

Kate looked at him with astonishment. "Me who moved away? Only after you'd kicked me out and moved my replacement in!"

"Yeah, OK, so I admit, I was a dick. I think I was going through some quarter life crisis or something. No excuse, I know. You have every right to be angry with me."

"I am."

"So you should be. But you can't deny you missed me, can you?" Alex looked at her with his puppy dog eyes. Kate laughed.

"You're such an idiot," she said, as he pulled her close to him. It was so long since anyone had held her, she nuzzled into his chest, breathing in the scent of his expensive aftershave.

"So, what do you say? Should we give it another go?"

"I guess so. But I want to take things slowly. See you every other weekend for starters maybe?"

"Kate, if you're really serious about this, I'd need one hundred percent commitment from you."

Kate rubbed her forehead in confusion. Shouldn't it be her asking for one hundred percent commitment from him? He sounded genuine though, and isn't love about forgiveness?

"And what does this one hundred percent commitment look like then?"

"You need to move back to Bath."

"But what about this house?"

"Sell it. It needs a shit load of work doing to it anyway."

"I've just done a shitload of work to it!"

"What about that kitchen? Kate, you take a piss *outside*."

"Only when guests are here."

"And are those guests making you money?"

"It's low season. I'll be really busy come Easter."

"Really? Are you sure? I can't see why anyone would want to visit this town, it's a dump. And anyway, Easter's months away. What are you going to do till then? Take up knitting?"

Kate had been thinking of volunteering at the local charity shop, but thought that idea wouldn't go down well. "This was my grandmother's house. I don't want to sell it."

"Rent it then."

"I don't know..."

"Look, Kate, I get that I've treated you badly, I really do, but are you genuinely telling me you're happy living here with that random selection of strays you've acquired?"

"I hope you're not talking about my friends."

"Yes, Kate, I am. You need a reality check. The old woman will be dead in a couple of years, and as for that bloke Bob, he hangs around you like a stray puppy. You should be living your best life right now, not stuck in the back of beyond."

Kate couldn't face an argument, so let his comments about Joy and Bob go. "How do I know that if I move to Bath you won't suddenly need space again?"

"You'll just have to trust me."

"Trust has to be earned."

"You're right. How about we set a time limit on it. Give me two months to prove myself to you, and if after that time you're still not convinced, we'll go our separate ways for good."

"OK. And will we see each other in that time?"

"That's up to you. I'm pretty snowed under with work, but I'll make time for you, if that's what you want."

Alex reached across and cupped Kate's chin with his palm. He drew her towards him, their lips meeting for the first time in months. It was the moment Kate longed for. As his lips moved against hers she waited for the fizz of excitement she was expecting, but it never came. As he slipped his tongue in her mouth she felt a new sensation... repulsion? She whipped her head back and jumped out of bed.

"Sorry, I haven't cleaned my teeth yet today."

"Your breath is fine, come back to bed."

He was giving her the look she remembered from the first night they met. She'd been out in a bar and he'd smiled at her across the room. Such a cliche now she thought about it, but he'd given her the same lazy, come-to-bed smile he was giving her now. The only difference was back then it had sent her weak at the knees, now her legs were immune and leading her out of the room.

"Come back," called Alex.

"Just fixing us some breakfast." Kate called back.

Maddie came into the kitchen while the eggs were boiling looking worse than the day she arrived.

"Fancy some eggs? I'm just making us breakfast."

"Alex stayed in your room last night?"

"Yes, but nothing happened. We are thinking of giving

things another try though."

Maddie's face drained from cream to grey and she leant against the kitchen worktop.

"Are you OK?"

"Yes, just didn't sleep well at all last night."

"Oh, I'm sorry you weren't comfortable."

"It had nothing to do with the bed. I've got a lot on my mind. Look, Kate, I think we need to talk about Alex..."

"Did someone mention my name?" Alex walked through to the kitchen, hands tucked into the waist band of his pyjama bottoms, muscular chest on display.

"Urgh, put some clothes on," said Maddie, scowling at Alex.

"That's not what the ladies usually say."

"For fuck's sake," said Maddie, storming out of the kitchen.

"I don't know what's wrong with her at the moment. Do you have any ideas?"

"Not a clue." Alex ran his hands through his cropped hair and avoided Kate's eye.

"Are you sure?"

"Yes. How would I know what's going on with her?"

"Because I saw you arguing yesterday after you'd been out to the shop, and you were comforting her earlier in the day when she was upset."

"God Kate, you're so paranoid. Firstly, she was pissed off with me because I'd got us lost on the way to the garage. Secondly, I was trying to have a nap but could hear her bawling upstairs. Would you rather I'd left her to deal with it alone?"

"No, of course not, but are you seriously telling me you have no idea why she was upset?"

"She told me it's something to do with work, and I believed her. Now can we please drop it?"

"OK, sorry."

Alex pulled Kate into a hug and she ran her hands up

and down the firm skin on his back. "Perhaps I was a bit hasty getting out of bed..."

"I'm off."

"Maddie?" Kate let go of Alex and stared at her friend. Maddie had her coat on and a rucksack slung over her shoulder.

"I thought you were staying for a couple of days?"

"I was, but I'm shit company and it seems like you two could do with some space. I'll call you."

"Wait," said Kate, rushing after Maddie as she headed to the door. "At least let Alex drive you to the station. Busses will be too unreliable over the Christmas period."

"No, I'm fine."

"Come on Maddie, I'll take you," said Alex, ducking into the bedroom and throwing on a hoodie.

Maddie tried arguing, but it was two against one and she eventually relented. She gave Kate a brisk hug goodbye and carried her bag across to Alex's car. She climbed into the passenger side and Kate blew a kiss through the window. Maddie turned away, not before Kate could see her cheeks were wet with tears.

Half an hour later, when Alex returned, Kate was waiting in bed, ready to get their reunion off to the start it deserved.

"Kate?"

"In here."

Alex looked flustered as he walked into the room. He began gathering up the clothes he'd flung on the floor the evening before.

"Aren't you going to come back to bed?" Kate asked. "We've got the house to ourselves now."

"Sorry, Kate, another time. I had a call from work on my way to the station. Looks like I need to head back ASAP."

"What? But why? Surely everyone's still on holiday?"

"Exactly. A contract's been ballsed up and there's no

one in the office to sort it. I'm really sorry."

Kate felt the heat of humiliation rushing over her naked body. "Don't forget your toothbrush in the bathroom," she said.

"Thanks."

As Alex left the room, Kate leapt out of bed and flung on her clothes. She didn't want the added humiliation of him knowing how ready she had been to let him have his way, only for him to turn her down. Was there really a contract that couldn't wait? It seemed a weak excuse given most of the country were sleeping off their festive indulgences.

"I'll call you when I'm back in Bath," said Alex, zipping up his bag and heading for the door.

"You do that."

"See you," he said, and let himself out of the house. Only as he was driving away, did Kate realise he hadn't even kissed her goodbye.

Chapter 35

Idiot, Kate muttered to herself as she scrubbed the kitchen worktops. *Idiot idiot idiot.* It wasn't as though she needed the money. She'd accepted the latest booking request without even reading it properly, only realising afterwards that she had agreed to the use of her kitchen. That wasn't a problem in itself, except the guests were two men coming on a New Year's *shooting* trip.

Kate hadn't once felt threatened by opening her home to strangers, but this felt different. This felt *stupid.* A single woman, alone in a house with two men and their guns. Kate could picture the headlines now; *Murdered woman brought it on herself. Woman killed after inviting gunmen into her home.* It was bad enough she had no one to spend New Year's Eve with, but now she would be spending it locked in her room. Great.

Kate scrolled through the messages on her phone. Five messages seen by Maddie, all receiving no reply. As for Alex, he'd not been answering his phone since his surprise visit, claiming he was inundated with work and would be in touch after the holidays. Then there was Bob. He'd at least answered the phone to her, but sounded harassed, saying *now isn't a great time* while Kate could've sworn she heard the sound of breaking glass in the background. Joy was busy with friends and WI commitments, leaving Kate utterly alone.

And so, she found herself waiting for two strangers on New Year's Eve, with no plans and no friends. Perhaps Alex's idea of moving back to Bath wasn't such a bad one. At least Flo was there, and Kate could try and figure out what was going on with Maddie. Kate picked up the framed photograph of her grandmother. She didn't look the type of woman who'd give up so easily. *I'm not sure I'm enough*, said Kate. *I'm not sure I can honour your wishes for the house. I tried at Christmas, I really did, but there were more scowls than laughter and I still can't work out what I did wrong.*

Kate replaced the photo on the windowsill and looked out on the grey day. She thought back over the guests she'd had since she opened. How would Rissa and Jeff be spending New Year's Eve? Kate pictured them surrounded by their girls, a family full of love, pushing away sadness to enjoy another *last*. Would Ryan be in Hong Kong with his Dad? Kate hoped so. And Gloria, where would she be? Wherever it was, Kate was certain she wouldn't be moping.

Stuck in traffic. ETA 1 hour.

Right, so she had an hour until her home was invaded. Kate grabbed her laptop and curled her legs up onto the sofa. She began scrolling through her Facebook page, but it was full of excited faces captioned *Can't wait for tonight!* Kate was about to close the page in frustration when a post about New Year's Resolutions caught her eye. That would be a way to fill her time. She picked a pad of paper out of the magazine rack, and jotted down numbers one to five.

1) *Make more friends.*

2) *Grow the B&B business.* Kate paused, chewing on the end of her pen, before adding a caveat */or decide where to move to.*

3) Maybe two resolutions were enough? The conversation with Rissa floated through her mind, and in the end, number 3 was an easy choice. *Go back to university.*

Kate put down her list and returned to her laptop. She

googled the Open University and felt bewildered by the choice of courses they offered. She checked various entry requirements and learned her two completed years at Bath meant she had accumulated credits and would only need to complete one year. At least that was something. Going to a real-life university may help her attack number one on her resolutions list, but she didn't fancy being the token mature student, and besides, who knew where she'd be living when the course started.

The internet had its usual effect of pulling her down a rabbit hole, and Kate jumped at the knock on the door, struggling to believe a whole hour had passed. She tucked her notes between the pages of a magazine and went to open the door.

"Hello!" she said, trying to hide her terror at the long thin cases slung over the men's shoulders.

"Hi, good to meet you. You don't mind us bringing the guns in do you? It's not safe to leave them in the car."

It's not safe to leave them in here, thought Kate. "Not at all," she lied. "Can I help you with your luggage?"

"Fancy the feel of a gun in your hands do you?" asked one of the men.

Kate blushed and let out a nervous giggle that sounded more like a squeal. "I meant any other luggage."

"No, don't worry we only have small backpacks."

Kate showed the men into the living room. She wondered if they were brothers, both short, plump and balding. They grinned at her, and although her rational mind told her they were being friendly, she couldn't get the word *creeps* out of her head.

"I'll show you the kitchen first, it's through here."

Kate hated turning her back on the men. What if one of them pulled out a gun and she didn't have time to make a run for it? "So are you... shooting somewhere locally?"

"Up on the moor."

"Oh, right I see. And do you have any plans for

tonight?"

"Not unless you're having a party and we can come along?"

That was clearly a joke, they're just joking, they're just being friendly. "Unfortunately not. I've had a migraine brewing all day so will probably have an early night. There's a pub just across the road, I'm sure they'll have something going on if you're looking for entertainment."

"Nah, we're all good. We've got to be up and out by five tomorrow morning so it will be an early night for us too."

Kate didn't know if that made things better or worse. At least if they went out she'd have a few hours to relax. "OK, well let's head upstairs and I'll show you to your rooms." Kate led the men upstairs, wishing she'd worn a looser pair of trousers.

"This is brilliant, thanks," said one of the men, propping his gun against the wall. "It's really kind of you to take the booking. I know guns aren't everyone's cup of tea. We really appreciate it."

"Ah, no problem at all," said Kate. *It is a problem, it is, it is, it is!* "Well, I'll leave you to settle in, I hope you have a good stay."

"Thanks, we'll try not to disturb you when we leave in the morning."

"Thanks," said Kate, forcing herself to leave the room slowly, rather than sprinting away.

*

Back in her bedroom, Kate turned the key in the lock, leaned against the door, and breathed a sigh of relief. Her heart hammered in her chest, but she could feel it slowing to just above normal. Thank goodness she'd prepared, she thought, glancing over everything she would need for the night. Beside her bed lay a box filled with snacks, a bottle of wine, and an empty ice cream tub. She knew she was being ridiculous, but planned on staying in her bedroom until morning when the guests had left. The empty tub had its own particular use.

Are you free to talk? Although calmer, Kate could do with a distraction and hoped Bob would provide it.

Sorry, can't right now. I'll try and call tomorrow x

He'd been such a good friend over Christmas, but other than the occasional text, hadn't been in touch since Boxing Day.

OK, I'd like to try out my new waterproofs soon if you're free for a walk sometime next week? x

Maybe, I'll see.

He'll see? Wasn't he still on holiday for a few more days? Kate viewed him as a close friend, but perhaps she'd mis-read the signals. That was definitely one of her talents after all. Kate sighed and threw her phone down on the bed. Her watch told her it was six p.m. Jules Holland wouldn't be on TV for hours yet. She wandered over to her bookshelf and thumbed through the spines. There were none she'd not already read. Kate picked up her phone and dialled Flo's number.

"Hello?"

"Hi, who's that?"

"It's Kate."

"Kate? Sorry, I don't think I know anyone called Kate."

"Oh, sorry, I must have got the wrong number."

A burst of laughter crackled down the line. "It's me, you idiot. I was just making the point you've not been in touch for forever."

"Sorry," said Kate. "Every time I try and call your phone is off."

"That's Sylvia that is. Do you know she now confiscates our phones at the start of each shift? The sooner I can get out of there the better."

"I didn't think it could be any worse. Sounds like I got out at the right time."

"Yeah, you lucky cow. Anyway, how's life in sunny Cornwall?"

"Um, not sunny. It rains more than Bath."

"Oh. I was planning on coming for a visit next month but I might head to Spain instead."

"Noooo, come, come, I'd love to see you. I didn't think you had any holiday left?"

"I don't, but I'm so close to walking out of that dump I may be on a permanent holiday soon."

"Well you're welcome any time."

"Cheers, mate. Look, I'm sorry but I've got to go. I'm waitressing tonight and if I'm late Sylvia will dock some of my wages."

"OK, speak soon. Love you."

"Love you too."

Kate hung up and wished she'd been a better friend to Flo. Flo worked so many shifts it was hard to pin her down, and eventually it became easier not to bother. Kate grabbed the piece of paper she's been writing on earlier and added another resolution- *spend more time with Flo*. Above Kate's head the floorboards creaked as her guests moved around. Kate sighed, climbed under her duvet and switched on the laptop.

Chapter 36

Kevin and Jason crept down the stairs, Kevin cursing under his breath as his gun bag knocked against the wall. The door to the kitchen creaked and they stood still, listening for any signs they'd woken their host. Jason gave a nod and they entered the kitchen, closing the door behind them. Kevin set about making a flask of coffee while Jason boiled eggs.

"You have remembered lunch is provided?" whispered Jason.

"Yeah, mate, of course, but it's so bloody hilly we might need a bit extra."

"Fair point."

"Right, pack these into your bag and let's get going."

The two men crept out of the house, clicking the front door behind them as quietly as they could.

"That was a nice place," said Jason relieved to be in the car and able to talk at a normal volume.

"I think we freaked the woman out a bit though."

"Yeah, you with your stupid jokes."

"I was trying to relax her."

"I think all you managed was to freak her out. Poor girl was probably thinking you'd attack her in the night."

Kevin laughed and tapped the steering wheel. "She kept herself locked away all night. She must have been peeing in a plant pot."

Jason looked over at his brother. It was good to see him smiling after the shit year he'd had. "Thanks for coming with me. It's fun doing this together."

"A good way to remember the old man too," said Kevin smiling at his older brother.

They drove on in silence, each lost in their memories. Things had been so different when their dad had been alive. For starters, they would have spent the night in five-star accommodation rather than an Airbnb in Bodmin. Dad always saw to it that their New Year's break was just the right mix of sport and luxury.

"What do you think Spanner's doing for New Years?"

Kevin chuckled at their nick name for their evil stepmother. "Probably sleeping off a champagne hangover after working her way through Dad's collection of Bollinger."

"I reckon the wine cellar's already been drunk dry. Not that it will be a problem for her to replace it."

Jason sighed and watched as the town turned to rolling countryside outside the car window. He hoped today's shoot would be worth it. It couldn't compare to the shoots of their youth, but it had good reviews for a bargain basement option. He watched the tense muscles in Kevin's neck twitch as he drove. Jason would do anything to help his big brother, and that included watching him like a hawk to make sure he didn't do anything stupid.

Jason had seen the fear in their host's eyes as Kevin had tried to win her round with his stupid jokes. He wanted to tell her about the Kevin he knew, kind-hearted, generous, confident, attractive. But he saw his brother through her eyes, and knew she'd never believe him. Kevin was a husk of the man he'd once been. It was scary how you're ever only one run of bad luck away from handsome hero to feared middle-aged creep.

Kevin was so closed off these days, only Jason saw the

man behind the mis-placed humour and hard outer shell. He knew Kevin still cried himself to sleep over the loss of his family. Jason couldn't imagine the humiliation of losing your entire family to your supposed best friend. It had done more than rip away Kevin's self-respect, it had broken him. Coming on the back of their dad's death, Jason wouldn't put it past Kevin to do something stupid.

Perhaps a day surrounded by guns was a bad idea. But Jason knew Kevin's respect for the sport and was ninety-nine percent sure he wouldn't do anything to jeopardize its reputation.

"Have you got any New Year's resolutions?" Jason asked his brother.

"Get myself out of that shit bedsit and start living again."

"Wow."

"What? Too ambitious?"

"No, not at all. I just can't remember the last time I heard you sound so positive."

"New Year, fresh start, and all that bollocks. I've spent too long letting life happen around me, it's time I took a bit of control."

Kevin pulled the car into the driveway of the shooting lodge, both brothers feeling that today was a turning point in their fortunes.

*

Kate woke early needing a wee. The ice cream tub was full from the night before and she had no other suitable containers to use. She heard the creak of a floorboard as the guests crept downstairs, heard them pottering around the kitchen and finally, just as she was sure she'd wet herself, heard them leave.

"Thank God," said Kate, unlocking her bedroom door and rushing outside to the loo. Relief washed over her as she emptied her bladder. How crazy had she been to have peed in a plastic tub last night? Hadn't Bob once called her brave? Yet she was too scared of her guests to even go out to the bathroom.

Kate finished up and rushed back into the warmth of the house. She made herself a coffee and wandered upstairs to see how the guests had left their rooms. To her surprise the rooms were spotless. Both the bed and sofa bed's bedding had been stripped and neatly folded. Any crockery they used had been washed and replaced, leaving her to wonder if they'd really been there at all.

Beside the bed in the double room sat a large bunch of flowers and a card. Kate pulled the card from the envelope and read the message inside.

Thank you so much for our stay. We understand the thought of two men with guns is less than appealing and apologise if we made you feel uncomfortable in any way. This trip is an important one for us, and we had struggled to find anyone who would accommodate us. We wish you a healthy and happy New Year. Kind regards, Kevin and Jason.

The saying *never judge a book by its cover* felt very real all of a sudden. Kate thought back to when she first met Bob, who must be a similar age to her guests. Hadn't she thought him a bit pompous? A bit old? Both had proved far from the truth. What was going on with Bob? Kate went down to the living room and took out her list of New Year's resolutions.

5) Find out what is wrong with Bob.

She would start on that resolution this morning, whether he wanted her to or not.

Chapter 37

It wasn't difficult to find out where Bob lived. Kate sat with a map of the town in front of her piecing together the clues he'd dropped over the course of their conversations. She narrowed it down to two possible streets. It wouldn't take long to spot his car and identify the exact house. Kate prayed he wouldn't take it as an invasion of privacy. Her intentions were good, she knew something was wrong and was determined to help.

The rain began hammering down as Kate took the last bite of her toast. She pulled her new waterproofs and wellies from her bag and tried them on. She looked ridiculous but at least she'd be dry.

Whether down to the rain, or hangovers from the night before, Bodmin was deserted. Rain splashed in fat dollops against her waterproofs, running down the road in rivers and bubbling up through drains. It was hard to see a meter ahead due to the fast-moving grey curtain in front of her eyes. Ice cold water stung her face as it torpedoed into her skin and Kate pulled her hood tighter around her.

At the bottom of the hill the hulk of St Petroc's church stood formidable against the black sky. Kate took a left at the church, feeling warmth return to her body as she pushed herself onwards uphill. This area of town felt a world away from the closely packed terraces of her own street. Here, the houses were mostly detached, a mix of old and new sharing a common thread of money.

Light glowed from behind curtains and smoke rose from chimneys. Kate paused at each driveway, searching for Bob's car with no success. At the top of the hill Kate paused to catch her breath. The view would be magnificent on a clear day, but as Kate looked across the town, even the omnipresent Beacon monument was hidden by low hanging cloud.

Kate retraced her steps, turning onto a smaller lane half way down the hill. She passed four houses before spotting Bob's car, parked beside a Mercedes on a large gravel driveway. Kate stood beside a tall hedge questioning the wisdom of turning up unannounced. The faded grandeur of the house made her feel small and insignificant. She wasn't made for places like this. Where her thin terrace felt homely, this house felt cold and unwelcoming. A light was on downstairs, but most of the windows were dark.

Kate thought of her gun loving guests and remembered not to judge a book by its cover. Perhaps Bob and his parents were in the back of the house. Maybe the smell of freshly baked cakes filled the rooms. Looking at the building in front of her, Kate struggled to imagine such a homely scene.

With a deep breath, Kate crunched across the driveway and hit a metal knocker three times. She heard muffled voices coming from the house, but no one came to let her in. She tried again, tapping out a jaunty rhythm so they'd know their surprise caller was a friend. The muffled voices grew in volume and Kate felt sure she heard a scream.

She knocked again, then noticing a rusty bell hanging from the door frame, pulled its metal chord. The door opened with such force Kate jumped back. Bob stood staring at her, a tissue hanging from his nose, his eye various shades of purple.

"What the fuck are you doing here?"

Kate took another step back. Despite his words, his

voice was quiet, as though he wanted to be angry but couldn't quite muster the energy.

"Sorry for just turning up. I was worried about you."

"Worried about me? Why?"

"Um...because you haven't wanted to chat or meet up." Her words sounded ridiculous even to her own ears. It was only a week since she'd last seen him. Was she really so needy she couldn't leave him in peace?

"I said I'd speak to you soon."

"Yes, I know. I'm sorry, I shouldn't have come."

"How did you know where I lived?"

"I figured it out from a few things you said."

"If I wanted you to know where I lived, I would have told you my address."

"Sorry."

"I'd like you to leave please. I'll call you."

Kate flinched as the door slammed in her face. Anger seeped through the shock as she considered how he would feel if he received that kind of welcome at her door. Kate stepped forward and knocked again. No one answered. She continued knocking and knocking until she heard heavy footsteps pounding along the hallway.

"Why can't you just leave me alone?" Blood had escaped Bob's tissue and was dripping on his shirt.

"I'm worried about you. Why won't you tell me what's going on? Why don't you want to answer my calls?"

"This is all about you isn't it?" Bob's voice was no longer quiet, growing louder with every word. "I tried to help you when you first got here, tried to help you get a bit of independence, but no. You can't even manage by yourself for a week. A WEEK! I'm not a babysitting service." He slammed the door once more and this time Kate didn't try knocking. She turned from the house and ran all the way down the hill until she reached the church. She found the ruins of a chapel in its grounds, and sat against its walls, her tears mingling with the rain that streamed down her face.

Kate pulled out her phone and dialled Maddie's number. *This is Maddie Price, sorry I can't get to the phone right now…* Kate hung up and tried again. *Please leave a message after the beeeeep.* Maddie's chuckle made Kate long for her friend. Her tears intensified as she scrolled up to Alex's number. Her finger hovered over the call button. No, she didn't want to talk to him. The realisation shook her. Why didn't she want to speak to him, weren't they supposed to be trying to rebuild their relationship?

Kate looked down at the puddle forming around her. Alex should be the first person she'd wanted to call. She thought back to when her mum died. He'd been great then, hadn't he? In her mind, she went back to that time. She remembered Maddie bringing round meals to heat up, even though Maddie hated cooking. Then there was that time Maddie had stayed up all night listening to Kate crying over Mum. Why wasn't Alex there? Oh yes, he had an essay deadline looming. *So had Maddie,* said a little voice in her head. Then there was graduation. She'd gone along to support Alex, but he was having a boys' night out to celebrate and Kate hadn't been invited. But Maddie had organised a tea party and mock graduation, telling everyone who would listen that Kate would be graduating with a first as soon as she was back on her feet. She even bought Kate a cap and gown so she didn't feel left out.

Kate scrambled to her feet, the memories leaving her dazed and unsteady. She staggered her way up the hill past closed shops, the occasional drunk lurking in a doorway and presuming she was a kindred spirit. Gasping for breath, Kate collapsed against the door of Joy's house. She had always been curious to go inside, having only ever waited on the doorstep, but right now Kate didn't care what it looked like, just that her friend was home.

Joy answered on Kate's second knock.

"Oh my goodness, girl, what's happened to you?"

"Everything's a mess," said Kate, wiping her nose on the sleeve of her waterproof jacket.

"Right, dear, come in, but take those wet things off first, will you? They'll leave a lake on the floor."

Kate stood in the lobby, peeling off her wet clothes. Joy appeared with a towel and began patting down Kate's hair. "No one's dried my hair since I was a little girl," said Kate, tears falling uncontrollably. Joy mopped them up with the towel. "Mum used to do that when I got out of the bath. It was one of the few times I felt I had a proper mum."

"Come on, come and sit down. You're not making much sense. Take some deep breaths and I'll get you a drink."

Kate sat on Joy's armchair and looked around the room. It was nothing like she'd expected and for a moment, Kate forgot why she was crying and took it all in. The floor was made up of enormous pieces of slate. All the walls were white, even the furniture was white. An enormous flat screen TV filled one wall, while the others were dominated by large, colourful abstract paintings of naked women.

"Here you go, dear," said Joy handing Kate a large glass of wine.

"Your house is incredible," sniffed Kate, managing a small smile.

Joy beamed at her. "It is rather special, isn't it? I decorated a couple of years ago after seeing this look in a magazine. I wanted it to be as far away from an old lady look as I could get."

"Well you've certainly achieved that," said Kate, dabbing at her eyes with her cuff.

"Now what's going on with you?"

"Everyone hates me."

"Well, I know for a fact that's not true. I don't hate you for starters, and I can't imagine why anyone else would. Who are you talking about?"

"Bob and Maddie... maybe Alex too."

"Right, let's start with Bob. What's happened?"

Kate explained about her surprise trip to his house and repeated their frosty exchange. When she finished, she looked at Joy, who had her arms folded and was gazing out of the window.

"I'm sorry, dear, you need to understand Bob has a lot on his plate at the moment."

"You've said that before, but no one will tell me what. All I want to do is be there for him, isn't that what friendship is for?"

"It's really not my place to comment on his private life. All I'll say is that he *does* and *will* need you. He'll come to you in his own time. And I can guarantee he'll be hating himself for the way he spoke to you. You need to be patient, and understanding."

"That's what I was trying to be!"

"Yes, I know. I suspect your turning up caught him unawares. He probably felt trapped, like he'd be forced into telling you things he isn't ready to share yet."

"I don't understand what you mean?"

"You will in time, dear. Now, what's happened with your friend Maddie?"

"I don't know. She was really weird when she came to stay and hasn't been answering any of my calls since she went home."

"Oh, don't take it personally, dear. It will be all the hormones racing around her body that's causing her to act out."

"Hormones?"

"Yes, the early stages of pregnancy are always the worst for mood swings. I was a nightmare when I was pregnant with…"

"Wait. What? Pregnant? What are you talking about?"

Joy flushed a deep red and looked at Kate horrified. "She didn't tell you," she said.

"No! But she told *you*?"

"No of course not. I just thought it was obvious. You

know, the mood swings, grey face, throwing up, not drinking."

"But she was drinking!"

"Hardly. She had enough to stop any questions but I saw her tip her wine in the plant pot a couple of times."

"But she was hungover!"

"Is that what she told you, or what you assumed?"

Now Kate thought about it, Maddie hadn't actually said it was a hangover. But why wouldn't she have said anything? Why keep something like that from your best friend? Kate took several large gulps of her wine.

"I'm sorry, Joy, I have to go."

"But you only just got here! Why are you rushing off home?"

"I'm not going home, I'm going to Bath."

Chapter 38

It had taken a taxi driver prepared to break the speed limit, and a small fortune to get Kate on the direct train from Bodmin to Bath. She'd called the taxi on the way from Joy's house and just had time to nip into her own for a change of clothes and her toothbrush. It felt like late evening but in reality, it was still only three p.m. It would be a rush to check in to the room Flo had arranged for her at The Sunbeam, and make it over to Maddie's before it got too late.

Throughout the journey Kate played questions around her head on a loop. How many weeks gone was she? Why had she kept it a secret? Who was the father? Why hadn't Kate met him? None of the answers Kate came up with were satisfactory. If Maddie was unsure of going ahead with the pregnancy, there'd be no reason not to share that burden with Kate. They may disagree on certain things, but Kate would never judge someone else's choices. OK, maybe she'd expressed her disapproval over Maddie's heavy drinking once or twice, but should be forgiven that given her background.

Lost in her own thoughts, the journey passed in a blur and Kate was shocked to find the train pulling into Bath Spa station. She walked the short distance from the station to The Sunbeam, to be greeted in typical fashion by Flo.

"You took your time. What's it been, six months?"

"Not quite," laughed Kate, pulling her friend into a hug.

"So, what's the emergency? I'm guessing it must be an emergency for you to book in here. No time to find somewhere else, was it?"

"Actually, I wanted to be somewhere familiar, and see you. I promise I won't leave my room in a mess."

"You'd better not or I'll make you clean it yourself. So, come on, spill the beans."

"I can't Flo, it's a personal situation Maddie's going through. Even I'm not supposed to know about it."

"Oooh, trouble in paradise is there? You and Maddie going to have words?"

Kate noticed the glee on Flo's face at the thought. "We're not going to have words. I'm here to offer my support, that's all."

"OK. Well, don't forget you have other friends here too."

"I won't. What time are you working tomorrow?"

"Ten."

"Fancy meeting for an egg McMuffin at nine?"

"Are you paying?"

"Of course."

"Count me in then." Flo carried on chatting all the way to Kate's room. Kate could've found the room blindfolded, but Flo was enjoying the chance to chat and take a few minutes break from her relentless work. "Alright, I can't string this out any longer. I'd better get back. See you tomorrow at nine."

"See you," said Kate, letting herself in her room and thinking Flo more than made up for the crappy accommodation.

Kate checked her watch- seven p.m. Maddie should be back from the office by now. Kate could do with something to eat, but hopefully if she cleared the air with Maddie they could go out somewhere together. Unlike Bodmin, in Bath the sky was clear and Kate enjoyed strolling through the city, the rush hour traffic subsiding yet still seeming like the M25 compared to what she'd grown used to. There was no doubt Kate missed parts of her old life, the beauty of the city for starters.

It was only as she drew closer to Maddie's house that Kate felt the first tingle of nerves. She pushed on, knocking on Maddie's door before her nerve failed. Maddie opened the door so fast, Kate wondered if she had been waiting for someone. She looked even worse than she had at Christmas. Her skin was blotchy with a greasy sheen to it. She had scraped her hair back into an unflattering ponytail, and was wearing a pair of old joggers and food stained hoodie.

Maddie actually groaned when she saw it was Kate at the door. "Great," she said shuffling towards her living room in the assumption Kate would follow.

"Lovely to see you too, old friend," said Kate under her breath.

Maddie flopped down into one of her squishy armchairs and pulled a blanket over herself.

"Aren't you going to ask me why I'm here?" said Kate, moving some old magazines so she could find a space on the sofa.

"I can guess."

"So, it's true is it? You're pregnant?"

"Unfortunately, yes, it is. I can't believe Alex told you." Maddie's voice contained a mix of what Kate assumed to be exhaustion and defeat.

"Alex? What's this got to do with him?"

"Nothing, nothing, don't worry about it. So, who was it? Not my mum, surely?"

"It was Joy."

"Joy? How the hell did she know?"

"She recognised the signs. You shouldn't be so dismissive of her, she's a pretty sharp cookie."

"So I see. Look, I'm really sorry I didn't say anything

when I was down there, it's just... complicated."

"I must admit I'm a bit hurt that you didn't tell me. But I get that it's a huge thing for you to get your head round."

"Yeah, I've not been dealing with it too well, as you can tell."

"You're feeling rough?"

"Throwing up at least four times a day. I've been off work the past few weeks. Everyone there thinks I'm dying, it's the first time I've taken a day off sick in the ten years I've worked for the firm." Maddie managed a small chuckle and for the first time since she arrived, Kate recognised her as the Maddie she knew and loved.

Kate didn't think it was possible for Maddie to look much worse, but as the doorbell rang her face drained of all remaining colour.

"Do you want me to get that?" asked Kate.

"No, no just leave it. It won't be anyone important."

The doorbell rang again and Kate stood up. "I'll get it for you, don't worry."

"No," said Maddie, pushing past Kate on her way to the door. She opened it a crack, but whoever stood the other side pushed the door open wider.

"Alex?"

"Kate?" Alex looked between the two women, blind panic in his eyes.

"It's OK, I know," said Kate. "Aren't you going to let him in Maddie?"

Maddie moved aside, looking as though she might throw up. Alex didn't look much better. His usually tanned skin was pasty, his hair, normally his pride and joy sat greasy and limp against his forehead. He walked through the hallway, adjusting his tie like he needed more air.

"So, you know then?" he asked Kate as he followed her into the living room.

"Alex," said Maddie, but he ignored her.

"And you're not tearing strips off me? Why?"

"What do you mean? Yes, you should've told me, but I get that you were respecting Maddie's privacy."

"Wow, um, OK. To be honest I thought you'd be more bothered."

"I am a bit miffed that you've been keeping things from me, but I'm not totally deranged. A baby is exciting, however I happened to find out."

"God, Kate," said Alex, pulling her into a tight hug. "Thank you. Thank you so, so much. You know I never meant for it to happen. I always thought if I was going to have children, and it was a big if, that it would be with you."

Kate felt the ground move from under her. If Alex hadn't been holding her so close she would've collapsed. Her head was spinning, and as Alex let her go, she stepped back, looking from Maddie to Alex and back again.

"Kate?"

"She didn't know," said Maddie, her voice little more than a whisper.

"What?" said Alex, spinning round to face Maddie.

"She didn't know." Her voice shook, her hands wringing in front of her stomach.

"Fuck," said Alex running his hands through his hair. "But you said?"

"I meant, I knew about the baby," said Kate, her voice sounding like it was coming from somewhere far away. "Maddie hadn't said anything about the father." She looked over to Maddie, who was staring at the floor. "Look at me," Kate hissed. Maddie kept her eyes down. "LOOK AT ME!" she screamed. Maddie started to shake, and took a step back towards the door. "Look at me," pleaded Kate, tears brimming in her eyes. She wanted Maddie to say it wasn't true, that she would never betray her best friend that way, but Maddie had tears running down her grey cheeks, arms wrapped round herself like she wanted to disappear.

"Kate?" Alex reached out for her arm but Kate snapped

it away. "Kate, calm down."

Kate's breaths were coming too fast, she was taking so many but couldn't drag air into her lungs.

"Kate, you need to take slow, deep breaths," said Alex.

Something in Kate snapped. Without giving it any thought, her arm shot out, clenched fist meeting Alex's nose with a satisfying thud.

"The bitch hit me," he squealed, looking to Maddie for help.

Kate shoved past Alex. Maddie reached out her hand as Kate passed her, but Kate pushed it away.

"Kate, please let me explain. Kate, please, Kate..."

Kate could still hear Maddie's wails as she ran onto the street. She stumbled past rows of houses till she reached an alleyway where she sat down, trying to calm her breathing. Maddie and Alex? When? How? Was Maddie really going to have his baby? There were so many questions Kate needed answers to, but she wasn't ready to face either of them to get them. Kate pulled out her phone and dialled the only person who still had her back in this God forsaken city.

"Hello? Kate? Is that you?"

"Ye... yes..."

"My God, Kate, what's happened?"

"Mad...Al...babe..."

"Babe?"

"Baby...having... baby... together." Her last word came out as a wail.

"Where are you?"

"Don't know... near Maddie's house."

"Meet me at the Horse and Groom. That's probably your nearest pub. I'll be there in half an hour."

"Thank you," said Kate through her tears.

*

Kate waited outside for Flo to arrive. She couldn't tell if she was shivering through cold or shock, but whatever the cause, her arms and legs shook like someone was zapping her with a taser. The tears returned as soon as she saw Flo running along the road, resembling a teddy bear in her faux fur jacket and fake Ugg boots.

"Darling, come here," Flo cooed, pulling Kate towards her and letting her friend's tears matt the jacket's fur. "You poor thing. I couldn't understand much on the phone, but I got the gist. I can't believe what those dick heads have done to you."

"They were my friends," sobbed Kate.

Flo held her tight and gently rocked her back and forth. "There are two things you need right now. Neat vodka, and a tissue. I'll never get the snot out of my coat at this rate."

Kate managed a small smile, taking the tissue Flo offered and blowing her nose so loud it made Flo jump.

"Just so we're clear before we go in, I'm still getting my egg McMuffin tomorrow, right?"

"Promise."

"Come on then, let's get some booze down you."

Chapter 39

Kate lifted her head from the pillow and peeled a damp tissue from her cheek. Blowing hair away from her eyes, she looked around the room. Where was she? Her hand reached for the lamp beside the bed and in the sudden burst of light she realised she was in a bedroom at The Sunbeam. Kate groaned, and fell back to sleep.

When Kate woke for the second time, weak wintry light penetrated the threadbare curtains. Her phone showed eight a.m. Only an hour till she had to meet Flo for breakfast. Kate threw back the duvet and dragged herself over to the kettle. She filled it from the tap in the bathroom, and climbed back under the covers to wait for it to boil.

Memories of the previous evening came flooding back as the kettle bubbled away. It still hadn't sunk in. How could two people she considered family betray her like that? Flo had been amazing in a typical Flo way. She'd shifted Kate from sadness to anger in a matter of minutes, only interrupting the flow of insults and exclamations with the odd *mmm, yes, fuck them, dick heads*. Kate had no idea how many vodka's she'd drunk. The pounding in her head suggested it was at least three, though with Flo in charge of keeping her topped up, you could never be sure.

The kettle clicked off and Kate made her way across the room. On the way she caught her reflection in the mirror and gave a grim smile. Her hair stuck up in all directions, the odd strand stuck to her face. Her eyes had disappeared into red pouches, her lids so heavy it was tricky to see out from behind them. She was still wearing clothes from the night before and the button on her jeans had left an imprint on her stomach.

Each step sent a wave of pain through her head, and Kate retreated back to bed with her coffee, stopping to grab two painkillers from her bag. She rested the coffee on the bedside table, and picked up her phone. A notification told her she had twenty-five new messages. She opened the safest message first.

How's your head? We can push breakfast to nine-thirty if you want. Flo xxxxxxx

Twenty-three of the messages were from either Alex or Maddie, and Kate deleted them without reading. She couldn't bear to have any contact with either of them yet. The only remaining unopened message was from Bob. It was a risk to open it. She couldn't face another rejection. Curiosity beat fear, and Kate opened the message.

Kate, I'm so ashamed of the way I spoke to you. Please know it had nothing to do with you and everything to do with me. Joy called me and told me how much I'd upset you. She also made me realise it's time I was honest about what's going on with me. I know you're in Bath, but when you're back, can we meet up? I'm so sorry for the way I've been. Bob x

Kate smiled at his message and tapped out a reply.

Thank you for saying sorry. I never meant to pry, I only want to help. I'm coming home today, things haven't gone well. I'll explain when I see you. Speak soon x

With a message sent to Flo to say she'd make their original time of nine o'clock, Kate downed the dregs of her coffee and forced herself into the shower. Of all the things wrong with The Sunbeam, water pressure wasn't one of them. Kate stood beneath the torrent of hot water, letting it wash away the smell of stale alcohol and sadness. As she wrapped a towel around her, she didn't quite feel a new woman, but at least now she was a clean one.

With dry hair and a change of clothes Kate felt more human, the painkillers doing wonders for her headache, and her swishy, clean hair rebuilding a fragment of the self-esteem last night had stolen away. She packed her clothes away in her backpack and gave the room a quick clean. The least she could do for Flo was make her shift a bit easier.

Kate handed her key into reception and wondered if she'd be back in The Sunbeam again. Aside from Flo, the reasons to visit Bath were few and far between. Her fragile strength couldn't take the inevitable battering of seeing Maddie and Alex play happy families.

Flo was already waiting for her when Kate reached McDonald's. The smell of the place made her feel queasy, but a bit of grease would do wonders for her hangover. Flo didn't notice Kate come in, and sat flicking through a brochure of some sort. As Kate drew closer, she saw pages full of smiling, young faces. One lad had a hard hat on, a girl was holding a stethoscope up to a dog's belly.

"What are you reading?" asked Kate, sitting down opposite her friend.

"Nothing," said Flo, shoving the booklet into her bag and letting her braids fall over her flushed cheeks.

"It's not porn is it?" asked Kate and Flo giggled.

"You think I'd be looking at porn in McDonalds?"

"I'm sure some people do."

Flo shuddered. "That's gross."

"Come on, what was it? I promise not to laugh."

"I'm not worried about you laughing. I just don't want to rub my happiness in your face when things are going so wrong for you."

"Oh, come on, I need cheering up."

"OK, fine," said Flo, pulling the booklet out of her bag and sliding it across the table to Kate. It was a glossy brochure for a local college. "So...um... I've sort of been taking night classes."

Kate looked up at her friend in surprise. "Night classes? In what?"

"The basics at first. I didn't have a single GCSE to my name when I left school."

"And now?"

"Passed them all last year." Flo's brazen grin had been replaced by a shy smile. Kate took her hand and squeezed it.

"Flo, you did all that on top of the crazy shifts you work? That's seriously impressive."

"It's only GCSEs."

"It's not *only* anything. It's brilliant, that's what it is."

"Thanks. Well anyway, my tutor said I should look into this college. I've been putting it off till I've saved a bit more cash, but I'd like to go for it."

"What will you study?"

"Hospitality. I spend most of my shifts at The Sunbeam dreaming up all the ways I could improve it. I think...you know...maybe it's something I'd be good at."

"What an amazing plan! Let me know if I can help in any way. I still have some inheritance sitting in the bank if you need help on that front."

"No!" Flo's face had crumpled into a frown. "Sorry, I don't mean to sound ungrateful, but I want to do this by myself. I want to prove all those fuckers who said I'd never achieve anything with my life wrong. If I took a handout it would feel like I'd cheated."

"I get that. But don't ever feel you can't ask for help. God knows you've helped me plenty over the years."

"How are you anyway?"

"I feel like shit, but I can't tell if that's from the shock of what's happened or the vodka you plied me with last night."

"I still can't believe they did that to you."

"Me neither. Do you know the weirdest thing though?"

"Tell me."

"I'm kind of relieved about Alex. It's like I've been hanging onto the hope of being with him for so long, but now he's been such a massive arsehole, I'm finally free to move on. That's not to say I'm not also massively heartbroken," Kate added with a wry smile. "The stuff with Maddie feels way worse. I'm not sure I can, or want to ever forgive her."

"I never got what you saw in Alex if I'm honest. He's so slimy."

"Slimy?"

"Yeah, those shiny suits, slicked back hair. It's like he's trapped in the eighties."

"You can't deny he's gorgeous though."

"Maybe a bit *too* gorgeous. Men like that are alright for a while, but I'd get so bored looking at that face long term. I mean, there's nothing interesting about it is there?"

"I'm not sure I get what you mean."

"Who's your celebrity crush?"

"Daniel Craig."

"Exactly. His eyes are a bit wonky and his ears stick out. He's *interesting* gorgeous, not *boring* gorgeous like Alex."

"You really are one of a kind," said Kate. "I can't think of anyone who could cheer me up like you can."

"Well if you love me that much, why haven't you shoved an egg McMuffin in front of me yet?"

*

"Here you go," said Kate putting a tray of food down on the table. "You know I never eat crap like this except when I'm with you."

"It's 'cause I'm common. You can be your common self when you're with me, rather than trying to fit in with your upper-crust mates."

"I don't think you're common!"

"OK, working class then, is that more PC? I'm just

saying that we get each other, we're on the same page. I think you forget that sometimes."

"Sorry," said Kate, wondering why she'd overlooked Flo for so long.

"It's fine," said Flo, a piece of egg sticking to her chin. "Just don't go forgetting me again when Maddie comes begging for forgiveness."

"My God, you're a witch," said Kate, frozen to the spot.

"A witch? That's a bit rude."

"I didn't mean it, but it's like you conjured her up or something. Shit, hide me!"

Flo turned around and saw Maddie standing in the entrance, scanning the restaurant. Her eyes settled on Kate. "Sorry, mate, too late, she's clocked you."

"I can't talk to her. We have to get out of here."

"Remember how you felt last night? Hold on to that anger. She has no right to drive you out of anywhere."

"Um...hi, Kate, hi, Flo."

Flo ignored Maddie, picking a piece of cheese from her muffin and moulding it between her fingers.

"Kate, can we talk?"

"No."

"Please, Kate. Just hear me out, then I'll leave you alone. Five minutes is all I ask."

Kate looked at Flo, who shrugged and said, "Five minutes to get that bitch out of your life seems like a price worth paying."

Maddie winced, but said nothing.

"Fine. Five minutes."

"Flo, do you mind if we talk in private?"

Flo laughed. "I'd hardly call this place private. If you mean *without me here*, you should have the balls to say it."

"OK, if you wouldn't mind Flo, I'd like to talk to Kate alone. *Without you here*."

"I'm late for work anyway," said Flo, shoving the last of

her muffin in her mouth and walking round the table to give Kate a hug. "Call me any time," she said, then turned and walked away.

Maddie flopped down in Flo's seat and put her head in her hands. "I don't know where to start," she said quietly.

"Well, you'd better think quick because those five minutes are counting down."

"There's no need to be like that."

"I'd say there's every reason to be like that," said Kate, noticing Maddie's blush with pleasure.

"Look, I need you to know it only happened once."

"When?"

"At the office Christmas party."

"But Alex doesn't work in your office?"

"Yeah, remember I told you there were lots of different companies going to be there? Well his was one of them."

"How long had you wanted to sleep with him?"

"I hadn't! Oh fine, anyone with two eyes in their head can see he's gorgeous."

"Boring gorgeous."

"Sorry?"

"Doesn't matter."

"Anyway, looks aside, I've always thought he was a right dick for the way he treated you. I don't know what came over me that night. The only excuse I have is that I was pissed out of my skull. I don't even remember it happening. I only knew when I woke up and he was lying beside me."

Kate sat in silence, waiting for Maddie to go on.

"Well, anyway, he didn't remember much either, so we agreed to pretend like nothing had happened. But then my period was late."

"Did you know you were pregnant when you came to stay with me at Christmas?"

"No, not for certain. There were a few signs and I was going out of my mind, but I hadn't done a test at that point."

"You made me feel like *I'd* done something wrong!"

"I know, I'm so sorry. I hated myself, and that hatred turned me into a grumpy cow."

"When did Alex find out?"

"I told him that morning he drove me to the station."

"So that's why he rushed off home early. You do know he'd been talking about us getting back together?"

"I'm sorry."

"Don't be, you're welcome to him. He might not have known about the baby, but he knew he'd slept with you, and still tried to get into my knickers. Bastard."

"Kate, I know I've hurt you, but..."

"Sorry, I don't think I can hear any more. And anyway, your five minutes is up. Good luck, Maddie. Please don't contact me again."

Kate stood and walked out of the restaurant with her head held high. It was only as she stepped into the cool winter morning that the tears began to flow.

Chapter 40

"You look worse than Moira the morning after her twenty first," said Joy, walking into Kate's living room. "Goodness me, girl, it stinks in here. What is that smell?"

"Me."

"Right, well I'm going upstairs to run you a bath."

"I don't want a bath."

"You need one. How many days have you been rotting in here now? Four?"

"Five."

"You youngsters don't know you're born. In my day there was no choice to mope around in a pool of self-pity. We had to get on with things. We had responsibilities."

"I don't have any responsibilities."

"Oh yes you do, girl. You have a responsibility to yourself not to let those bastards win. I bet that sleaze Alex isn't pining in his pyjamas. And if you won't get moving for yourself, think about the other people who need you."

"No one needs me. I'm all alone."

"Well, thank you very much," said Joy. "I thought we were friends, but perhaps I'm just a nuisance to you."

"I'm sorry," said Kate. "Of course you're my friend."

"Then start treating me like one. And what about Bob? The poor chap's got enough on his plate without worrying about you. You should be up at his house offering him support, not wallowing over your own petty dramas. What's it they call it these days? I know, a pity party. You're having a pity party for one and it's damned right disgraceful. Your grandmother would be ashamed if she could see you now."

"That's a bit harsh," grumbled Kate, pulling the blanket up around her chin. Did she really smell that bad? It had been a few days since she'd washed so it was possible.

"You need a good talking to, so don't expect an apology from me. Now, I'm going to run that bath, and if you won't get in it of your own accord, I'll carry you up there myself."

Kate smiled in spite of herself. "Fine. You win."

"I always do," said Joy as she headed up the stairs.

*

Kate climbed into the hot bubbly water and felt every muscle in her body relax. It was a classy bathroom, thought Kate, admiring the handiwork she rarely got to enjoy herself. She should make the most of this time alone, the calendar was filling up with bookings from Easter onwards. It was going to be a busy summer.

Bubbles erupted from her nose as Kate plunged beneath the water. It felt good to be clean again and Joy's no-nonsense speech had the desired effect of snapping her out of it. She wasn't completely sure what *it* was, only that she had been smothered by a feeling of despair ever since she set foot on the train back from Bath. Until that point she had been holding it together well by anyone's standards.

The anger Flo helped her access was soon replaced by hopelessness. Alex and Maddie had been in her life for over a decade. Even her own father hadn't stuck around that long. Part of her wished she hadn't blocked their numbers, for her phone lay silent without Alex's stupid videos and Maddie's regular chit chat. If Kate were honest, she missed Maddie far more than Alex. He had been more a fantasy than reality she now realised, but Maddie had been the sister she never had.

Kate scrubbed shampoo into her scalp, fingertips working out dirt in a way she wished she could do with her soul. There had been many times over the years when she and Maddie had daydreamed about having children. They'd promised to appoint each other godmother, agreeing to live close enough for their children to attend the same school. At least they'd been right about one thing, thought Kate bitterly. Alex had indeed turned out to be the father of one of their babies, just not with the mother Kate expected.

A twinge of guilt raced down Kate's body as she remembered the promises she'd made her best friend; the first trip to Mothercare, the standby birthing partner, the baby-shower organiser, the babysitter. Guilt seeped into envy. At least Maddie had family who could do all those things. Maddie's actions left Kate with nobody.

A gentle knocking on the door reminded Kate she wasn't alone, even if in that moment she'd like to be.

"Are you decent, dear?"

Kate pulled bubbles over herself to protect her modesty. "Yes, come in."

"I thought you might like this," said Joy, handing Kate a chilled glass of wine. "Oh no, dear, there's no need to cry."

Kate hadn't realised she was crying, but lifting her fingers to her face, felt warm drops of water running down her cheeks. "I'm not sad," she said, brushing the tears away. "I mean, of course I'm sad, but right now I'm just so incredibly grateful to have you as a friend."

"Likewise," said Joy, sitting herself on the toilet seat. "Now, I know you're not feeling quite yourself, but I really think it would be a good idea to pay a visit to Bob. I could come too. It's been a long time since I had a proper chinwag with his mum, and I'm sure she could do with a bit of company."

"Are you sure Bob wants us to go round? He wasn't very happy about it the last time I tried."

"I gave him a call earlier. He said it's fine. There are things the two of you need to talk about."

"Alright. I'll finish up my drink then pull myself together."

"That's the spirit," said Joy, standing up and shuffling to the door. "I'll be waiting downstairs. See you shortly."

*

If the walk to Bob's house in the rain had seemed a mission, it was nothing compared to the painful walk up the hill with Joy. Kate battled nerves and adrenaline to keep to Joy's snail pace, linking arms in case she fell. *Patience is a virtue*, Kate told herself as they stopped for the twentieth time so Joy could catch her breath.

"Me and your grandmother used to cycle up this hill. You can't imagine the fun we had whizzing back down. Neither of us could afford a motor car, so riding down here at full pelt was the closest we could get. It's a wonder neither of us were injured."

"I bet that was lots of fun," said Kate, smiling at the image in her mind.

"It was, and not half as many cars around as you get these days."

Joy chatted on until they found themselves outside Bob's house. They paused, neither taking the first step onto the driveway.

"You're not nervous too are you?" Kate asked.

"Hmm, well Bob's mother is a bit of a closed book. My popping round could go either way."

"And you didn't think to tell me that before? Are you sure Bob knows we're coming?" Joy looked everywhere but at Kate. "Joy?"

Joy ignored Kate's question and marched across the drive, far sprightlier than she'd been up until that point.

She rang the doorbell and Kate hovered behind her shoulder, anxious about the welcome they might receive.

"I don't think anyone's home," said Kate, after Joy had rung the bell for a third time.

"Let's look round the back."

"Joy! No!" Kate chased after the old woman, who was already reaching over to unlock the side gate. "Joy, this is trespassing! They could call the police!"

"Don't be such a worry wart, dear." Joy led the way along the path that ran the full length of the house. "Wait," she said, putting a hand on Kate's arm. "Listen."

The two women stood and listened. What sounded like a scream reached them, followed by the sound of breaking glass.

"You go first," said Joy, squeezing behind Kate.

"Wow, thanks, so kind of you," said Kate, glaring at her friend.

They continued along the side of the house until they reached a conservatory. The conservatory backed on to an enormous garden which had seen better days. Overgrown flowerbeds spilled on to grass that was in some patches knee-high, in others reduced to mud.

Joy gasped as they looked through the conservatory windows. An older version of Bob was throwing cushions around the room. Kate yelped as he lifted a plant pot above his head and smashed it to the ground. A woman cowered in a corner of the room, protected by Bob, who stood in front of her, as if on guard. The man picked up a photo frame and held it high above his head. At that moment he caught Kate's eye.

The transformation was instant. Kate looked on as the man placed the frame carefully on a shelf, smoothed down his hair and walked to the door. He stepped into the garden and Kate gripped onto Joy as he headed their way.

"Good afternoon. You must be my two-thirty appointment. What is it? Divorce? Boundary dispute? I'm

Robert Carter. Pleased to meet you." The man held out a hand to Kate, and she took it, feeling as though she had little choice in the matter. "Apologies, but I can't remember your name?"

"Katherine," said Kate. "Katherine Trenain, but please call me Kate."

"A pleasure to meet you Miss Trenain. Now, come through to my office and I'll get my secretary to make us some tea."

Kate followed the man into the conservatory. She looked at Bob but his eyes fell to the floor.

"Dad..."

"Shush, boy. Don't you have homework to be getting on with? Up to your room. Now!" Turning to his guests, he offered them a seat, scratching his head as he took in the jumble of cushions and soil on the floor. "Dearie me, you can't get the staff these days. Goodness knows what's happened here."

"Dad," said Bob his voice gentle. "You're at home, remember? These are my friends, Kate and Joy."

Robert Carter looked at his son. His eyes clouded with tears and he looked suddenly frail. "Home?"

"Yes, Dad, you're at home. Come on, sit down."

"Where are Mama and Papa?" he asked, clutching a cushion to his chest.

"Don't worry, Dad, they're upstairs."

"Why are you calling me Dad?"

"Sorry, Robert, I'm Bob, and this is Sheila." Bob moved his body so Robert could see his wife.

"Sheila?" Roberts voice was full of wonder as he stepped towards his wife. She flinched and pushed herself further into the corner of the room. Robert's eyes clouded again, and he looked around the conservatory like a lost little boy. "Where am I? Who are you?"

"This is..."

"I'm tired," Robert interrupted. "I'd like to go to bed."

"Come on, Dad," said Bob, taking his father's hand. "I'll take you to your bed."

Kate's throat tightened at the site of Bob leading his father from the room. It was the most heart-breaking sight she had seen. Joy moved towards Sheila, holding out a hand for her to take.

"How about you and I make a nice cup of tea," said Joy. "It's been an age since I last saw you at the WI and I'm sure we've got lots to catch up on." Sheila grabbed Joy's hand, and pushed herself up to standing. With meek resignation, she leaned against Joy and headed towards the kitchen.

Kate sat herself down in an armchair. How could she have been so unaware of what was going on in her friend's life? Bob walked into the conservatory and slumped down beside her, leaning his back against the wicker leg of the chair. Neither of them spoke for what felt like an age. It was Kate who broke the silence.

"I'm so sorry."

Bob looked up at her. "What on earth do you have to be sorry about? It's me who's been the arsehole."

"I should've made more effort to help."

"You didn't know what was wrong."

"I knew *something* was wrong."

Bob put his head in his hands. "I didn't want to bring you into all this. You've been my sanctuary these past few months."

"Well I'm here now, so you might as well tell me what's been going on."

"I don't know where to start."

"The beginning."

Chapter 41

Bob lay his head on Kate's knee and she ran her hands through his thick hair. With every stroke she felt him relax, until finally he was able to talk.

"When I first moved back here after Ellie died, Mum and Dad were amazing. They pieced my shattered heart back together, both emotionally and practically. They decorated the spare room so it felt like a fresh start rather than a backwards move, held me when I cried, listened for hours as I talked and talked. Dad got me a job at his solicitor's firm. He even took me camping, I think to remind me of happy times before Ellie. Not that they wrote her out of history. Mum put photos of her up around the house, and brought her up regularly in conversation. They were amazing." Bob looked up to be sure Kate understood. She smiled at him, and he lay his head back down.

"We were good for a few years. I felt no shame being back with my parents, because in truth, they were my best friends. It was more like a house share than a parent child relationship. It was a couple of years ago when things started to go wrong. You have to remember, I was living and working with Dad, so it was natural, given how much time we spent together, that I was first to spot the signs.

To begin with it was little things, losing keys, forgetting clients' names, things Mum could pass off as tiredness or stress. But soon it became impossible at work. I was covering for him, smoothing over mistakes, sitting with him in meetings. Effectively I was doing the job of two people, and I couldn't handle it. It was a long, nasty process getting Dad to leave work. It was his company after all. Plus, he was still sharp enough to figure out what I was trying to do. Eventually I got the diagnosis and power of attorney I needed, but I paid a heavy price for it. It ruined our relationship and precipitated the start of the anger.

I've told myself over and over that anger is a symptom of his condition, it's not personal. But it feels bloody personal when you've been screamed at and hit. He's never once hurt Mum, but I'm worried it could happen."

Bob took a deep breath and his shoulders started a slow heave up, down, up, down. Kate felt the wet of his tears seep into her trousers and reached her arms round him.

"It's OK," she whispered, "it's OK."

"Somehow I've managed to keep it to myself. I know some of the people I work with guessed, they're not stupid, but we all went along with the farce. The retirement party, the gold watch, as if retiring was Dad's idea all along."

"What was the diagnosis?"

"Dementia."

"Bob, I know it's not my place to say, but don't you think you need professional help?"

"I have carers coming in when I'm at work, or can't be in the house. But they're struggling to cope and it's increasingly hard to find someone who will come. He's starting to need round the clock care, but Mum won't hear of him going into a home. She doesn't want to lose him."

"That's understandable."

"Yes, but the reality is he's already gone. I mean, there are flashes of the man he used to be, like the way he was when he first met you. But they're few and far between. God, Kate, I wish you could have met him before. He was the most incredible man, clever, kind, funny, generous. He would have loved you."

"And I'm sure I would have loved him. I can't believe you spent so much time helping me settle in when you had all this going on. I feel a real arse for taking you away from your dad."

"Kate," said Bob, brushing away his tears and looking up at her. "Don't you get it? I wanted to do those things. You gave me the chance to forget all this shit even if it was just for a few hours."

"And the calls you kept getting? All the times you had to rush home?"

"From the carers when they couldn't cope."

"Oh, Bob, why didn't you tell me sooner?"

"I've been trying to protect him, or the memory of him at least. I want people to remember him as he was, not the man he is now. This is a small town, Kate, and he was always such an important part of it. He'd hate people to see him like this. I thought I could manage between me and the carers, but it doesn't feel like I'm managing right now."

"Well, now you've told me, I'm here to help."

"You've got enough on your plate already."

"Yeah, well my own mess feels completely utterly insignificant right now. So, I've lost a couple of friends, in the grand scheme of things that's not such a big deal. I have you, Flo, and Joy. You're all so amazing wanting any more friends would quite frankly be a bit greedy."

Bob looked up at her and smiled for the first time since she'd arrived.

"Bob? Kate?" Joy's voice held a note of panic and they ran through the house to find out what was wrong.

Joy and Sheila were stood at the bottom of the stairs, worry etched across their faces. "He's in the bathroom," said Sheila. "Bob, can you help him? I think he's had an accident and I'm not strong enough to lift him."

"Sure," said Bob, squeezing his mum's hand. "Look, I think it might be best if you two go now, but thank you so much for coming and being such amazing friends. I'm sorry

I've not opened up to you sooner."

Kate pulled him into a hug. "Call me any time," she said. "And if you ever need a break, you know where to find me."

*

A week later, Kate and Bob strolled arm in arm down the camel trail. "Is it ever going to stop raining?" she asked, a tiny circle of face visible beneath her waterproofs.

"This is Cornwall, it never stops raining," laughed Bob. Kate loved that he was smiling. "Seriously though, spring is just around the corner. You'll see Bodmin in a completely different light once the leaves come back and green shoots start popping out of the ground."

"I love it already."

"Really?"

"Yes, don't sound so surprised. It feels like home, and I'm always a sucker for an underdog."

"I'm not sure I'm happy with you calling my hometown an underdog."

Kate laughed. "It's a good thing. Let all those tourists squish themselves into Padstow and St Ives. We'll keep this place to ourselves."

Bob laughed. "We could cycle to Padstow one day if you like? It will be busy even at this time of year, but not unbearable like it is in summer."

"I'd love that. Anyway, how's your mum and dad?"

"Same old, except Mum's agreed to come with me to look round some homes."

"Really?" asked Kate, stopping to look at him. "That's a massive U turn, isn't it?"

"Yes, and I've got Joy to thank for it. I don't know what she said to Mum when you came around, but that evening she was looking up care homes on her iPad."

"Good old Joy. She's a marvel that woman."

"She certainly is. Anyway, how have you been? You said you had news?"

"You might think I'm an idiot doing it at my age... but I've signed up to the Open University to finish my degree."

"That's brilliant!" said Bob, grinning at her. "When does the course start?"

"Not till September, which is good as I'll be run off my feet with guests till then. There's something else too." Kate shuffled her feet, kicking up mud and leaves with the toe of her boot.

"Come on, Kate, what is it?"

"I'm going to start counselling."

"That's a great idea."

"So, you think I'm nuts?" said Kate, smiling at him.

"No, not at all. I just think you've had more to deal with than most, and counselling is never a bad idea. Is it someone local?"

"No, it's with a rather lovely lady who came to stay. I'll do it over Skype as she's in India for a few months."

"Well I think that's brilliant. Have you heard from Maddie at all?"

"Urgh, no. I've blocked her number."

"Maybe the counselling can help you find a way to heal the rift between you?"

"You think I should forgive her? After the way she betrayed me?"

"Look, I just don't think you should write her off completely. Yes, she did a nasty thing, but it was one stupid decision that has affected the rest of her life."

They walked along in silence, each lost in their thoughts. The rain intensified and became so heavy it was hard to walk, let alone hear. They stopped to shelter under a bridge until the rain eased off.

"It's so cold today," said Kate, wrapping her arms round herself and shivering.

"Come here," said Bob, pulling her closer towards him. His wet waterproofs did nothing to help with the cold, but there was something so comforting about being held by him.

"Bob," she said, lifting her face until it was inches from his. He held her gaze, a shot of electricity passing through them. A drop of rain fell from his hood and landed on Kate's nose. She smiled, but didn't look away.

"Kate," said Bob, his voice thick with some unexpressed emotion. "Can we meet back here, under this bridge in a few months' time, when things with Dad are more settled and you've had time to work things through with your counsellor? I don't think either of us are in a great place right now, and quite frankly, my heart is too fragile to risk it breaking again."

"Yes," she whispered, looking up at her *interesting gorgeous*, kind-hearted friend. She stood on tiptoes and placed the lightest of kisses on his rain soaked-cheek. Bob took her hand, their fingers linking together. They turned and headed out into the rain.

Five Years Later

"This is a world away from The Sunbeam," said Kate, as they walked across the marble floor to the polished oak reception desk.

"Good morning, how can I help you?" asked a chirpy young woman, sleek blond ponytail swinging as she spoke.

"Hello, we'd like to check in please, Mr and Mrs Carter." Bob was using his posh solicitor's voice, and Kate smiled at him in amusement.

"Right, let's see..." the woman clicked her mouse, checking the computer screen for their reservation. "You're in room number..."

"I'll handle this." A woman in a tight-fitting jacket and pencil skirt, complimented by a rose-pink silk shirt, clicked across the lobby in a pair of patent heels. Her corkscrew hair bounced against her shoulders and a wide grin spread across her shiny pink lips.

"Flo!" Kate squealed and rushed forward to embrace her friend. "My God, you look incredible. Let me see," said Kate, holding Flo at arm's length.

"Watch out, Kate, you'll undermine my authority if you go on like this." Kate let go of her arms, then hugged Flo again when she realised she was joking.

"It's so good to see you again," said Kate, beaming at her friend.

"Wow, Kate, anyone would think it had been years. It's only been three months."

"Well it felt like years," said Kate, pouting and making Flo laugh.

"Right, Tia," said Flo, leaving Kate and marching behind the desk. "These are VIP guests, let's upgrade them to the Mortimer Suite."

"There's really no need," said Bob, not wanting to cause a fuss.

"There's every need. Now, let me make a fuss of you and stop interfering, Bobby."

Flo winked at Kate. Bob pretended to hate Flo's use of Bobby, but Kate knew no one could be annoyed at Flo for long.

"Here you go," said Flo, handing them a key card. "Your room's on the top floor, I'd take you up there myself but I've got a million and one things that need my attention. Tia here will take good care of you if there's anything you need. She's an angel."

Tia smiled adoringly at her boss and nodded her head in agreement.

"Thanks, Flo, this is so kind of you," said Kate. "We're still on for dinner?"

"Of course, why do you think I'm running around like a blue arsed fly? I need to make sure everything's sorted so I don't get called in later."

"Thanks," said Kate, thrilled at the thought of spending time with her friend.

Tia gave Kate and Bob instructions to find their room, and offered to fetch someone to help with their luggage. Bob insisted there was no need, picking up a case in each hand to show he could manage. They stepped into a lift and emerged moments later on the top floor.

"Wow," they said in unison, staring at the wall of windows that looked across the city.

Their suite was at the farthest end of the corridor, and

both were lost for words as they stepped inside. An entire wall was made of glass, its doors opening onto a wide balcony. The middle of the room was dominated by the biggest bed Kate had ever seen. Next to the bedroom was a dressing room, and beyond it a bathroom bigger than the entire downstairs of their house.

"Look at this," said Bob, staring at two love heart shaped towels on the bed, a bottle of champagne nestled between them. "Fancy a glass?"

"Better make it really small," said Kate, smiling at her husband.

"Are you feeling OK about being back in Bath?" he asked, pulling her on to the bed and wrapping his arms around her.

"Yes, I am. Everything that happened feels so long ago, like it happened to someone else. And besides, I'd be happy anywhere as long as it's with you."

Bob leaned over and kissed Kate. "You're telling me you haven't enjoyed your solo city breaks?"

"They weren't city breaks, they were for work!"

"Yes Mrs Carter, whatever you say."

Kate picked up a towel and flicked him. He grinned and she snuggled back down.

"How long till you meet Maddie?"

"An hour. Why?"

"Oh, I don't know," said Bob, running his fingers up and down her back. "I thought you might need some help relaxing." He turned her over so she was facing him.

"Oh… did… you… now…" said Kate between lingering kisses.

*

It wasn't until Kate stepped out of the enormous shower half an hour later that nerves began to take hold. The massage setting on the shower hose had eased some of the knots in her shoulders, but nothing could stop the churning in her stomach.

"Are you OK?" asked Bob, pouring them each a small measure of champagne.

"Not really. I'll be glad to get this over with."

"You never know, you might actually enjoy it," he said, handing her a glass.

"I don't know. Things can never be how they used to be, can they?"

"No, of course not, but there's no reason they can't be good."

"Hmm," said Kate. Her feelings towards Maddie had softened over the years, mainly thanks to Rissa's counselling sessions and Bob's calm logic. But so far, their only contact had been via email. This would be the first time Kate had laid eyes on Maddie in five years.

*

Kate stepped out into the beautiful hotel garden and spotted Maddie straight away. She was standing on the manicured lawn, legs spread wide as a small boy weaved a remote-controlled car back and forth through her legs. Maddie looked up and Kate gave her a wave.

"We've got a table over there," said Maddie, jogging up to Kate and pointing to the far side of the terrace.

Kate followed Maddie to the table and sat down opposite her oldest friend.

"You look well," they each said, laughing and smiling nervously at each other.

Maddie did look well, thought Kate. She had tell-tale purple crescents under her eyes that came with being a mother to a young child, but she'd grown out her hair and more than anything, she looked happy. A small boy ran over to them.

"This is Fred," said Maddie, pulling the boy onto her lap. "Fred, this is your Aunty Kate."

"Hi," he said, before burying his head in his mother's neck.

"Sorry," said Maddie. "He's really shy around

strangers."

Strangers. The word made Kate catch her breath. Why had she allowed her resentment to go on so long?

"It's lovely to meet you at long last," Kate said to the boy. He peeped out from behind Maddie's hair. He'd inherited the best qualities from each of parent. Alex's clear blue eyes, Maddie's beautiful blond curls.

"Can I get you anything to drink?" A smart waiter stood holding an iPad poised to take their order.

"I'll have a diet coke please," said Kate.

"Same for me, plus a small orange juice."

"You're not drinking?" Kate asked, after the waiter had left.

"No, I hardly touch the stuff these days. Between work and Fred, there's not much time left for a social life." Kate detected a slight hint of regret in Maddie's voice.

"Do your parents help with babysitting?"

"Yeah, sometimes. But they're a couple of hours away so I mostly rely on the childminder."

"Does Alex help out much?" Kate felt relief that it no longer hurt to say his name.

"Didn't I tell you? He's moved to Dubai."

"Yes, you said, but I assumed he'd be coming back regularly to visit his son."

Maddie let out a joyless chuckle. "He's seen Fred once in the past three years. Fred's lucky to have his Gramps, or he'd have no male role model at all."

"What a bastard."

"Yeah, he is." They shared a knowing smile. "Look, Kate, I'm so sorry for what I did. I was a bit off the rails back then, but I know that's no excuse. I have to be honest though, I don't regret what happened. How could I?" Maddie looked at the beautiful boy on her lap and Kate understood exactly how she felt.

"To be honest, Maddie, it's me who should be saying sorry. I wasn't there when you needed me. I was so angry, but I think everything got a bit jumbled up, you, Mum, Dad, Alex. I'm much more sorted now."

"So I see," said Maddie, nodding towards Kate's wedding ring. "I always thought there was something going on between you two."

Kate laughed. "There wasn't really. Not for a long time. We both had so much to sort out in our own heads, we stayed friends for ages before anything happened."

"And it's going well?"

"Yes, really well. There have been a few bumps in the road, Bob's dad died last year and it hit him hard, but we've learned to face everything together."

"I'm really happy for you," said Maddie, sounding like she meant it. "How are things going with the B&B?"

"It's been tough since I started teaching, but it's going from strength to strength. Bob's building us a summer house at the top of the garden so we can start renting the whole house out during the summer holidays. We'll go back to B&Bing in the winter. I'd miss meeting all those interesting people if we stopped it completely."

"The house of many lives," said Maddie, smiling.

"Yes, it is. Anyway, tell me about your life. Anyone special on the scene."

"Fred, why don't you go and play with your car?" The little boy jumped off his mum's lap and ran across the grass. "There is someone at work, but it's early days. I haven't introduced him to Fred yet."

"Is he kind?"

"So kind," said Maddie, a far off look in her eyes. "He's dying to meet Fred, but respects my decision to take things slowly. It's tricky though, we don't get the chance to go out much, and I wonder how long his patience will last."

"If he's as kind as you say he is, he'll stick around. You know, we're in town for two nights and Bob will be busy with his conference. How about I babysit for you tomorrow night?"

"That's really kind, but I couldn't ask you to do that while you're on holiday."

"Maddie, it's what I should've been doing for the past five years."

Maddie looked at Kate with tears in her eyes. "You're amazing, you know that? Are you sure you're sure?"

"It would be good practice for me," said Kate, putting a protective hand against her stomach.

"You're not?"

"I am."

Maddie screamed, and Fred came running across to see if she was all right. She picked him up in her arms, and drew Kate into them. "Mummy's fine," she told him. "I'm just excited because you're going to have a new cousin."

Fred dragged Maddie off to play with his car, and Kate sipped her coke, stroking the small bump beneath her dress. *Fill the house with love and laughter.* Her grandmother's instructions floated through her mind. Kate thought about her family: Bob, the baby, Joy, Flo, Maddie, and the people who stayed at her home, sharing a little piece of themselves before they continued on their way. *I think I have, Moira*, she whispered, *I think I have.*

Acknowledgements

This book took me by surprise. The story came to me when I was between Historical Fiction projects, flowing out onto the page like it was desperate to be let out.

Inspiration for this book came from the many lock-downs, when we were forced to stay local and as a result explored Bodmin in a way we never had before. We discovered so many beautiful hidden gems in a town that can sometimes be dismissed too easily. When it came to the BnB stories dotted throughout the book, I drew inspiration from our many years hosting strangers in our attic room. Some of the stories contain a grain of truth, some are imagined, and some come very close to my own experience. I'll let you decide which you think falls into each category!

When my husband first read this book he called it my 'love letter to Bodmin'. Thank you to all my friends in Bodmin who make the town 'home'. Thank you to all those who work tirelessly to create new opportunities for the community here. The well-tended flower beds, cultural opportunities, youth work, behind the scenes decision making, and so much more don't go unnoticed.

Thank you to the readers of early drafts- Jo, Jen and Pete. Your suggestions and encouragement made refining this book a whole lot easier than it would otherwise have been.

Thank you to Audrey Davis, who tackled my pitiful understanding of grammar and punctuation and whipped the manuscript into shape. As well as being an excellent proof-reader, Audrey is also a very talented author, so do look out for her books.

Thank you to my family, who as ever put up with me being distracted, unavailable, and obsessed with getting this book finished for months on end.

Being an author can be rather lonely at times. I am very grateful to the online community of readers and writers, particularly on Twitter and Tiktok, who have welcomed me, encouraged me, shared wisdom, and made my writing life feel significantly less solitary.

Finally, thank you reader, for picking up this book and taking a punt on something quite different from the books I usually write. This book was great fun to write and I hope reading it provides as much escapism as I found when writing it.

One Last Thing...

If you enjoyed this book and have a spare minute or two please consider leaving a review or rating on Amazon. Reviews are the best way of helping other readers find my books, and as a self-published author it is hard to overstate how important they are!

I love hearing from readers, so if you would like to get in touch you can find me at-

www.lkwilde.com

Twitter- @lkwilde

Instagram- @lkwildeauthor

Tiktok- @lkwildeauthor

Facebook- @lkwilde

Or you can email me at

lkwildeauthor@gmail.com

Also by LK Wilde...

Forced from their island home, Clara and Jimmy join the east-coast herring season in a bid to survive. Their paths are dogged by war, injury, and misunderstandings... Will they ever find each other? And will they finally learn what it means to be 'home'?

Born into poverty. Sold to the fair. Will Barney Read and his world of illegal gambling offer Queenie a chance of happiness? Based on a true story.

Coming soon...

1840, Cornwall. A murderer, a victim, and the wives left behind.

Printed in Poland
by Amazon Fulfillment
Poland Sp. z o.o., Wrocław

30451635R00167